Hugh couldn't bring himself to look away.

If it was possible for ten years of hurt to be conveyed in someone's eyes, then Zoe had mastered it.

When she spoke, her voice was soft. "Hugh, it was all a long time ago. We're both very different people now."

He certainly hoped so. They were going to have to find a way to deal with each other without this massive lump of history coming between them every time their eyes met.

Hugh wanted to buy Waterford—that meant discussions, negotiations, meetings. Interactions he intended to conduct as an adult, not a broken-hearted seventeen-year-old.

Dear Reader,

Like many people, I really enjoy an occasional glass of wine. It's a reward after a hard day's work, or a way to mark a celebration—whether it's a birthday, an achievement or simply friends coming together to enjoy each other's company.

I'm lucky enough to have two close friends, Kim and John, who own their own boutique winery—and make a very delicious shiraz. I've had the opportunity to do a little work with them over the years, and have seen from the inside both the pleasures and sheer hard work that come with winemaking. I'd like to thank Kim and John for their help with the insight into winemaking and their patience with my frequent questions. Any errors I've made are my own.

In this story, my heroine, Zoe, says it takes people of "steely determination and unwavering passion" to succeed in the industry. She's right. I've visited wine regions in various parts of the world, and I will never forget the day I visited a winery where a frost had destroyed the estate's entire grape crop the night before. Can you imagine? I would be inconsolable. But the owner shrugged and said something like, "It happens. There's always next year."

In a way, writing is very similar. It is an art, but there is a little science to it, too. Things don't always turn out the way you think—characters sometimes have their own plans for themselves. And "steely determination and unwavering passion" are pretty much prerequisites for becoming a romance author!

I hope you enjoy Zoe and Hugh's story. They're two people with lots of passion and determination—they just need to find a way to apply it to what their hearts are telling them!

I'd love to hear from you. Visit me at www.emmiedark.com.

Cheers,

Emmie Dark

In His Eyes

EMMIE DARK

HARLEQUIN®

entertain, enrich, inspire™

Recycling programs
for this product may
not exist in your area.

ISBN-13: 978-0-373-60722-8

IN HIS EYES

www.Harlequin.com

Printed in U.S.A.

ABOUT THE AUTHOR

After years of writing press releases, employee newsletters and speeches for CEOs and politicians—none of which included any kind of kissing—Emmie Dark finally took to her laptop to write what she wanted to write. She was both amazed and delighted to discover that what came out were sexy, noble heroes who found themselves crossing paths with strong, but perhaps slightly damaged, heroines. And plenty of kissing.

Emmie lives in Melbourne, Australia, and she likes red lipstick, chardonnay, sunshine, driving fast, rose-scented soap and a really good cup of tea.

Books by Emmie Dark

HARLEQUIN SUPERROMANCE
1769—CASSIE'S GRAND PLAN

For the OC Babes,
without whom none of this would have happened.

CHAPTER ONE

ZOE WATERS DROVE UP THE long, rutted drive and noted that the pale green farmhouse ahead of her desperately needed a new paint job. But then, it had needed one for as long as she could remember. Only these days—more than ten years since she'd last been here—it was beginning to seem as if the flakes of paint were what was holding the crumbling weatherboards together.

Zoe wasn't sure whether she should feel comforted that so little had changed or disgusted by the neglect.

She pulled into the yard behind the house and climbed out of the rental car, stepping carefully to avoid the soft, squelching mud threatening her inappropriately delicate shoes.

The signs of dereliction were even more obvious here.

A strange, melancholy sense of déjà vu settled over her as she looked around. Now that she surveyed things closer up, it was clear that not only did little appear to have changed—

pretty much *nothing had*. Everything had just decayed a touch more. The scattered car bodies near the back fence had rusted a little redder and sunk a little deeper into the overgrown grass. The door to the shed that held the tractor and her grandfather's other old-fashioned and outdated farm equipment was crooked, the top hinge clearly broken.

Zoe sighed heavily and leaned against the car, warm from the two-hour drive from Melbourne. The task ahead of her seemed to grow exponentially as she surveyed the ruins of Waterford Estate.

The only building that still looked in reasonable condition was the tin shed and converted refrigerated shipping container that housed the winery. Well, what passed for a winery on the Waterford estate. She wondered if all those rich people in Sydney, California and France on the Waterford mailing list who so eagerly awaited her grandfather's vintage Shiraz each year would feel quite the same way if they could see where it came from.

She sighed again and ran a hand through her hair as the wind whipped the long strands into her eyes. Wrapping her light jacket more tightly around herself, Zoe shuddered—she'd forgotten the icy chill of the wind out here and how it could leach into your bones. Too much time in

California. Too used to the endless sunshine and warm breezes, unlike the capricious weather of this part of the valley—stinking hot in summer, subject to grape-endangering frosts seemingly out of nowhere in spring. Right now—winter— the weather was at least somewhat predictable. Cold. With a side of rain and wind.

She mentally surveyed the contents of the suitcase still sitting in the boot of the car. She was going to have to buy some new clothes.

A trip into town. Yippee.

The thought sent a different kind of shiver through her.

Turning away from her survey of the ruined outbuildings, Zoe shielded her eyes from the weak sun. The Waterford vines stretched out in long, bare lines to the north and east of the house, dormant for the winter yet still visibly neglected. It was a tragic state for any viticulturist to see—some of the oldest vines in the valley, planted by Zoe's great-great-grandfather and tended by a member of the Waters family for more than a hundred years.

Until now.

To her left, the well-tended vines of the neighboring Lawson Estate—her family's rivals for her whole life—grew just a few feet from the property line. Zoe made an effort not to look, to pretend that across the post-and-wire fence there was just a big, empty *nothing.* Just as she'd always done—at least when her grandfather was watching.

The only way she could get through these next few days was to pretend Lawson Estate didn't exist, the township of Tangawarra wasn't there and Waterford had a protective force field around it. She snorted at the fanciful idea at the same time she wished it could be true.

Zoe pushed her sunglasses to the top of her head as the sky clouded over. Heavy, slate-gray clouds waited on the horizon. Rain was definitely on the way. *More* rain from the looks of the sodden ground. She shivered again. Maybe even a storm.

At least that would give her a break. A few hours to sit and catch up with everything that had happened in the past few days. Perhaps even the chance to turn her brain to the task of working out what to do next.

The very thought started a headache throbbing at the back of her neck.

Just as she made a move to dig out her belongings and find her house keys, the sound of a vehicle reached her. A white utility truck bumped along the corrugated dirt track that led from the unsurfaced road. It had prominent signage along the side—elegant black script, a flowing red ribbon—unmistakably the Lawson Estate logo.

She swore under her breath.

She couldn't have had a day or so—a few hours maybe—to get her bearings before facing reality? It seemed the universe wasn't going to extend even that small kindness to her.

Zoe stepped toward the ute as it pulled up beside her own bland white rental car. The driver's face was hidden in the shadow of a straw, American-style cowboy hat. It struck her as odd—most men in the valley preferred the very Australian Akubra or a simple cap, most often embroidered with the logo of their winery.

The driver cut the engine and climbed out. Time slowed somehow, and Zoe was conscious of every moment. The scuffed R. M. Williams boots that hit the ground first. The tight-fitting jeans, worn almost white around the knees and crotch. The chambray shirt that had once been crisply ironed, but was now creased and loosened by a day's work. The stubbled jaw—not quite bearded, but wearing more than a five-o'clock shadow—that gave his familiar face a hard, almost savage edge. And last—but never least—those blue eyes, shocking, tormenting blue. The blue eyes she'd dreamed of for ten years; the blue eyes that had been her ruin.

"Well, if it isn't Zoe Waters," he drawled.

Zoe's knees turned to jelly, and as her vision began to blacken at the periphery she realized she'd stopped breathing. Through pure force of will she took in a deep lungful of air and strengthened her wobbly legs. Fainting now would be an unacceptable humiliation. From somewhere deep inside, from the core of steel that had been honed over a lifetime and never before failed her, she managed to paste a tight, unwelcoming smile on her face. She'd show him how little she cared, even if it killed her.

"Hugh Lawson, well, well," she managed to say, pleased that her voice conveyed exactly the right tone of distaste.

"So the old man finally let you come back." Hugh was smiling, but his eyes were cold. There was no hint of the warmth or humor she remembered from so long ago.

Was he angry with her? What on earth for? She was the one who had lost everything…her family, her reputation, the only real home she'd ever known.

She managed another grim smile. "The old man died yesterday."

He hesitated and his cool look faded as concern creased his brow. She felt an odd satisfaction at the knowledge she'd unsettled him, but she clasped her hands tightly to hide their sudden tremor. It had been ten years, for heaven's sake! She'd moved halfway around the world to escape from her past. She was over it. The mistakes she'd made as an infatuated sixteen-year-old little girl were not going to taint her whole life. She'd made sure of that.

"I'm…I'm sorry to hear that," Hugh said. His eyes lost their hard edge for a moment and Zoe remembered how easy it had been to fall for him, how easy to think herself in love and to be fooled into thinking he might love her in return.

Hugh took a step forward and reached out a hand. For a moment, she thought he was going to hug her and a mess of emotion washed over her. Mostly, though, she was filled with horror at the idea that she looked as if she needed comforting. She stiffened and took a step back.

Hugh's hand immediately dropped. Whatever he'd been thinking, whatever sympathetic gesture he'd been about to make was now hidden behind that impenetrable blue gaze.

"Yes, well…" Zoe flicked out her hands in a helpless gesture. Apart from anything else, she had no idea what to do with sympathy; it had been the same when the nurse at the hospital had expressed her condolences. Her grandfather's death still wasn't real. Even when it did eventually sink in—assuming that happened— she wasn't sure how she should feel about it. Sad? Relieved? Indifferent?

She straightened her shoulders. "Why are you here?"

That laconic smile was back, warmer this time, more like the Hugh she remembered, erasing the years from his face and making him look just as he had when they'd snuck away to be together. "Neighbors look out for each other around here, Zoe, don't you remember that?"

Irritation flared inside her at his veiled reminder. Just where had he been when she'd needed looking after?

And she was over this. Over him.

Yeah, right.

She couldn't help raising her eyebrows in disbelief at his comment. "Neighbors might. But you know as well as I do that that never applied to the Lawson and Waters families."

Hugh ignored her. "One of our groundskeepers saw the car," Hugh continued, gesturing to her white sedan. "We knew Mack was in the hospital, so I thought I'd check it out in case... you were up to no good." He grinned slyly.

Zoe swallowed her storm of emotions somewhat unsuccessfully, frustrated with herself for feeling them in the first place. The only way to deal with this was to appear as unaffected by their reunion as he seemed to be. As unaffected as she *wanted* to be. "Thank you so much for your concern," she said, putting on a sarcastically polite tone. "But there's no need. You can leave now."

"Ah, Zoe. Still the angry little firecracker, I see." He shook his head, then his expression softened. "Are you okay, though, really?"

His condescension made her emotions burn brighter. The fact that he could still see through her, that he remembered anger was her default defense mechanism, was the final straw. "You can leave," she repeated. "Now." Zoe dug her fingernails into her palms as she struggled to rein in her response. She must surely be drawing blood.

His gaze swept over her, a lingering glance that created an entirely different kind of heat. When his eyes met hers again, they were subdued, a little clouded. She'd have given anything to know what he was thinking.

"It's…good to see you again, Zoe. To see you looking so…*well*."

Well? What was that supposed to mean? Before she could ask, he turned on his heel and climbed back into the ute. With a short, salute-like wave against the brim of his hat, he was gone. Zoe let out a long, relieved breath and refused to think about the disappointment that washed over her as she watched the car disappear down the track.

At least that was over. Seeing Hugh Lawson

again was the thing she'd been dreading most. Now she was just left facing a small town that had always hated the sight of her, dealing with her grandfather's funeral and his estate, and single-handedly producing the last-ever Waterford Estate vintage. Compared to facing the love of her life who'd abandoned her when she'd needed him most, all that should be easy.

Pushing those thoughts away, Zoe headed toward the house, intent on getting started with the seemingly impossible tasks in front of her.

THE FIRST JOB TO TACKLE was organizing her grandfather's funeral. In comparison to her day-job of managing the production of a multi-million-dollar wine vintage, that was a snap. And not just because her grandfather's controlling nature hadn't receded an inch, even right at the end. She should have expected that a man like Mack Waters would have made all the arrangements himself. Especially once it had become clear that the cancer wasn't going to let him escape.

A simple melanoma on his balding head, burned away like the many others he'd had in his life. Only this one had grown, burrowing below his epidermis, reaching out its ugly tentacles and infiltrating his skull. Once it reached his brain stem it had been only a matter of days.

Mack was too stubborn to leave his funeral to chance—or to risk someone else mucking it up. He wanted what he wanted. And at the time, he'd probably thought it unlikely that his granddaughter would come home to do it for him.

Hadn't stopped him calling her, though. Zoe wasn't sure who'd been more surprised—herself when she took the call, or Mack when she'd answered. She'd always made sure Mack had a phone number for her when she made one of her frequent moves, but he rarely used it.

Besides, by the time she got here—still reeling from the shock of her unexpected, and still impossible to explain, decision to take leave from work, pack a suitcase and jump on a plane—he was lucid only in short bursts. It hadn't stopped him from loading her up with guilt and forcing her to make promises she'd had no intention of keeping. But Zoe had stayed and held his hand at the last.

Mack had opted for a church service, a shock to Zoe since she'd never known him to set foot inside one. Apart from her sightseeing visits in Europe, neither had she. Certainly not this modest, clinker-brick, slate-roofed building that sat on a grassy slope just on the outskirts of Tangawarra township.

The storm that had threatened yesterday still hung low on the horizon. For now, the sun was shining through the stained-glass windows, sending beams of colored light crisscrossing through the dusty air of the church.

As per Mack's instructions, it was a private funeral—invitation only. And the list consisted of one person: Zoe. She couldn't help a rueful grin as she surveyed the half-dozen mourners behind her as she sat alone on the front pew. She didn't recognize any of the other mourners—all women, she noted. They were probably professional funeral-goers, women the minister had asked to attend against Mack's wishes, just so the church wasn't completely empty.

Mack wouldn't be happy about that. His exclusive funeral was his final joke on the town he loved to hate—and who loved to hate him. That the valley's most prestigious wine was made by a grumpy, antisocial misanthrope wasn't lost on the tightly knit community of Tangawarra.

The plain, dark wood coffin at the front of the church stayed silent. No more complaints from Mack. Not anymore.

Zoe swallowed a suspicious lump in her throat.

She was actually grateful for her grandfather's unsociable wishes—no public announcement of the funeral, no notice in the local paper. Because if they'd known, Zoe was sure that more members of the Tangawarra community would have turned up—just out of curiosity and that bizarre schadenfreude that was part of small-town life. They'd nod knowingly with superior looks on their faces. The thing of most interest to them wouldn't be the coffin or the service, but Zoe herself, sitting alone in the front row. She could just imagine them critiquing her hairstyle, her makeup, deciding that her gray pencil skirt and beaded red-and-gray knit sweater weren't somber enough for the occasion. The fact that she'd worn red lipstick would be a scandal talked about for weeks.

Because they knew the true reason behind Mack Waters's sad and miserable existence. Although he'd never gone out of his way to make friends, everyone knew his life had been ruined when he'd been saddled with his hell-raiser of a granddaughter to bring up.

Zoe gave an inner shrug—she could understand why he hadn't wanted the judgmental, gossipy town at his farewell. Neither did she.

Thankfully, the minister kept the service short. One of the anonymous churchgoers read a short passage from the bible. Again, Zoe had no idea why. The minister's eulogy was polite and for the most part accurate—praise for Mack's wine making, including a glowing quote from a prestigious wine reviewer, a short note about the tragic loss of his wife and then his daughter, an unexpected mention of his pride in his granddaughter's success in the California wine industry. Zoe guessed the minister had to say *something* about her, since she was sitting right there.

So far, so good. The first promise she'd made to Mack—to give him a private, low-key funeral—was almost over. Pity it was the easiest promise of them all.

When she walked outside into pale sunlight, following his coffin, she realized she should have known better. Dozens of people stood around, women with grim smiles aimed at her, men with hats held to their chests.

Tangawarra was an impossible place to keep a secret—she should have learned that years ago. It was also an impossible place to tell the truth, but then that was the dichotomy of small-town life.

"Zoe?"

A woman in a pale blue fleece windbreaker stepped closer as the undertakers pushed her grandfather's coffin into the hearse. She appeared to be in her mid-fifties, and had the sun-weathered look of someone who worked outside. Zoe frowned, searching her memory to try to put a name to the face.

"My condolences," the woman said. "Mack

was a stubborn old coot, but it's always hard to lose a loved one."

Loved one? She and her grandfather had tolerated each other; that was about as far as it went. Zoe just nodded. "Thank you."

She wished, once again, that she'd thought to pack a winter-weight coat. The morning's chill still hung in the air. She'd clearly acclimatized to the California weather far more than she'd thought. Zoe was finding the valley colder than she'd ever remembered—a deep, gnawing ache that had gone away only last night when she'd soaked herself in a steaming hot bath. Of course, she'd had to clean the tub first, which had helped warm her up a little, too.

"I'm Patricia Owens. From Long Track Estate—just up the road from Waterford."

Zoe had seen the sign to the vineyard, neighbors to Waterford on the side opposite to the Lawson Estate, but the woman still didn't seem familiar.

"We bought the property about eight years ago. Mack was a good neighbor. We used to chat—sometimes shared pickers and the like. I liked to look out for him—especially in the past year or so when he was beginning to get frail."

Zoe tried to push away a stab of unwanted guilt. Mack hadn't phoned her until it was too late—there was no way she could have known that she needed to be home. And even if she had…

At least she'd come back in time, so he hadn't been alone at the end. She'd given the old man that much, at least.

"Thank you," she said, giving the other woman a genuine smile. "I really appreciate that."

Patricia gave her arm a squeeze. "Mack talked about you—he was so proud of what you were doing. You must come by and visit us—are you staying at Waterford?"

Zoe nodded, holding her surprise inside at the unexpected repetition of the words the minister had used in the eulogy. *Mack? Proud of her?* Zoe was an award-winning winemaker with a reputation—spanning two continents—for quality, perfectionism and an innate talent for bringing out the best in grapes. But she'd never considered what people back in Tangawarra—including her grandfather—thought of her. She'd run so fast to get away from the tiny town, in her mind it was still just as it had been ten years ago. Complete with her own starring role as the town's one and only teen rebel. She'd never stopped to think that they might see her differently now.

"Come around for dinner one night, then. It would be lovely to get to know you."

Zoe battled a sudden swell of emotion. "That's very nice of you. Thanks."

The funeral directors motioned to Zoe—the procession was ready to head to the cemetery. Zoe would ride in one of their cars. She stepped forward, but Patricia reached out again to place a tentative hand on Zoe's arm.

"Um, Zoe, would it be okay if we came to the cemetery to pay our respects?"

Zoe looked around; several people in the small crowd were hanging on every word she and Patricia exchanged. Her grandfather couldn't have been more explicit in his wishes for privacy at the funeral. She figured he meant the interment, as well, but the cemetery was a public place. Zoe couldn't exactly lock everyone out.

Maybe if she explained.

"Mack was pretty clear—" she began. She stopped short when the slam of the hearse door made the flowers on top of the coffin shudder, as if Mack himself was banging on the lid in protest. Zoe bit back a peculiarly hysterical urge to laugh. A little of her old rebellious streak reared up inside her. *You know what, old man? These people want to say goodbye. I'm gonna let them and there's nothing you can do about it.*

She shrugged. "Sure. If you want to." Although a quick look around the crowd had her instantly regretting her capitulation. It wasn't just about what Mack would have wanted—or not. She didn't particularly want to spend a great deal of time with the Tangawarra towns-folk.

Patricia gave her a small hug and pulled back with a sweet, sympathetic look. "Thank you. I'll see you there."

From the plush interior of the car, Zoe watched as the small town passed by. She had plenty of time to take in the details; the car was travelling slowly, following the hearse, and the guy from the funeral home made no attempt to speak. Everything seemed unreal, like a David Lynch movie—the colors somehow wrong, some things too bright, others unfocused, as though she existed in a fissure in reality that kept her remote from the world.

Nothing much about the township had changed. Some of the shop fronts were differ-ent; a few buildings seemed more modern. The milk bar where Zoe had bought cigarettes—old Mr. Bond sold them to underage teenagers if they paid extra—had become a café with tables and chairs set out on the footpath. The chem-ist's where she'd been caught shoplifting was the same, only its sign was brighter and louder, and it had expanded to take over the next-door premises.

An old council building was now the most well-tended and attractive store on the main street—it had become the winemakers' center, a tourist information spot to help visitors find the various wineries in the valley. The Lawson Estate logo was prominent, and Zoe turned away.

All the worst things that had happened in her life had happened in, or because of, Tangawarra. She didn't want to notice the changes in the town, the fact that it seemed prosperous, the people friendly, the buildings neat and well maintained. No, she wanted it to still be the dark, miserable place she'd found it as a teenager—it was easier to hang on to those old impressions than integrate new ones. Then it was easier to understand why she'd never wanted to come back.

Just before they left what passed as Tangawarra's city center, Zoe spied a couple of teenagers hanging around outside the supermarket. The hearse had caught their attention and they stared unabashedly at the pitiful two-vehicle cortege. Both kids were dressed in head-to-toe black; one had shocking pink hair, while the other's head was half shaved, half long greasy black locks. Zoe peered closer as the car drove past—leather straps encircled their wrists, multiple piercings ran up their ears and one had a heavy-looking crucifix around his neck. *Lots of eyeliner on both of them.*

Emos, or neogoths, or whatever they were calling themselves these days.

Up to no good is likely what the townsfolk of Tangawarra would call them.

Zoe's car crawled past and the kids were left standing aimlessly on the footpath, staring after the funeral procession with the world-weary expressions that only teenagers are capable of.

At least there are two of you.

At the cemetery she followed the coffin and the minister over the uneven ground on autopilot. Her attention was mostly focused on walking without stumbling—her impractical heels sank into the ground with every step and she wished she was wearing her usual wine-stained work boots. She was sure Mack wouldn't have minded.

A tall, granite headstone was already in place, the open grave in front of it lined with eye-wateringly green artificial turf, ready to accept its latest occupant. The headstone hadn't yet had Mack's details engraved, but there was a blank space ready for him. Above that was her mother's name, Margie Waters, dead at thirty-two when Zoe was just ten.

Funny, she didn't remember her mother's funeral at all. That was strange. Surely she should remember something as significant as that event. Maybe Mack hadn't let her attend. But she couldn't remember that, either.

At the top of the stone was her grandmother's name; she'd died when Zoe was six. All Zoe had of her were some disconnected memories of hugs, scones hot from the oven and Mack smiling. She was pretty sure he hadn't smiled ever again after Rachel Waters had died.

The minister began reciting the usual prayers. The wind had picked up and it snatched the monotonous drone away, which was fine with Zoe. She couldn't seem to concentrate on the words, anyway.

Slowly, something entered in the periphery of her vision. She turned her head, expecting to see Patricia, and realized with a shock that there were at least half a dozen people already standing behind her and more filtering in through the cemetery entrance.

Mack would have hated this. The thought made her smile and a lump grew in her throat that she fought against. She hadn't cried for ten years—no way was she starting now. Not over this. Not over anything—she simply couldn't risk it.

Zoe had lived with Mack for nine years, two with her mother, seven more just her and the old man. He'd never really been a parent to her;

they'd simply struggled through life together, working it out as they went along. They'd kept in touch sporadically in the decade since he'd sent her away in disgrace a few months before her seventeenth birthday. But Zoe had made her peace with that—it had been the only option he thought available to him.

"Zoe?" The minister gestured to her and she realized she'd missed her cue to throw dirt into the grave. One of the undertakers had removed the floral arrangement from on top of the coffin and Zoe was glad that the lush, lively flowers wouldn't end up under the ground.

She quickly bent and scooped up a handful of dirt, fertile but thick and claylike, remembering as she did what her grandfather had taught her about terroir and the impact the soil had on the grapes that were grown in it.

It was one of the lessons that had since allowed her to build a career as one of the most renowned up-and-coming winemakers in California's Napa Valley.

"Goodbye, Mack," she whispered. Her breath misted in the icy air, floating eerily over the open grave before the wind carried it away. And then the coffin disappeared from sight.

The minister completed his final words and walked over to Zoe to shake her hand and squeeze her shoulder. There was a murmuring then, people began talking and even laughing—telling stories of the old days, she was sure. A shiver of dread ran down her spine. The last thing she wanted to share with this town was memories.

Patricia materialized at her side, cupping her elbow and steering her back toward the cemetery gate. She treated Zoe as if she were fragile, as if she were grief-stricken. Zoe definitely did feel zoned out, but she put that down to tiredness and lingering jetlag. And when had she last eaten? She couldn't remember.

Overwhelmingly, she was just thankful this task was behind her. Boneless with relief, actually. It probably looked similar to grief, she figured; grief was no stranger to her, and neither was that numb and empty feeling that accompanied it. When she was seventeen and had lost everything, she'd understood what true grief was. This wasn't even close.

"I'll make sure she gets there."

A male voice broke into her thoughts, but Zoe was still finding it difficult to focus on the world around her. Basic senses were returning slowly; she was aware that the wind had become almost a gale, she could smell eucalyptus as people walked over the leaves on the ground and crushed the oil out of them. People were chatting loudly now, getting into their cars with raucous farewells and banging of doors.

"Are you sure?" Patricia asked. "I can go with her in the undertaker's car. Bert can drive my car over."

"No, it's fine, she can come with me."

Zoe was barely conscious of the fact that Patricia's soft touch on her arm was replaced with a strong masculine hand and she was being steered assertively toward a European sports car.

"See you there."

Zoe blinked and found herself sinking into buttery-soft leather seats as the powerful engine purred to life. And next to her sat Hugh Lawson, a grim look on his face. *How could she have been that out of it?* They were in his car and pulling out of the cemetery car park before she pulled herself together enough to protest.

"See us where? Where are we going?"

"Lawson Estate."

"What? Why?" The last place on earth she wanted to go.

"Because Mack Waters deserves a decent send-off."

CHAPTER TWO

"EXCUSE ME?" ZOE PROTESTED, just as Hugh expected her to. She reached for the door handle, but he reversed and drove off quickly before she could get out.

He flicked a glance at her as he steered the car away from the cemetery and back toward the road to Lawson Estate. She sat rigid, staring straight ahead. Her head was slightly bowed, and waves of dark hair fell forward hiding her expression, hiding eyes that Hugh knew were velvet brown. Brown eyes that could flash with fire when she was angry, darken with passionate intent late at night.

"Put your seat belt on," he said.

She cooperated without a word. Well, he hadn't expected her to be grateful, had he? He'd been an utter pain in the ass at their unexpected meeting yesterday, and he knew it. It had unsettled him just *how* unsettled he'd been by it. Looked as though today wasn't going to be any different.

At least now he could direct that emotion

at its rightful target instead of his poor staff. They'd tiptoed around him the day before.

"Are you really so bitter about Tangawarra, Zoe? You didn't think that the people of this town would want to attend Mack Waters's funeral? That they wouldn't want a wake for its most famous winemaker? For a man from the family who more or less put the valley on the map?"

"I...I..." Zoe stumbled for words, and Hugh was surprised. But then the old Zoe returned and her eyes flashed at him as she twisted in the seat. There was that spark he remembered too well.

"You think I made that decision? I'd have invited the whole town—it'd be better to get their rubbernecking over and done with in one go. But I was following Mack's instructions. He wanted it private, low-key."

Hugh deliberately didn't turn away from the road, but he rolled his eyes and knew she'd see. "Anyone with an ounce of sense would know that what Mack wanted and what Mack needed were two different things. Besides, funerals aren't for the dead—they're for the living."

"I had to do what—"

Hugh didn't let her finish. "I'm hosting a wake at Lawson Estate. The word's gone out, so I figure we'll have half the town there within an hour or so."

Her protest died on her lips. She shut her mouth with a snap and sank back into the leather seat. From the corner of his eye, Hugh watched her hands clasp over her stomach, pressing tight enough against her belly to crease her sweater and turn her fingernails white.

"No, no," she said, shaking her head. Hugh wasn't sure how, but he could sense the struggle inside her. Then he dismissed the idea. *Ridiculous.* He knew next to nothing about the woman sitting beside him. They'd been lovers a decade ago when they were practically children. Parted under the most miserable of circumstances. But high school was a long, long time ago. He was a different person now—she surely was, too. A person he had to get to know if his plan to take over Waterford had any chance of success.

"I…we…you can't. Mack wouldn't have wanted it. He would hate it. And I'm not prepared for it."

There was a quiver about her mouth and he noticed that her legs were trembling, too. He fiddled with the controls on the dash and sent a rush of warm air through the car.

He adopted his best authoritative tone. The one he used at Lawson Estate all-hands meetings and at the Tangawarra chamber of com-

merce breakfasts. The one that convinced other
people to listen. "Zoe, this has nothing to do
with what Mack would have wanted. It's about
Tangawarra celebrating the life of one of its
most famous citizens. It's the right thing to do."

"The right thing to do? What would you
know about that?" Zoe suddenly blurted, biting her bottom lip with her front teeth as if she'd
like to swallow the words.

Oh, that was too much. He'd thought the
wake would be a good way to thaw the ice between them—show that the whole Lawson-
Waters feud thing was ancient history and had
no bearing on the present. In fact, he'd hoped it
would become the opening round in his negotiations for Waterford. Not that he'd be so crass
as to push Zoe for a deal on the day of Mack's
funeral. But he'd thought she'd at least be grateful. Perhaps even conciliatory. He hadn't expected Zoe to be so violently opposed—had
actually thought she might enjoy going against
her grandfather's wishes. But he wasn't going
to put up with bullshit like that. "Going to give
me a lecture on right and wrong, are you, Zoe?"
he asked.

"*Need* a lecture, do you?" she bantered back.
Her tone was all careworn insolence, bringing
a sudden, long-forgotten memory to the surface
despite his determination to focus on the pres-

ent. Hugh could picture her, clear as day, fronting up to a teacher at school, all fierce bravado and defiance, before being sent to the principal's office for insubordination. Hugh had admired her, even before the summer they'd gotten together. Her "take no prisoners" approach had appealed to the rebel inside him—the one buried deep under layers of family responsibility and community duty. But that was all in the past. All he was concerned about now was seeing both their signatures on a deed of sale for Waterford.

"I suppose you do," she continued. "You talk about what the community needs, but from what I hear you've become Tangawarra's own little corporate raider."

Hugh clenched his jaw to prevent himself from responding hastily. Her criticism made him want to bite back, just as he would have years ago. But she wasn't the only one who'd changed. Hugh had grown up, too, and he wasn't about to give her the satisfaction of letting her know the barb stung.

"Is that what you hear?" he asked blandly. He needed to remember that he had a larger purpose here. He'd dealt with all kinds of people over his years in business, and Zoe Waters wouldn't be the most difficult by a long shot. He had a strategy and he'd pursue it logically and methodically, like any other business deal. Hugh had the Lawson Estate legacy to honor and the prosperity of Tangawarra to consider. Waterford was too valuable to fall into the hands of a competitor—or be left to fall to ruin. Not to mention the fact that securing Mack Waters's vines would be an indisputable coup. The two estates had been rivals for decades, and seeing Waterford vines become part of Lawson Estate would be eminently satisfying.

So far, negotiations were not off to the best start, but he could recover from this. He'd been in worse situations before and come out on top.

"Mack told me you were buying all the grapes in the valley—pushing out the smaller players. Even buying up their vines if you could get your hands on them."

He wondered how far she was going to push him. He soon got his answer.

She waved a careless hand. "I suppose you had to find a way to make sure that watery stuff you call wine gets around the world."

His knuckles whitened around the leather-wrapped steering wheel and all his good intentions vanished. "You'd know all about that, would you, Zoe? From what I understand, despite the accolades you've managed to garner, you never stay anywhere long enough to make a decent career."

So much for his strategy. He didn't want to give Zoe the impression that she was anything other than a minor annoyance. Showing her that he was vulnerable to her criticism was a mistake.

He wasn't Tangawarra's mayor, or its mythical defender riding in on a white stallion to save the day. But he was, as his father had been, a community leader. And today he was doing what a community leader was expected to do: honor the passing of one of its most famous citizens.

And make some inroads into an important business acquisition at the same time.

He waited for her comeback, but she didn't have one. She shifted in her seat, and Hugh hated himself for noticing the whisper of her stockings as she crossed her legs, her perfume. She smelled different now—subtler, more complex. But then, her perfume of choice at sixteen had been some generic store brand that she'd more than likely shoplifted.

He glanced her way when she stayed silent. To his surprise, he laughed at her tightly pursed lips.

"What?" she asked.

"I never thought I'd see the day. Zoe Waters lost for words. What happened to that smart mouth of yours? Never short of an insult and never short of an attack. What happened to you?"

"I grew up," she snapped. "Ever thought of doing it yourself?"

ZOE CURSED HER IMPETUOUS tongue just as Hugh let out a long breath that sounded a little like a wistful sigh. "Ah. There she is." A quick grin shot across the car at her. "Good to see."

She pressed her lips into a taut line. *This* was why she hadn't wanted to come back to Tangawarra. Hugh Lawson had known her better than anyone. He'd seen into her heart—at least, at the time she'd thought he had—and he still expected her to be the delinquent, impertinent teen who had been the town's number one trouble-maker until she'd been shipped off in a cloud of shame. How would it be facing other townspeople? Maria from the chemist's shop where she'd been caught shoplifting, Frank from the hardware store she'd vandalized... Oh, God, what if the school principal was still around? Her stomach did another unsettling swoop at the very thought.

"Who's coming to this...*thing* you've arranged?" Zoe asked, waving her hand around in a way she hoped looked dismissive. She found herself grinding the heels of her shoes into the pristine carpet of the car, leaving behind some of the mud she'd collected at the cemetery. The sight of Hugh's beautiful car messed up, even this tiny way, was a small satisfaction.

"I don't know. You know how it works out here. Bush telegraph."

Ugh. That's exactly what she dreaded. Anyone and everyone would be coming. Anyone who even vaguely remembered the tear-away teenaged Zoe, the girl who had caused her grandfather all that grief, would be champing at the bit to stare at the creature she'd become. What were they expecting? A Mohawk hairdo, top-to-toe tattoos, a sneer and a gutter mouth? Probably.

The best Zoe could offer them was the fact that her right ear was pierced at the top as well as in the lobes and—not that anyone was going to see it—she had a tiny winding grapevine with a bunch of plump purple grapes tattooed on her right butt cheek, which she couldn't quite bring herself to regret. Sure, she could still swear with the best of them, but she'd long since learned to control herself. By many standards, she would be considered civilized, well-mannered. Polite, even.

She hated the fact that Hugh's presence seemed to make her regress ten years in her manners. She resolved not to let it happen again—well, at least *try* not to let it happen again.

The car pulled into a reserved space near the entrance to a huge, architecturally impressive building full of hard edges and angled planes that somehow still seemed totally in tune with its surroundings. A large sign announced it as the Lawson Estate tasting room and restaurant. Tall sheets of glass that made up much of the building's walls reflected the gum trees whipping in the wind, and the native garden and vineyard beyond provided a romantic view for the diners inside. The building was just one of the many improvements Hugh had made to the estate after taking over the reins from his father.

Right now the view was spectacular—the dark gray clouds that had skittered across the sky during the interment now loomed overhead, providing a ghostly backdrop for the skeletal vines.

Hugh turned off the purring motor and turned to face her. The silence was deafening. Zoe maintained her stony expression, staring straight ahead, refusing to feel intimidated by him.

But, oh, she did.

Always had, really.

When Zoe first left Australia, a naive and wide-eyed eighteen-year-old, she'd sworn she'd never let anyone make her feel like a second-class citizen again. But then she'd also sworn to never set foot in a winery again. All she'd wanted was a complete break from her past. Easy in theory, but when she needed to earn a living, it was common sense to turn her hand to the tasks she knew so well. Since then, she'd made her own way in wine-making, a male-dominated industry, holding her own against some of the toughest, roughest characters imaginable. Wine-making seemed so civilized from the outside, all *la-di-da* and French words, but within it was just like any other kind of farming: backbreaking physical labor, absolute dependence on the whims of the weather and no guarantees of returns at the end. It took people of steely determination and unwavering passion to succeed.

Why, then, did she feel so weak now? Hugh's presence in the tiny car was overwhelming. His broad shoulders filled the car seat; his solid thighs were disturbingly close to her own. His scent surrounded her, some expensive musky cologne, but underneath the smell that was all his own, one that had called to her sixteen-year-old inner self and made her want to crawl into his arms and seek shelter there. Back then, he'd been her safe harbor.

At least, that's what she'd thought.

Zoe's hands were still primly and tightly folded against her stomach. She took the risk of glancing in his direction. He was frankly staring at her, and she could have sworn there was melancholy in his blue eyes, an expression that exactly reflected her own mixed feelings about the past, but he covered it so quickly she wondered if she'd imagined it. It was replaced by a look of cool indifference. He looked for all the world as if he was sitting beside a business colleague, not a woman he'd shared the most intimate of experiences with.

The chill shocked her. But she wasn't sure what she should have expected instead. Sympathy? Pity? Ugh. Anything but that. But she realized she'd definitely expected some kind of recognition of what she'd gone through. She was the one who'd been run out of town. She was the one who'd lost her home. She was the one who'd been broken beyond repair.

He'd been allowed to continue his privileged life as normal.

"What?" she asked, eventually breaking the uncomfortable silence, interrupting his unsettling examination. "Not what you expected?"

He paused for a moment and Zoe realized she cared far too much about what his answer might be.

But then, instead of speaking, he reached

across and took her left hand, pulling her arm towards him.

"What—?" Zoe started in reflex. His fingers curved around to hold her in his grasp, reminding her of how much bigger he'd always been. His hands were different now, though—harder, more weathered. Calloused and scarred from physical labor. If he was a lord, he wasn't one who sat in the manor directing others to do the dirty work. It was clear he got stuck in himself.

Zoe had no idea what was going on. He gripped her palm with one hand, while he pushed up her sleeve with the other.

Zoe tried to pull her hand from his grasp, but it was futile. "Let me go!" she protested as she struggled.

His finger traced a path down the inside of her arm, marking a light trail from her inner elbow to her wrist. Zoe gasped at the tingling sensation his fingertip left behind and at the way her pulse leaped in response.

Then his touch slowed, repeating the stroke, this time becoming feather-light as he reached the faded scars on the insides of her wrists. Barely noticeable anymore unless someone looked closely, the fine white lines were permanent reminders of a past that Zoe did her best to ignore. In fact, she couldn't remember the last time she'd specifically examined them. It had been such a childish thing to do, a silly, attention-seeking stunt. She'd never really intended to end her life—just to get Mack to notice her. He'd noticed her long enough to take her to the clinic, then things went back to exactly the way they had been before. The whole thing made her feel embarrassed to remember, now.

But Hugh…Hugh had always been a little awed by her scars, a little scared by them, too. He used to kiss them and ask her to never do anything like that again. It hadn't been a hard promise to make. Or keep.

He sucked in a breath and then sighed heavily. In annoyance or regret? Zoe didn't trust herself to guess.

"I wish…" he began, before trailing off.

"What?"

Before he could answer, another car crunched on the gravel and pulled up beside them. Zoe ripped her hand from Hugh's grasp and pushed her sleeve down, feeling suddenly exposed. Her scars—physical or metaphorical—were no longer any of his business, and they were certainly not the business of any other Tangawarra townsperson who might look through the window. Townspeople who were turning up to honor her grandfather's memory, even though it was against his explicit instructions.

Righteous—and very welcome—anger flooded

through her, but before she could explode again about this betrayal of Mack's wishes, Hugh was out of the car, walking around to open her door. Her new neighbor, Patricia, was standing right there to greet her.

Another three cars arrived and people began climbing out.

She needed to control her responses. She was an adult now, and she'd left that angry teenage Zoe behind long ago. Even if anger was still her default defense mechanism, she'd since learned to control it better.

Just not when Hugh Lawson was around, it seemed.

Screaming at him might help let off some steam, but even if Tangawarra had changed since she'd left, she bet it was just the kind of thing that the gossip-hungry townsfolk would still love to watch.

"Hugh, it is so kind of you to do this." Patricia stood on tiptoe and gave Hugh a peck on the cheek.

"I'm sure Mack would have really appreciated it." Patricia smiled sadly and then walked over to a small gathering of women to chat.

No, he wouldn't! Zoe wanted to yell. Somehow she kept the words to herself. How was it possible that the people who had known Mack for years, lived with him in their community, had so little understanding of how the man worked? She'd shared a house with him, sure, but they'd never shared their inner selves. Even still, it just seemed so *obvious* to her that this was wrong.

"Shall we head inside, Zoe?" Hugh took a step closer to her and Zoe refused to move back, even though she wanted to. "I need to make a few arrangements."

Then his hand was on her arm again, leading her up a long ramp to the entrance. She was sure that from an observer's perspective it seemed perfectly correct—yet another example of saintly Hugh comforting the grieving granddaughter. They couldn't see that his fingertips were ever so slightly stroking the inside of her elbow. She wondered if he was even aware that he was doing it himself. And if so, was he doing it only to rile her? She still couldn't help the physical response of her body. It had been trained too well to respond to his touch.

The next hour passed in a blur. Accosted on every side, Zoe could barely catch a breath as everyone wanted to pass on their condolences and, more subtly, find out what the naughty Zoe Waters had been up to these past ten years.

"So you didn't end up in jail, then." An older man she didn't recognize had remarked with a laugh. The woman next to him laughed, too, and Zoe figured she was supposed to think it was a joke. Very funny. Not.

"Or did you?"

Zoe didn't dignify the question with a response.

Other people were nicer—asked about her life in California, made sincere-sounding comments about Mack's passing.

On the one hand, she was genuinely surprised. She wondered if her gruff, antisocial grandfather had had any idea just how many people cared enough to turn up to say farewell. Or perhaps they were here for the free Lawson Estate wine on offer, her more cynical side couldn't help thinking. She did note that it was their table wine being poured, not their premium label, but even still.

She shook her head in bewilderment at some of the stories people were telling—her grandfather turning up to repair fences when George Armino had his tractor accident, donating wine as an auction prize to raise money for the primary school, sending his pickers to spend an extra day helping out the DiAngelos when they hadn't had enough cash to pay for their own.

Surely they were making it up? None of that sounded remotely like the grandfather she'd grown up with. Other stories—Mack turning the hose on a particularly persistent person who'd come to help him when he was sick—seemed more familiar.

People were curious about her, but again Zoe was surprised—Mack seemed to have shared some of her various moves and achievements with a couple of people. Which, in Tangawarra, meant everyone knew. He had talked about her current position as winemaker at the Golden Gate Estate in Napa; mentioned her work at wineries all around the world. When they'd had their occasional phone calls every year or two, he'd responded to her tales of what she'd been doing with little more than a grunt. If he'd been proud of her, she'd had no idea.

On the other hand, there was no mistaking her appeal as a novelty here today. The sly glances and hushed conversations where people looked at her, then looked away when she caught them staring. The constant stream of people wanting to talk to her, each subsequent person interrupting to ask the same round of intrusive questions, the same gleam in their eye. *How did a girl like you make it?* They all seemed to silently ask. Or maybe it was just her own paranoia. From an outsider's perspective it probably looked like pretty average curiosity about the naughty teenager who'd been sent away to get straightened out. And some of the people had been genuinely friendly and sweetly concerned for her. It was just so hard to let go of her ingrained memories of Tangawarra—and of the people who'd watched her live through some of the most miserable years of her life.

It was exhausting. Not only the nonstop chatter, but the constant second-guessing of herself. The only good thing was that Hugh Lawson had turned invisible—he'd organized this thing, dumped her in it and then disappeared. It annoyed her, even while she knew she should be grateful that he wasn't around to further upset her equilibrium.

Patricia appeared just as Zoe's polite smile was growing ragged around the edges.

"Zoe? Why don't you come over here with me and take a seat?"

Zoe could have hugged the woman in gratitude. She'd worn her heels—still thick with mud—figuring she'd be on her feet only an hour or so for the funeral. But now, after three hours, her toes were blistered and the balls of her feet were burning. Patricia steered her to a padded-leather bench seat that ran along one wall of the restaurant.

"Have you had anything to eat or drink?" Patricia fussed around her like a mother hen. Usually the attention would have made Zoe uncomfortable, but for the moment she was immensely grateful.

Zoe grimaced. "I haven't had a chance. Too many people want to grill me."

Patricia gave her a frowning look. "Grill? I don't think—"

Before she could finish, the crackling sound of a PA system interrupted. Someone blew into a microphone and the din of conversation in the room hushed.

"Hello? Hello? Is this thing on?"

A chorus of people yelled out that it was, in fact, on. A rotund man Zoe vaguely recognized struggled to stand on a chair and everyone turned to face him. Grateful for her seat, Zoe stayed where she was.

"We're here today to celebrate the life of Mack Waters."

A muted cheer went up and everyone held their wineglasses aloft.

"Mack kept himself to himself, but as many of you know, the Waters family were the original trailblazers of wine-making in this valley— a trail that many of us here today have followed. Mack carried on his family's tradition in his own way. He only ever sold his wine by mail order because, in his own words, it meant he'd never have to deal with any bloody customers." The portly man laughed at his own wit and an answering ripple of laughter ran around the room.

"We also know that although he wasn't a joiner, Mack was a part of this community in his own manner. He helped out his neighbors— well, some of them, anyway…"

The man paused for the wave of hushed tittering at his unsubtle reference to the long feud between the Lawson and Waters families—a matter that was widely known but rarely discussed publicly.

"…although I guess today goes some way to seeing *that* put to bed." He gestured to their surroundings. He didn't have to say anything more. A member of the Waters family being farewelled on Lawson Estate property spoke volumes in itself.

Zoe watched everyone nod. The lump in her throat rose again to block her windpipe, surprising her with its intensity. *No crying.* She tried to take deep breaths to hold the emotion at bay, but her chest just wouldn't expand properly.

"Mack also raised his granddaughter, Zoe, after Margie was killed in that awful car accident."

Zoe tried hard to ignore the fact that almost everyone in the room turned to look at her as they tut-tutted in what could only be fake sympathy. No one in Tangawarra had liked her mother, either.

She swallowed again, but the lump didn't move.

"We all know Zoe gave him a run for his money." He paused for a hearty chuckle that a few in the crowd joined. "But we also know that once she found her way onto the straight and narrow he was rightly proud of her. Mind you, she tested him—and most of us—along the way." Another jovial laugh. "I remember when she was fifteen and she was caught spraying graffiti on my store…"

That's where she knew him from. Frank from the hardware store. He'd just put on a lot of weight and aged ten years.

The room closed in. Her lungs seized. There was no air.

Whatever Frank said that caused another wave of laughter in the room passed her by as her ears buzzed with growing panic.

"Zoe, are you all right?" Patricia whispered nervously at her side.

"Now, Zoe," Frank boomed. It was clear he had no need of a microphone—that voice of his resonated in Zoe's bones without any kind of amplification. "It's your turn to come up and say a few words about your grandfather."

Zoe tried again, unsuccessfully, to take

a deep breath. She waved him off, even as a spattering of applause began, encouraging her to take the microphone. Zoe had done plenty of public speaking, led talks in front of many large groups—wine appreciation societies in the main. But now? Invisible bands tightened around her chest and her heart skipped and thudded as if it were about to grind to a halt.

"Come on, Zoe. Everyone wants to hear from you. Just a few words. Come on, lass."

"I—I have to get out of here…" she stammered to Patricia. "Fresh air…" She couldn't breathe; the temperature in the room had just gone up ten degrees.

"Leave the girl alone, Frank," Patricia called out. "She's had enough to deal with today."

She had to get away. Escape from the staring and the accusations and draw a breath. Zoe rushed from her seat and took a hurried step toward the nearest door. That was when the room blackened around her and her knees buckled.

CHAPTER THREE

Hugh had been watching proceedings from the sidelines. It had taken him a while to calm down his hot-tempered chef, furious that Hugh had sprung catering for a crowd of at least fifty on him with about ten minutes' notice. And right before a fully booked dinner service, too. As the chef had railed about the insanity of the idea, Hugh had been on autopilot, placating him while at the same time he was internally agreeing with him.

He'd made up some rational-sounding reasons, but the whole thing *was* crazy. Why was he doing this? As a tactic to warm Zoe Waters to the idea of selling Waterford to him, it had already failed miserably—her reaction in the car had told him that as much as her forced smile from across the room did now. He couldn't pinpoint why he'd thought it might work in the first place.

Mack Waters and he had certainly never been friends. The bitter enmity between Mack and Hugh's father, Pete Lawson, hadn't ended at his father's death—it had simply been transferred to Hugh. And, if anything, Hugh had even more reason to dislike the stubborn old goat. The cantankerous-but-kind-at-heart-if-you-look-hard-enough man people were speaking of today was not someone Hugh had ever known. Mack Waters had been cranky, vengeful, rude and argumentative.

Hugh had gone out of his way to try to move on from the past, to offer assistance as it became clear that Waterford was foundering under Mack's failing health. Mack hadn't even pretended to listen.

It didn't help that whenever he and Mack had tried to talk business they seemed to be stuck in a time warp. When they were forced to interact, Mack always treated Hugh as if he was still seventeen and Hugh found himself responding in kind. It frustrated him no end that no matter what he'd achieved in life—the money he'd made, the wine he'd created and sold around the world—as far as Mack was concerned, Hugh was still the boy who'd taken his granddaughter's innocence.

Hugh had never bothered to correct him, but in truth it had very much been the other way around. Zoe Waters had been like a thrilling adventure park in comparison to Hugh's sheltered upbringing and good-boy persona. She'd

introduced him to sex, drugs and rock 'n' roll—
not necessarily in that order. Mack Waters had
made it clear that he blamed Hugh for Zoe's
troubles. How the old man didn't see that those
troubles had begun long before Hugh had come
on the scene—and that Mack himself had had
a significant role to play—Hugh would never
know.

He gritted his teeth and surveyed the room of
people cheerily drinking his wine, toasting the
old man whose presence just across the fence
line had cast a shadow over Hugh's whole life.
He wouldn't be joining in the celebration. He'd
get on with his life, just as he had all these
years. And maybe now his long-held plans to
possess the Waterford Estate would finally
come to fruition.

There was just one fly in the ointment. She
was sitting across the room from him right now,
a strained smile on her face.

Watching Zoe, he was again struck by the
difference between the wild child he'd known
and the woman who appeared before him. A
woman who, if she'd been anyone else, Hugh
could admit he found attractive. Very attractive.

Her hair was its natural shiny brunette, none
of the bright purple or fire-engine red she'd
experimented with from time to time back at
school. There were some lighter streaks in it

now, probably the result of the California sunshine. Her makeup was restrained, no dark circles of kohl. She'd once liked to draw those on him, as well. She'd insisted it looked cool and that all the male rock stars wore makeup, but Hugh knew Tangawarra and knew that the town wasn't ready for boys in eyeliner. He'd always washed it off before anyone else had seen.

A smattering of freckles had appeared across her nose—they were new. Otherwise, her skin was still the pale creamy porcelain that he remembered.

Very pale.

A surprising stab of sympathy for Zoe shot through him as Frank appealed to her to get up and speak. He knew she'd hate doing anything of the sort. When he looked across at her, the stark terror on her face sent an unexpected wave of protectiveness through him. Even as he told himself to stay out of it, he found himself stepping forward, about to take the microphone from Frank to save Zoe from the spotlight.

But then she stood up and the blood drained from her face. Hugh knew what was going to happen a moment before it did. It was just like that day right before she'd left town when she'd had fainted in the corridor—only this time he wouldn't be carrying her to the school nurse.

In a few quick strides he was by her side,

scooping her into his arms as her knees collapsed and she fell.

Hugh took no notice of the collective gasp or the mutterings of concern in the room. Heading straight for the side door, he carefully maneuvered them out onto the small walkway that led into the Lawson Estate homestead and to his personal suite of rooms at the back.

He was aware of footsteps following him, but he didn't pause until he had carefully lowered Zoe onto the navy blue quilt of his bed.

"Is she all right?" Hugh turned and saw that Patricia was watching nervously from the doorway. She seemed to have adopted her neighbor for the time being.

"I think she's just fainted," Hugh said. "I'll just get Morris to—"

"I'm here." A burly man with a weathered face, Lawson Estate cap and graying beard appeared in the doorway clutching the estate's sizable medical kit. Morris was Hugh's foreman, in charge of the day-to-day operations of the Lawson Estate vineyards and had been for as long as Hugh could remember. He'd tended every kind of emergency Hugh could imagine, from tractor and machinery accidents to the scrapes and bumps of guests who'd overindulged and overbalanced. The man had also been witness to all the ins and outs of the Lawson family—from the minor to the traumatic—over the years.

Hugh stepped back to let Morris look over Zoe, while Patricia nattered on about Zoe not eating and having had a stressful day.

Hugh's stomach churned with a concern he didn't want to admit to. He sucked in a breath and blew it out, hating the faint nausea that had begun to stir in his gut.

He'd honestly thought he'd put everything to do with Zoe Waters and their tempestuous relationship behind him. The strength of his reaction to her was a surprise. Maybe he hadn't been so successful at processing all that history as he'd thought.

On one level it was impossible to comprehend that Zoe was lying on his bed, her hair on his pillow, her skin against his sheets. She was no longer the sixteen-year-old girl he'd seen lying like this in the nurse's office. She'd gained weight in the past ten years, but that wasn't quite the right way of putting it. It was more like she'd filled out—the curves that her teenage body had hinted at were fully developed now. A lush, hourglass figure was outlined by her clingy top and tight skirt, cinched at the waist with a skinny, patent leather belt. The skirt had hitched up as he'd carried her and a set of stunning legs in black stockings were on display.

Part of him wished she was just another customer—someone who'd overindulged on chardonnay or stayed out in the sun too long. He could patch her up, get her on her feet again, then ask for her phone number. They could go on a date and have the kind of short-lived, intensely physical relationship he preferred.

He cursed under his breath. He shouldn't have brought her to his bedroom—he wouldn't have brought any other guest here.

"She'll be all right," Morris declared matter-of-factly, bringing Hugh back from his daydream. "I'd say her blood sugar's a bit low. Just needs to eat and drink something when she comes 'round. I'll get the kitchen to organize something."

"Good," Hugh said, feeling a genuine rush of relief at Morris's words.

"You need me to hang around awhile?" Morris asked. There was a strange inflection in his words and Hugh looked at him sharply.

"Why?"

"No reason. Just askin'. You look like you—"

"Everything's fine," Hugh interrupted harshly. He had no desire to hear what Morris thought. Unusual, because Morris was one person whose opinion Hugh trusted implicitly.

Thankfully, Morris didn't do more than twitch an eyebrow at Hugh's imperious tone before giving a short nod acknowledging his boss's bidding.

"You must be busy, Hugh. I'll sit with her," Patricia offered.

"No." He ran a hand through his hair, frustrated to be once again losing his usual cool because of Zoe Waters. "I mean, it's fine. Patricia, please go back and tell everyone that Zoe's okay, but that it's time for the party to come to an end." He turned to his foreman. "Morris, once you've placed the order with the kitchen, show everyone out and then organize the staff to get the dining room cleared and reset before the dinner crowd arrives." The world calmed a little as he gave orders and took control.

"Of course." Patricia shuffled out with a pleased look on her face. Hugh knew she couldn't wait to get back to the restaurant and have her little moment of fame as everyone hung on her news. Patricia meant well and did a lot for the town, but sometimes her tendency to gossip overwhelmed her common sense.

Morris gave a brusque nod and went off to carry out his orders.

Hugh pulled up a chair and sat heavily. He waited for a moment, watching Zoe's breasts rise and fall, trying hard not to wonder whether they'd changed, too. He made his voice as unaffected as it could be. "It's okay, they're gone now."

Zoe blinked, and after a moment shuffled on the bed a little, rearranging her skirt more modestly and propping her head up on the pillow. "How did you know?" she asked, not looking at him.

"You started holding on." She'd been a dead weight until they'd reached the bedroom, then she'd stirred against him; the arm that had been thrown around his shoulders had gripped him tightly.

"Ah." She didn't sound surprised.

"It's just like last time," he said, not understanding the impulse.

She stiffened. "No, it's not."

One of his staff members appeared with a tray. "Mr. Lawson? Morris asked me to bring this up. Is the lady awake? He wanted to know if she was still unconscious."

"I'm awake," Zoe answered before Hugh could.

"Leave it and get out," he ordered.

"Uh, fine." The waiter looked startled at the harsh words from his usually friendly boss, put the tray at the end of the bed and beat a hasty retreat.

"Drink this."

Hugh reached for the coffee mug on the tray

and handed it to Zoe. She sat up and pushed a pillow behind her back, accepting the cup meekly.

She grimaced after taking a sip. "Ew, too sweet."

"You need the sugar. Drink it."

Zoe took another few sips and Hugh was relieved to see some color return to her cheeks. She reached for a plate of biscuits and nibbled on a chocolate chip cookie.

"I guess you're right," Hugh said, returning to the conversation that had been interrupted when the waiter had arrived.

Zoe's forehead crinkled in a frown. Was she deliberately avoiding the topic?

"It's not like school," he said. "After all, we're adults now. Grown up. Responsible for our own actions."

Her frown deepened. Hugh himself wasn't even sure what he was trying to say.

Zoe's eyes dropped from his and she shifted uncomfortably. "Well, I'm fine, so I guess I'll—" She threw her legs over the side of the bed and began to stand up, staggering almost as soon as she was on her feet.

Hugh jumped up and put a restraining arm around her shoulders. Now he knew exactly what he wanted to say. "Don't be an idiot. You fainted a minute ago. Sit down." He pushed her back down, but he didn't need to use much force. She was trembling and as weak as a kitten. Once she was leaning against the pillows again, she drew a shaky breath.

Hugh tugged his chair closer to the bed and sat. Anxiety was still unsettling his gut, although he couldn't put his finger on why.

She managed a weak, mocking laugh. "Don't worry, Hugh, I'm not about to throw a tantrum or pull out a razor blade."

He cursed himself for being so easy to read. But then, to her, he always had been. He'd just thought he'd learned to hide his inner thoughts better in the intervening years. "I want…I want you to be okay," he finished lamely.

She smiled then, sad and sweet. "You always were too nice," she said, almost to herself.

"Not really," he said.

She studied him curiously for a while and Hugh couldn't bring himself to look away. If it was possible for ten years of hurt to be conveyed in someone's eyes, then Zoe had mastered it.

When she spoke, her voice was soft. "Hugh, it was all a long time ago. We're both very different people now."

He certainly hoped so. They were going to have to find a way to deal with each other without this massive lump of history coming between them. He wanted to buy Waterford—that meant discussions, negotiations, meetings. Interactions he intended to conduct as an adult, not an angry and broken-hearted seventeen-year-old.

But despite his best intentions, a flash of fury from back then revived itself somewhere deep inside him. It was wrong, so wrong, to be angry with someone for something they couldn't control. Zoe had been sick. Mental illness was a disease just like cancer—intellectually he understood that. Emotionally, the idea that she'd tried to take her life again after she'd *promised*...

"Mack told me you were lucky to survive," he said. *So much for leaving the past in the past.*

Her eyes became glassy. Not with tears, but with a sadness that was beyond crying. "That's not quite true. It took a few weeks to recover, but I was eventually okay—healthwise."

He noted her modifier, didn't know what to say about it. "Good. I'm, uh, glad to hear it." *Cringe.* Hugh scrubbed a hand across his mouth. His business goals evaporated. Suddenly, more than anything, he needed to talk about it. Let her know how hard it had been on him—how doing the right thing had felt like the worst thing possible. He wasn't sure if talking would make it any better, but it would be something.

"Zoe? I..." He blew out a breath. "Christ, this is hard."

"Don't say it." She looked almost...*frightened*.

Of what? "What?"

She looked down at her hands, her fingers twisting together. "Don't apologize. I couldn't bear it. Not now."

Apologize? No, that wasn't what he'd been about to do. "But I—"

She didn't let him finish. "It's too late," she said simply.

His shoulders slumped. "Yeah, I know." She was right. They should leave it alone.

A thick silence fell over the room.

"Why?" Her voice was barely more than a breath.

"Why what?"

"Why didn't you come for me? I called so many times, wrote letters when my emails to your account bounced..."

He ignored the email comment—he'd deactivated his account on instruction from his father and Mack. But letters? "I didn't get any letters."

"You didn't..." She sighed heavily. "Your dad."

Hugh nodded. Pete Lawson would have made

sure that any mail from Zoe didn't reach Hugh. He'd probably thought he was helping. "Yeah, I guess."

"But I called." Her voice held no accusation; it was a simple statement of fact.

"I know. But, Zoe, I was doing what I thought was best. They told me it would be better for your recovery if I didn't speak to you. And…" Oh, this was hard. On a scale of one to ten, this sucked pole.

"You still believed what Jason told you."

It sounded so juvenile now. Hell, it had been juvenile at the time, he'd just been too young to realize it.

"What is Jason up to these days?" Zoe asked mildly.

"Accountant. Married, with a kid, I think. Lives in Melbourne. I don't see him much. He came out here a couple of years ago to visit the winery—that was probably the last time."

"You guys were best friends."

"Yeah." The friendship hadn't survived Zoe's betrayal—fictional or otherwise. And it certainly hadn't survived Hugh's guilt. He and Jason had stopped being friends the day after Zoe's collapse.

"I didn't, you know. Not with him. Not with anyone else when we were together. Just in case you were still wondering." She sounded so calm.

Hugh managed a tight smile. "I wasn't." Although, if he was honest he'd never been completely sure. Jason was full of shit, but Zoe had earned her bad-girl reputation. And she'd been the first—and only—girl Hugh had lost his heart to. Even the *idea* of her infidelity had been enough to send a blood haze over his vision. His teenage rage had been a scary thing—to both himself and Zoe, he was sure.

"But you were fine," he said, deliberately not making it a question, ready for this conversation to end. Zoe's still countenance and her calm, monotone voice were becoming unnerving.

She gave a strange, bleak laugh. "Oh, I don't think I was ever *fine* again, actually. But I get by."

Ah, shit. Had he intended this conversation to make him feel better? Because that hadn't happened so far.

"Did you cut yourself again? Or was it something else?" The question blurted itself out without Hugh's conscious permission. "Sorry, you don't have to answer that."

For the first time, her Stepford-wife-like composure seemed to slip. "What do you mean?"

"Nothing. Sorry, I shouldn't have asked."

Zoe sat up straighter in bed. "No, no. This is important. Why did you ask that?"

Hugh sighed what felt like his hundredth sigh for the day. He kicked himself yet again for starting down this path in the first place. "I guess…I guess I asked because it's been bothering me, not knowing what you'd done." That was part of it, but he couldn't quite put his finger on the true source of his unease about Zoe's disappearance. Let alone express it.

She swung her legs over the bed to sit up, her face a picture of the kind of deadly seriousness that had always made Hugh's heart pound. She'd worn that expression when she'd talked about her plans to get away from Tangawarra, from her grandfather, when she'd talked about her first suicide attempt at thirteen, when she'd told him she loved him.

"Hugh—we had a fight, right?"

"Yeah." Ten years ago and he still remembered it in high definition. Jason had just dropped his bombshell. Then Zoe walked up, all urgent and panicked looking. *I need to talk to you.* Oh, he'd needed to talk to her, too. He'd needed to yell. The fight had been momentous. Zoe had denied everything so vehemently she'd worked herself into hysterics.

"And then you passed out."

"You took me to the nurse."

Hugh nodded. "And then, after Mack took you home, you…you did it again. He wouldn't tell me how. But I guess I figured…" He gestured towards her wrists.

Zoe shook her head, eyes wide. "Oh, no."

The ground shifted under Hugh's feet at her expression. "What?" he asked nervously.

"Is that what Mack told you? That I tried to kill myself again?"

The weird anxiety in Hugh's belly stepped into high gear. He had a feeling that whatever was coming, it wasn't going to be good. "That's what both Mack and my father told me." He paused. "You didn't?" he asked, not entirely sure he wanted to know the answer.

"Oh, Hugh. Mack sent me away because I was pregnant."

SHOCK MADE THE TRUTH come tumbling out before Zoe could reel it in. The full weight of the grief and distress of those twelve months after she'd been banished from Tangawarra crashed down on her all over again. And Hugh hadn't even known?

"Pregnant?" Hugh blurted. He was gripping the seat of his chair as if he might fall off.

She couldn't speak, so simply nodded. A hot tear spilled down her cheek. It surprised her so much she swiped at it and stared at the telltale moisture on her fingertip. Tears? Really? An edge of panic rose inside her. She couldn't cry. Not now. Not ever. Because if she did, Zoe genuinely feared she might not be able to stop.

"What? But...*what?*" His eyes popped as his voice rose.

She struggled to calm her ragged breathing, blinked up at the ceiling to force the treacherous tears away. "You didn't know." It wasn't a question.

If someone had told her that a five-minute conversation could shatter some of the foundations on which she'd built her life, Zoe would never have believed them. But here she was....

"Of *course* I didn't know." His anger began to surface again, knuckles white against the chair. "Why didn't you tell me?" he demanded.

"I tried!" she protested. "What do you think I needed to talk to you about that day? But you started in on me about cheating on you with Jason. You didn't give me a chance and I..."

She threw her hands in the air at the futility of at all. Too late. It was all just far too late.

That last day was a blur. She'd fainted at school after working herself into a state arguing with Hugh. Hugh, ever proper, had carried her to the nurse's office. After he'd gone back to class, the nurse—a stern, severe woman—had asked a lot of questions. Zoe's confession prompted the scowling woman to make Zoe take a pregnancy test, confirming her own suspicions. Then her grandfather had been called in and she'd been taken home, the older man stony silent in the car beside her.

That night, Mack locked Zoe in her bedroom, the first time he'd ever resorted to such a measure, even though she'd given him plenty of reasons before then. She could have climbed out the window if she'd wanted, but fear kept her captive.

Instead she lay there, rigid with terror, listening to her grandfather make phone call after phone call. Then Hugh's father arrived and the two men had spoken, too quietly for Zoe to overhear. Strange, because usually they yelled at each other, if they spoke at all.

The following morning Mack made her pack a bag as she sobbed her protest, and next thing she knew she was on the train to Sydney. Her great-aunt Maureen's disgust and heavily worn martyrdom had been waiting on the platform for her when she arrived.

"Mack and my father told me you went to a…to somewhere to get psychiatric care," Hugh muttered, almost to himself. "And then you were going to a girls' school in Sydney that was designed to help girls like…" He trailed off. When he spoke again his voice was firmer.

"They told me that after you recovered you ran away, overseas."

"Well, that bit was true." Why the lies? The sweet tea and chocolatey biscuit she'd consumed formed a solid ball in her stomach. "That must have been the story Mack and your dad agreed on. What on earth were they thinking?" She didn't understand how Mack or Pete Lawson could think a suicide attempt less scandalous than a teenage pregnancy.

Hugh still looked stunned. "The suicide part of it was a secret—they told everyone else you went to a girls' school in Sydney. But why would they tell me you tried to kill yourself?"

Zoe shrugged, just as baffled as he appeared, still too deeply in shock to reason out past motivations.

"Pregnant," Hugh said again. His eyebrows drew together and he leaned forward. "Does this mean you...I...we have..." He broke off and swallowed hard. "Where's the child?"

His voice was strangled and Zoe couldn't interpret the look in his eyes. Panic? Longing? Fear?

Zoe's mouth compressed in a tight line. "You don't have anything to worry about, Hugh. There's no illegitimate Lawson offspring running around out there, waiting to make a claim on your fortune." It took every ounce of her dwindling strength to get the next words out without shattering into tiny pieces. "Our baby died."

Hugh recoiled as if she'd slapped him, but just as quickly his face shuttered down into its usual mask of impenetrable cool.

Zoe battled against a rising tide of panic. Breaking down now—or ever—would be of no help, but this conversation had her feeling like she was on the edge of a very high precipice. What she had to do was get through the next few weeks then sell Waterford and get the hell out of town. She'd endeavor to do that with as little contact with anyone else as possible.

"I can't believe they lied to me. I can't believe they kept us apart," he said under his breath.

Hugh stood and paced over to the French doors that led out to a small terrace and showcased the vines beyond. His impressive silhouette made something inside Zoe clench.

"I know why Mack and my father came up with that story," he said bitterly. "They knew I'd go after you," he added more quietly.

Why didn't you? A tiny, traitorous voice inside Zoe wanted to wail. *Why didn't you come for me when I needed you most? You weren't there when our beautiful daughter was born, when she was laid in my arms, not breathing, but exquisitely perfect.*

When I was so alone.

The dangerous thoughts made her shudder, even as she shook her head in quiet denial. She'd known, by then—even not knowing what lies he'd been told—that he wouldn't come. After her unanswered calls, after her desperate, unsuccessful attempts to reach him. If there was one thing she'd already learned, it was that even in her most desperate hour, the only person she could rely on was herself.

And by then, she'd reached a kind of peace with his silence. In a way, it was almost better that she'd never spoken to him—because at least then she could secretly cling to the hope that he *might* come—than to know he'd rejected her, just as her grandfather had told her he would.

Hugh stood ramrod straight. "Your disappearance was big gossip at school for a while, as you can imagine. I kept up the pretense, just said you were sent to a girls' school in Sydney. Everyone was speculating on the reasons." He barked a short, black laugh. "No one went with 'pregnant,' though."

"No, I guess they didn't. According to what I heard out there, most people were betting on jail." She tried to sound as if it didn't matter, but knew she failed. It was time to get out of here—away from this hellish reminiscing.

Zoe stood up gingerly, testing her weight, but the dizziness had passed.

Hugh didn't so much as turn around to see if she was okay.

She swallowed hard and willed her voice not to waver. "Thank you for the first aid and thank you for the wake, although I know Mack is turning in his grave at the very idea."

Hugh could have been carved from granite. He acknowledged her thanks with a grunt. Zoe wasn't sure what to do. A silly, juvenile part of her wanted to throw herself into his arms and sob, to cry with him over the loss of their child, to have him hold her again, to be surrounded by his scent and cradled in his protective embrace. A stupid instinct—it wouldn't change anything.

She stared for a moment at his frozen posture. What was going through his mind right now? She'd been living with the knowledge for ten years and the sharp edges were as jagged as ever. She couldn't imagine what it would be like to have it dumped in one blow.

He deserved some comfort.

Pity she had none to give.

Zoe slipped her still-aching toes into her stilettos and made for the door. She wanted to get out before everyone left, beg someone to give her a lift back to Waterford. There was no way she could cope being in that little sports car with Hugh again.

CHAPTER FOUR

NOT LOOKING BACK TO see whether Hugh turned away from the windows, Zoe headed down the corridor. Her pace increased as a strange kind of panic enveloped her until she was almost running, desperate to escape. By the time she made it to the empty car park, her breath was coming in pants.

"Damn." She swore as she glanced around. The only vehicles left were Hugh's coupe and a couple of Lawson Estate utes.

"Need a lift?" Morris appeared from around the side of a building. He'd been Lawson Estate's foreman as long as she could remember, and it was somehow comforting that he was still around. He wore jeans, a checkered blue shirt and a Lawson Estate cap pulled low on his forehead. His graying, unkempt beard covered most of his face, but his eyes were as bright and shrewd as they'd always been—she'd guess he didn't miss much.

"Yes, please." Zoe hated asking for favors, and didn't want to be any more indebted to

Lawson Estate than she already was with this farce of a wake, but Tangawarra didn't have a taxi service. And although Waterford was next door it would be a painful twenty-minute walk in her stupid shoes. Not to mention in the rain that had finally begun to spatter from the dark clouds overhead.

"Jump in." Morris tilted his head toward one of the utes and Zoe gratefully clambered in. She was even more grateful when he started it up and drove her home without speaking. Polite small talk was beyond her.

"Thank you." Zoe reached for the door handle.

"Zoe?" Morris broke his silence just as she was about to open the door and jump out. She paused a moment.

"Yes?"

"I remember you from when you was a kid."

Zoe sagged with the physical and mental exhaustion of the past few days. She didn't have the energy for any further trips down memory lane. "I'm sorry," she said, her tone resigned. "For whatever it was I might have done to annoy you."

"Nah, it wasn't like that. Do you remember when I caught you and Hugh?"

A wash of memory flooded through her. "Oh, God. The tractor shed." Her cheeks burned. *So embarrassing.* She folded her arms over her chest, feeling as naked now as she'd been then.

"Been wondering all these years whether I did the right thing by not turning you kids in."

"We… I was very grateful that you didn't."

He shot her a quick, avuncular smile. "I always liked ya. You had spunk. Weren't gonna let a small town grind away your individuality."

That was one way to look at it, Zoe guessed. Just a pity no one else shared his perspective. "Uh, thanks, I suppose." She opened the door and climbed out, holding on to the vehicle for balance as she found her feet on the muddy ground.

"You were a good influence on the boy," Morris said, raising his voice to be sure she heard him.

At that, Zoe started in genuine surprise. "I'm pretty sure you're the only one who thought so."

Morris's eyes were kind. "He was in danger of being a spoiled little brat, if you ask me. Being friends with you changed that."

Zoe's fragile composure began to crack. She stared down at the grass and took a moment's pause, to be sure her voice wouldn't betray her. "I guess our…*friendship* changed both of us," she said eventually.

"Hugh ain't the one to blame, Zoe. Don't take it out on him."

Zoe looked up from watching her Italian leather heels sink slowly into the soggy ground, startled. Of course, anyone from the Lawson side would be defending Hugh. Morris had no idea what had really happened. Although it was long past the time for blame games, Zoe hated the twist in her gut that reminded her of her outraged teen self.

It might not be Hugh's fault, but it wasn't *her* fault, either.

"Right," she managed to say through gritted teeth. A teenage impulse urged her to yell and insult this man who'd butted in where he didn't belong. But she was too tired, too emotionally drained to be bothered. "Thanks for the lift," she muttered, before giving the door a solid shove to slam it shut, expressing herself physically instead of verbally. She marched into the house, slamming that door, as well.

As the ute drove off, the storm broke and a deluge of rain hit the tin roof of the house. She sank to the floor, curling up against the cold, cracked linoleum. She shivered and just tried to remember to breathe.

AND THE HITS JUST KEPT ON COMING.

The conversation Zoe had had with Stephen Carter, her grandfather's accountant rang in her ears for the next two hours.

Waterford was on the verge of bankruptcy.

The options the accountant had presented still burned in her belly. Sell up now, or find some extra money—from somewhere—if she wanted to bottle the final Waterford vintage as she'd promised Mack. Stephen was strongly in favor of selling—he had a buyer all lined up and everything.

That buyer just happened to be Hugh Lawson.

Zoe should have known.

Holding the wake for Mack hadn't been some altruistic community gesture on Hugh's part. It had been a ploy, a gambit to butter her up so he could get his hands on Waterford, just as his father had been trying to do for decades. As a tactic it hadn't been successful—Zoe had hated every minute of it and Hugh really didn't know her anymore if he hadn't realized that.

Seemed like Hugh had grown up to become the spitting image of his dad: an ambitious, heartless, money-grabbing industrialist, more interested in the financial rewards than the art and science of viticulture and wine-making.

Zoe sighed as she put the groceries away and leaned against the counter, surveying the decrepit kitchen.

When she'd first arrived back in Australia everything had seemed so clear. Say goodbye to her grandfather. Organize his funeral. Settle his estate. Get back to California as fast as possible.

Only she hadn't bet on the old man hanging on for a few days. Long enough to extract promises from her. Promises that even at the time she hadn't wanted to keep. Why she felt she owed Mack any loyalty at all was a mystery she hadn't yet unraveled.

And yet now that she was here, standing on Waterford soil once again, something deep inside her railed at the idea of directly countering his instructions. Could she sell Waterford to her grandfather's lifelong enemy in direct contrast to his wishes? See it swallowed up by Lawson Estate, disappear as if it had never existed, the way so many other smaller vineyards in the valley had been?

Not to mention the more immediate issue: would she be able to fulfill Mack's request to finish his last-ever vintage before she sold Waterford? He'd been under no illusion that Zoe had returned to take over from him. Just begged her to please see the last of his wine into bottles. Then sell up and leave, finish Waterford on a high.

Her grandfather had been specific about that, too: the Waterford name was not to be sold, only the property. Waterford would not be Waterford without a member of the Waters family at the helm. At least that was something Zoe could agree with.

More than a century of her family's heritage, gone at the stroke of a pen. Even if it was a family she felt no real connection to, it was the only one she had.

Maybe that was why she felt so conflicted.

After putting the groceries away, Zoe grabbed a coat and headed outside. With a notepad and pencil, she walked around the property and all its rickety sheds, taking an inventory of everything she found. She quickly realized that she could have made the list from memory. Nothing had changed in ten years. A couple of pieces of machinery had been updated—there was a new pump and a new pile-driver attachment for the tractor—but otherwise everything was the same. Only older, more run-down, more rusted and decayed.

The shed that housed the winery was chilled and held the sharp smell of young wine, oak barrels, acid and bleach. Her grandfather had been a stickler for cleanliness in the winery. He'd been in the hospital for several weeks before he'd died, and no one had tended to anything in that time. But unlike the house, which Zoe had spent some hours that morning scrubbing, the winery still seemed pristine. Old-fash-

ioned and worn out, like the rest of the place,
but clean.

Zoe stood and stared at the rack of wine
barrels that lined one side of the shed. Waterford had never made a fortune, Zoe had always
known that. She'd never gone without the ba-
sics as a child, but she'd never had luxuries or
indulgences, either. Partly because there wasn't
a lot of money to go around, partly because her
grandfather was frugal to the point of mean-
ness. No wonder she'd shoplifted nail polish—
Mack would never have bought something so
frivolous and the ten dollars a month for "wom-
en's things" that Mack allowed her certainly
didn't stretch to treats.

The winery was Mack's priority. Every dol-
lar went back into it. Although his wine was
critically acclaimed as one of Australia's best,
Waterford was run on a shoestring. Mack refused to irrigate his vines to increase his grape
crop, claiming it would water down his wine.
He never did any of the marketing or publicity
that would allow his boutique Shiraz to become
an "investment" wine. He refused to open a
cellar door to passersby to increase his trade.

Mack's fans said it was because he was a pur-
ist, interested in nothing but making the perfect wine.

Mostly, Zoe reckoned, it was because the old

man simply didn't like people, and by keeping things small he didn't have to bother with having employees or advisors.

Waterford's Shiraz was sold by mailing list to a discerning group of loyal buyers who, Zoe was sure, had no doubt they were getting a bargain. They sold out every year.

And yet, the place was practically bankrupt.

"The income from each vintage just paid for the next one," Stephen Carter had explained. "Mack had some savings, but those were eaten up by medical bills. There's nothing left, and there are more than a few outstanding debts, including the mortgage on the property that your grandfather took out back when your grandmother was sick. And, for example, my bills with regard to his estate." Stephen had had the good grace to look slightly embarrassed. "I'm sorry, Zoe, but once you sell and pay off the debts, there won't be anything left over."

Zoe ran a hand along the smooth surface of one of the oak barrels. "Oh, Mack." She sighed, her voice echoing dully from the concrete floor and tin walls.

She grabbed a glass pipette and tasted each barrel carefully. As the ruby red liquid swirled around her mouth, she smiled in rueful amazement. She had no idea how her ailing grandfather had managed it, but he'd created yet another magnificent wine. A pang of family pride and professional jealousy rushed through her as she found Mack's notebook and flicked through his meandering scribbles.

The wine needed to be racked off—the barrels emptied and cleaned before the wine was returned to them—and then bottled. It wasn't impossible to do on her own, but it would be difficult, dirty and time-consuming.

It was a reminder of her dilemma.

There was no money to hire help, no money to pay for the bottling. The existing debts made further borrowing impossible. And Zoe had no nest egg of her own to reach into. She lived from paycheck to paycheck and was perfectly okay with that. As long as she had enough for food, shelter and an occasional bottle of good wine, she didn't care. She never stayed anywhere long enough to put down the kind of roots that would require significant purchases.

She rested a hand on the smooth oak barrel, the wine flavor lingering in her mouth. Her only option was to sell immediately, but that meant breaking her promise to produce one last Waterford vintage for her grandfather.

The grandfather she'd barely tolerated during her teenage years, and barely spoken to since. What did it matter? Mack was dead. He would never know.

There would be no last Waterford vintage. It was just impossible.

Zoe sighed. Heading back to the kitchen to put on the kettle and make a cup of tea, she tried to rationalize the decision that for some reason sat uneasily within her.

It's not your problem.

It's not like Waterford means anything to you.

It's not like Mack will know. And even if he did—she imagined him peering down at her from the clouds, that familiar disapproving frown etched on his face—*why do you care?*

Zoe sat on the back step of the farmhouse, her hands clasped around her mug of tea for warmth and comfort.

She shivered as a gust of wind whooshed through the yard, making the shed door bang and a tangle of litter rise in a dusty whirlwind before settling back over the unkempt ground.

Zoe drained the last of her tea, standing up and wrapping her cardigan tighter around her as she headed back inside the dilapidated house.

Decision made. She'd instruct Stephen Carter to sell up, pay out Waterford's debts and give anything left over—however measly—to charity. Something to support teen mothers, just for the hell of it. And she would book a plane ticket back to California and leave all of this behind. In the past. Where it belonged.

IT WAS A NORMAL DAY on the Lawson Estate, which meant that by midday Hugh had already been working for more than six hours.

He started the morning checking his stocks on the internet and talking with his trader in Sydney. At eight, Morris and the operational crew for the vineyards held their weekly meeting—this morning the hot topic was security, and how to stop enthusiastic and/or drunken visitors from wandering around the vines, potentially damaging them or, worse, introducing pests to the vulnerable plants.

Then his advertising agency had come to present a campaign for the new Lawson Estate sparkling rosé—a light and pretty wine they were targeting squarely at the female market. The hope was to have it out in time for the Melbourne Spring Racing Carnival, when the whole country gorged itself on celebratory bubbles. After that there'd been a distribution bungle to sort out, a complaint from one of their largest buyers—an airline—about lopsided labeling on the last shipment. And, just now, an intoxicated winery visitor angry about being refused service.

Hugh headed back to his office after escorting the staggering man out to the car park. The man's friends had been embarrassed, and once

Hugh had been sure that he wasn't driving, he'd left them to sort it out.

Usually Hugh strode through the day with energy and confidence, seeing any challenge as a hurdle to be overcome with perseverance and charm.

But not today.

He'd yelled at the trader for missing a deal, dismissed the concerns of the operational staff with a wave of his hand and sent the ad agency back to the drawing board. He'd left the bottling company in little doubt as to his fury about the labeling mistake, and had barely managed to rein in his temper when dealing with the visitor. Drunk before noon from wine tasting—Hugh had trouble hiding his disgust for the guy.

He sank into his executive leather chair and let out a sigh. Someone had placed a steaming caffe latte on his desk and disappeared—apparently word about the boss's foul mood had circulated fast.

For a multimillion-dollar business, Lawson Estate still operated with a relatively small staff, and Hugh liked to think that they were a good team. Usually he ended each day with a glass of wine and the satisfaction of a job well done.

But not anymore, it seemed.

Yesterday his world had been turned upside down. Everything that had seemed so clear was suddenly fuzzy and out of focus. He still had no idea how he felt about Zoe's revelations about the past and what, if anything, the whole thing meant.

He was angry, that was for sure. But with whom?

Last night, as sleep eluded him, Mack Waters had been his main target. Even though his father was just as culpable, Hugh wasn't ready to face that betrayal. Instead he'd spent the night wishing his misanthropic old neighbor could come back from the dead, just so Hugh could look him straight in the eyes as he sent the traitorous old git back to his lonely grave with his bare hands.

"Boss?" Morris knocked on the open door before walking in. Hugh was certain that was the first time the man had ever knocked. He made an effort to arrange his face into a blank mask.

"What's up?" He strove for pleasant, rather than annoyed, but was fairly sure he didn't succeed.

Hugh had fought and lost the battle over Morris calling him "Boss." The man was at least twenty years older and had been almost a second father to him. "Boss" was what Morris had called Pete Lawson, and when Hugh had taken over, a gradual process that had begun when he was eighteen and reached its conclusion when he was twenty-four and his father had suffered his stroke, Morris had transferred the title to Hugh.

"Just wanted to let you know that the kitchen's all set for the lunch service, though we're only half booked. Hopefully the sunshine'll bring us a few drop-ins. And the fencin' around the dam's done, so I let the guys go early."

Hugh gave a short nod of acknowledgment. "Good. Thanks."

He expected Morris to leave, but instead the foreman dropped into the chair opposite his desk with a groan. "My knee's giving me curry," he said, wincing.

"You should get it looked at."

Morris flicked a hand dismissively. "The doc says it's just 'cause I'm getting old."

Hugh couldn't help but smile. "Surely you're not doing anything like that."

"Doin' my best not to."

Hugh didn't want to think too much about it. Morris was the one person who'd been there through most of his life. And although they maintained a careful employer/employee balance, the relationship went a lot deeper than that—for both of them, Hugh was sure.

"I saw you lookin' at the photos this morning."

"Yeah?" Hugh tried to sound as if he didn't

care that he'd been caught. This morning, in the wine-tasting room, he'd found himself stopping to look at the carefully arranged wall of framed photos surrounding the bulging trophy cabinet.

The display was for visitors, depicting the history and achievements of Lawson Estate. Hugh couldn't remember the last time he'd really looked at it.

There was a photo of his mother in the early days of the vineyard, a soft, gentle woman who'd died from breast cancer not long before he and Zoe had gotten together. She'd been sick for so many years, Hugh didn't have many memories of her healthy.

There were photos of his father: community leader, businessman, autocrat, founder of Lawson Estate. He'd suffered a stroke just after Hugh had finished university and then slowly declined until a second, massive stroke had killed him. The end had been a relief, mostly. Watching his powerful father struggling to take care of himself had been painful to watch.

"Your mum was such a lovely woman." Morris sounded a little wistful.

Hugh nodded. "Yeah, I still wonder how she put up with Dad."

As teenagers, he and Zoe had been able to bond over their shared parental pain, although their pain had different causes. Listening to

Zoe, Hugh had often gone home and been just a tiny bit thankful for his father's watchfulness, his *where have you been* inquisitions. Because Zoe didn't face anything like that when she got home. At first, Hugh had been jealous. Then he saw what it did to her—knowing no one cared.

"She loved him, I guess," Morris said. "That counts for a lot."

Hugh couldn't help a sad smile. "Yeah. She did." His mother had been warm and loving to the end.

"And he loved her, in his own way."

Yeah, that was probably accurate. Pete Lawson did everything his own way, even loving his family. "Dad was a pain in the ass sometimes."

As much as Hugh loved Lawson Estate, he often wondered how his life might have turned out if he'd had half a chance to make his own decisions. But Pete Lawson hadn't even considered that his son might have a mind of his own. After he'd died, when Hugh could have struck out and done something different, there were all these people to consider: Lawson Estate employees, customers, suppliers. So many people whose livelihoods depended on Hugh stepping up and making things right. So that's what he'd done. What he continued to do—build a business so strong that he was able to provide security for all those people and their families.

Owning Waterford was another important step in that strategy.

Morris shrugged one shoulder. "Pete, well, he just…wanted things the way he wanted 'em."

No kidding. Particularly when Hugh had been a teen. And right now, he didn't feel one little bit grateful or thankful for his father's interference in his life. Zoe had *not* been a fragile, mentally ill girl who needed help, and most importantly, distance from the boy who'd pushed her over the edge—the story his father had told. She'd been pregnant. With Hugh's child.

Just thinking about it made his stomach tilt.

His father may have intended to protect him, but Hugh only felt betrayed.

"Well, I'd better get movin'." Morris stood up, groaning and rubbing at his knee again.

"You really should get that knee checked," Hugh repeated.

"Is that an order?" Morris asked with a cocked eyebrow.

"Yes—but it's for your own good."

Morris gave a low chuckle. "Ah, that'd be one o' those things that line the road to hell."

Hugh started to object, but quickly gave up.

Morris turned to go, but paused at the door. "Oh, and Boss?" Morris quirked up one side of his mouth in what might have been a smile. "Might wanna try takin' it easy with the natives. Pr'haps you need an afternoon off, too. Go sort out a few things."

Hugh's lips tightened into a straight line and he watched the other man retreat. Morris had a way of getting straight to the point.

Hugh drained the hot coffee, relishing the burn as it went down.

Without conscious thought, he reached for the set of keys on the side of the desk and headed for the car park.

CHAPTER FIVE

THERE WAS NO SIGN OF ZOE when Hugh pulled up behind the farmhouse at Waterford. Her car was there, so he knew she'd be around, perhaps in one of the sheds or out checking the vines.

He made a quick reconnoiter of the buildings, calling her name once. No answer. He knocked at the farmhouse, trying the door when he got no response. It opened and he leaned inside, calling out Zoe's name again, but again there was no answer.

Where could she be?

He regretted not changing into the casual Lawson Estate "uniform" of jeans, boots and a branded button-down shirt after his meeting with the ad execs, but there was no helping that now. Hugh ignored the mud building up on his expensive leather loafers and the splatters on his suit trousers and headed into the rows of grapevines.

In hibernation for winter, the precious plants were nothing but dried, twisted sticks; desiccated and dead-looking, they held no hint of their ability to produce plump fruit and lush green foliage when spring returned.

The vines had thick trunks and had been artfully trained, testament to their age, hardiness and the skill of their now-deceased caretaker. Hugh ran a hand over a rough, twiggy branch. They really were some of the best vines in the valley. They deserved to be protected as part of Lawson Estate's holdings.

He scanned the vineyard. The bare vines left nowhere to hide. He still couldn't see Zoe. The paddock slanted down toward the creek then ran through both Waterford and Lawson Estate, hidden by the eucalypts and shrubs that grew along the bank.

No.

She wouldn't.

And yet Hugh found himself striding past the end of the rows of vines, ducking under a low-hanging branch as he drew closer to the creek. The sound of trickling water came to him over the rustle of leaves and the mournful calling of a crow.

This was their place. The place they'd hidden from their families and the prying eyes of Lawson Estate employees and visitors. A little nook by a bend in the creek, right at the fence line between the two properties. There, they'd hidden from both, wrapped up in a love he'd thought would last forever.

Even at seventeen he should have known better. Nothing lasted forever. Not even grapevines. Although, personally, Hugh was doing his best to make sure that Lawson Estate wine would be on the dining tables of generations to come. Something permanent in a temporary world.

A low roll of thunder echoed and the surrounding bush darkened a little as the sun retreated farther behind clouds. The ground was uneven and marshy in some places because of the recent rain. Hugh paid little attention to the mud, his focus on the strip of color he could see through the trees.

Zoe.

She was sitting on the bank. Waiting for him, just as if time had stood still. Ten years ago he might have tried to sneak up on her. He'd wrap his arms around her and bury his face in her hair, breathing in her subtle scent of roses and sunshine. She'd pretend to be cross, but her angry words would turn into laughter, her playful wrestling would become an entirely different kind of touching. By the time she let him kiss him, he'd want her with a hunger that scared him.

Now, ten years later, he could recall those

feelings with uncanny clarity, but was completely unable to pinpoint how he felt at this present moment. Zoe should have tried harder to contact him. It wouldn't have been *that* hard to get a message through. Even though the most obvious channels of communication to him had been blocked, she could have had a classmate pass on the news. And then he would have... *done what, exactly?*

He didn't know.

He still hadn't quite managed to wrap his head around the news she'd broken yesterday. *A baby.* It seemed impossible to grasp, yet it was obviously real. There was no mistaking the pain he'd seen in Zoe's eyes.

He wasn't entirely comfortable with his need to see that pain again. On the one hand, he simply wanted to *know* what had happened. If that hurt Zoe, well, that was a sad but inescapable consequence. On the other hand, he needed to punish someone for bringing all this upheaval into his life—and Zoe was far more than just the messenger.

A rustle nearby brought him back to the present. Some creature scurrying away from his determined strides. A gust of wind rushed through the canopy of leaves.

What would have happened if things had been different? What if they'd been together—

would he have been able to change things? Would they have been happy?

Through the shrubbery, he could see the set of Zoe's shoulders, the way her head rested in her hands.

One thing was for certain. Regardless of what had happened, Zoe wasn't happy now. And, he realized, now neither was he. His plans to take over Waterford had seemed simple and achievable, at first. He'd figured on some awkwardness, sure, but he'd been confident of his ability to overcome it. Now things were murkier and far more complicated than he'd ever predicted.

ZOE HEARD A TWIG CRACK a moment before she heard him speak.

"Zoe."

Her head snapped up, eyes focusing again and she ran a hand through her hair.

Had his voice always been that deep, that adult? She wasn't sure.

He appeared through the trees like a vision. Hugh, but not Hugh. He frowned when she met his gaze, but his eyes still sparkled. That was familiar.

He wore a charcoal-grey suit, finely tailored to emphasize his broad shoulders and narrow waist. A crisp white shirt and burgundy tie contrasted with the dark beard on his jaw.

That was *not* familiar.

It suited him. He looked comfortable, powerful, supremely confident. Even here, by the creek, dressed inappropriately like that, his shoes coated with a thick layer of mud.

He'd always been that way. Always sure of himself and his place in the world. Sure that he was loved; sure that he would succeed.

Zoe wished she had been half as sure of anything in her life.

His frown faded into a look of amused puzzlement as his eyes lit on the structure near where she sat. "It's still here?"

Zoe couldn't help smiling as she followed his gaze over the wooden structure set between two trees. It was their cupboard—they'd built it from leftover timber and hardware stolen from Lawson Estate. They'd stored blankets, food and even the occasional bottle of wine in it over the summer they'd spent at the creek. As autumn had set in, it had held raincoats, jumpers and pillows.

"I can't believe it lasted this long," Hugh said, walking a circle around it, a hand reaching out to brush over the top.

The doors were closed and fit together snugly; Zoe bet it was still weatherproof. "I can. There's about a thousand nails in it."

"Only because you kept banging them in

crooked." He shot her a teasing look and then tugged on one of the doors, but it didn't budge.

"Hey!" Zoe protested. "I think you'll remember it was you who couldn't hit a nail straight."

He shook his head, a ghost of a smile still playing about his lips. "I can't believe it's still here," he repeated quietly.

"You don't come down here much?" She wasn't sure why that should be a surprise.

His eyes moved from the cupboard to meet Zoe's. "Never. Not since…"

His gaze was like a physical touch; she was spellbound, captured by it, just like she had been as a teenager. Back then, he'd been the only one to see the *real* her, the hurt, lonely, frightened little girl that hid behind bravado and a sneer, who did her best to convince everyone she didn't deserve to be loved, because inside she was sure it was the truth.

Now, though, his eyes narrowed. Whatever he saw, Zoe had the distinct impression he didn't like it.

She tore her eyes away and shook off the fog that had descended as she'd stared sightlessly at the creek. Shifting, Zoe clasped her raincoat closer around her. A shiver went through her—regret that she'd told him her secret when it might just as easily have stayed buried, and the vain hope that he'd never mention it again.

It was pointless to hope for that, though. She knew why he'd sought her out, what he wanted to know. She also knew she wasn't ready to talk to him about it. Wasn't sure if she ever would be. But she was filled with a sense of foreboding. There was a reckoning to come.

She looked up. He was tall, towering over her. She could see more than a passing resemblance to his father—they'd always had similar coloring, but now Hugh had some of the same authority that Pete Lawson had worn as a mantle. The kind of attitude that she'd always found intimidating.

Zoe knew she should stand, to match him, but then he moved to a fallen log and, hitching his trousers as if he were about to take a seat in the boardroom, perched on the edge. Zoe stayed where she was, her every nerve singing with alarm.

"What brings you here?" he asked after a moment's silence.

"I had some thinking to do," Zoe replied. She looked around their little glade, stared at the water trickling past—the creek seemed lower this winter—but kept him in her field of vision like a gazelle who'd spotted a lion.

"This was always where you came for that."

His tone was soft again, as it had been in the car when he'd stroked her wrist. She couldn't afford to let that get to her. That soft voice seduced her, made her forget.

Zoe swallowed hard, forcing back the memories. "Yes, and I can do it better without company." Snark was always her best defense.

It worked.

He stiffened and his expression hardened. "I wanted to talk to you."

"I don't see any need for that."

"What?" Incredulity threaded through his voice. "Zoe, after what you told me yesterday, surely you can't believe that I don't have questions! That I don't deserve—"

Her stomach dropped, but she did her best to ignore it. "It doesn't change anything." She struggled to keep her face blank while inwardly she winced at her tone. She sounded like her bitchy, in-your-face, teenaged self. What was it about Hugh's presence that stripped away the maturity she'd striven hard to develop in her years away from Tangawarra? Sure, she still had moments when she couldn't stop her inner rebel from popping out, but she usually had better control.

He spluttered in disbelief. "Of course it does! It changes...well, everything."

She risked looking at him directly. "What, exactly, does it change, Hugh? The fact that we had a relationship when we were kids? That it ended badly? It doesn't really matter how it ended—it ended. You're just angry that you were lied to and you want payback. Well, sorry, but I can't help. I'm the wrong person."

The look of hurt and awareness that flashed across his face was so quick that Zoe almost thought she'd imagined it. Almost. She was right. His anger was all about the fact that he'd been lied to about something he should have been able to control. He'd been deliberately excluded, and for the most popular boy in school, the top of the class—now the CEO of Lawson Estate—that was unacceptable.

"Zoe, I want to know—"

She smiled grimly and didn't let him finish. "I know you do."

He growled in frustration and his knuckles were white where he gripped the branch.

"Look, Hugh," she began, playing with the cord of her raincoat, trying hard to look carefree, as if this conversation wasn't important. She wasn't going to talk to him about their history any more than she already had. She couldn't. "Raking over the past isn't going to do either of us any good. I've got more than enough to deal with in the present. And from everything I've heard, so do you. A multimillion-dollar business to run, wine to sell, small winemakers to buy out and squeeze off their properties…" She shot him a defiant look, as if she were back-chatting the principal. It felt… good. Somehow gratifying. And keeping him off balance stopped him from asking her the questions she couldn't answer.

He gritted his teeth. "I don't know where you get the idea—"

"Give it up, Hugh." Zoe cut him off again. Each time she cut in she made him angrier. Clearly Hugh wasn't used to people talking back to him, interrupting the big boss man. She got a jolt of satisfaction from seeing a vein pulse in his temple.

It was stupid, of course. It was the gazelle taunting the lion. But she couldn't stop herself.

"I know you're trying to buy Waterford." She met his gaze and held it, steeling herself to ignore the effect it had on her. She lifted her chin. "And I know you understand that I always thought Mack's rivalry with your dad was stupid. But I just want you to know that I wouldn't sell Waterford to you if you were the last buyer on the planet."

The words came tumbling out of her mouth before she could stop them. What on earth was she thinking? Hadn't she decided last night it would be easier to sell up and head home? Selling Waterford to Hugh would be the simplest solution to her problem. But just because he was the only one who'd made an offer so far didn't mean he was the only potential buyer. She'd still sell, just not to him. It might take a little longer but the satisfaction would be worth the wait.

Hugh puffed out a frustrated breath but then gathered his usual cool demeanor. He gave her that icy look again, but Zoe could see the anger ticking just below the surface. "Yes, I want to buy Waterford. Zoe, it just makes sense. I'm the only one in the valley who can afford to buy it outright. We can even talk about keeping the Waterford label going as a specialty line within the Lawson Estate range, if you want. It's your best option." His eyes narrowed. "I can write you a check and you can walk away."

Despite her newfound determination, his offer was appealing. Walk away from all this with the flick of a pen? Oh, it was so tempting. She refused to let him see that. She leaned forward, searching inside for her usual defenses. "You'd like that wouldn't you? Don't you dare presume to know what's best for me."

He stood, brushing his palms down the front of his trousers. There was a long smear of mud on the inside ankle of one of his pant legs, more spatters around the cuffs, but otherwise he was pristine. Zoe decided to stay where she was— mostly because she was trembling from head to toe and she wasn't sure if her knees would support her.

"You were always too stubborn to know what was good for you."

"And you were always too proud to admit when you were wrong," she snapped back.

He looked up at the trees and shook his head, a gesture of disappointment that Zoe had been used to seeing from adults when she was a teen. He only needed to add a tutting tongue for it to be a perfect replica.

She'd never thought Hugh would use it on her.

Suddenly she was small, and childish and so very, very alone. All her defenses seemed flimsy.

"Zoe…" he began, but then he didn't seem to know what to say next. He turned toward the creek, his back to her, stepping carefully onto a rock, its edges worn smooth by running water. Zoe wished the same thing could happen to her. Maybe if she just lay down in the creek long enough, all her harsh edges would be scoured away.

"I want to buy Waterford, but that isn't what I came here to talk about," he said eventually, voice soft again. "You know what I need you to tell me about."

Damn him. It was so much easier to argue.

"Tough luck."

He turned his head just enough so she could see his smile. "You know, I wasn't surprised when I heard about what happened with Pierre Renault."

Tangawarra was a small place, but the world of wine making, it seemed, was no bigger. Zoe didn't bother asking how he knew. "The man didn't know Beaujolais from botrytis," she said dismissively.

"But you were more than happy to teach him. A man who grew up in Burgundy, who makes one of the most renowned wines in the world."

She didn't miss his teasing tone. "He was a wanker."

"You lasted awhile there, though, didn't you?"

A year. A record for her up until her current almost two-year stint at Golden Gate. Somehow, despite her well-deserved reputation for problems with authority and tendency to move around, she always managed to walk into another job—because she was bloody good at what she did. "Your point being?" She didn't want to get into her patchy work record with Hugh.

He continued to stare out over the creek, hands hanging by his sides. He rocked, very slightly, from his toes to his heels and back again. "Funny, isn't it?" he said over his shoulder. "When we were kids the very last thing we wanted was to be like our parents. And yet that's exactly what we've become."

Given she'd just been thinking how Hugh had come to resemble Pete Lawson, there was some truth to what he said. But to think that Zoe was like her mother?

Zoe made a dismissive noise. "Yeah, right."

Hugh twisted around to face her. "You don't agree?" He raised his eyebrows in question.

"You're the perfect shadow of your dad, Hugh. Right down to those shiny shoes."

"And you're the rebellious nomad, just like your mother."

Zoe actually felt her blood pressure rise, felt her cheeks heat. "I'm *nothing* like my mother."

He opened his mouth, as if to protest, but clearly some better instinct took over and he stayed silent. Just as well. Zoe was itching for a good fight.

His lips thinned and she could tell his patience had, too. "Zoe, enough. Let's talk, properly—you know what I came here to find out. We can't dance around this forever."

Oh, yes, they could. "I buried my grandfather and only remaining family member yesterday, Hugh. Give me a minute, yeah?" Her tone was bitter on purpose. The sympathy card couldn't fail.

And it didn't. Hugh winced and looked down at his feet.

But when he looked up, his expression was cool. "It's not over, Zoe. I'm not going to let you off so easily next time."

The determination on his face sent a ripple of shock through her. Enough to force a crack in the armor she'd put up around her wounds. A flash of emotion, of the nights she'd cried herself to sleep after she'd lost everything, leaked out and almost overwhelmed her. But Zoe forced it away—years of practice had not been for nothing.

Without another word, he turned and walked back the way he'd come, disappearing through the trees.

CHAPTER SIX

ZOE SOAKED FOR AGES in a hot bath to warm herself up after sitting too long by the creek. Afterward, she stared into the mostly empty refrigerator for a while, but couldn't manage to feel hungry enough to cook anything. She knew she should—she knew that she had a tendency to faint when she didn't eat—but the effort seemed too great.

The sun had set while she took her bath, and Zoe decided to put off any further work until tomorrow. She'd brought firewood inside—tonight she'd light a fire, watch some TV and pretend everything was okay. She was good at that. She'd been pretending for years now.

In the living room, Mack's wall of ancient photographs stared down at her. Generations of the Waters family scowling in that way peculiar to old portraits. Disapproving. Unsympathetic, just as they'd always been.

The noise of a vehicle coming up the track startled her as she was screwing up newspaper for kindling. Her stomach dropped at the thought that it might be Hugh, but through the windows she caught a glimpse of a white Land Rover.

As Zoe stepped out the back door, Patricia, her neighbor from Long Track Estate, waved to her from the driver's seat and pulled up.

"Hello!" The older woman fumbled around with something on the passenger seat before jumping out of the car.

"Hi, Patricia."

"I made you a casserole. Well, actually, I made Bert and me a casserole and I brought you some of it. Wasn't sure if you'd had time to go to the supermarket."

Such a country neighbor thing to do. Zoe couldn't help but smile as Patricia held up a plastic container. Patricia bustled Zoe into the house and began organizing her a plate in a way that indicated she was familiar with the kitchen.

"Thanks, Patricia, this is lovely of you, but I—" Zoe tried to protest that she wasn't hungry, that the pity casserole could go in the fridge for tomorrow, but Patricia didn't appear to be interested.

"I also brought you a bottle of our wine—it's a Shiraz, too. Thought you might like to give it a try. It's not a Waterford Shiraz by any means." She gave a little self-deprecating laugh. "But we're still quite proud of it."

Patricia found a couple of wine glasses and Zoe could see it would be useless to protest that she didn't want any wine, either. The way the woman bundled around the kitchen made Zoe feel tired to watch. In the end, she succumbed to the inevitable and took a seat at her grandfather's battered kitchen table while Patricia prattled on.

"Quite the weather we're having, isn't it? Freezing cold yesterday, sunny today, even if those rain clouds are still hanging around. Still that's what you get in the valley. I moved down here from northern New South Wales eight years ago, you know, and I'm still not used to it. The four seasons in one day thing. Up there it was far more predictable. Okay, I think this is hot enough now. There you go."

Patricia removed the plate from the microwave and placed it with a flourish in front of Zoe, along with a glass of red wine. Strangely, although she'd have sworn she wasn't hungry, Zoe's stomach grumbled at the sight of the typical country meal: beef and onion casserole with chunks of carrot, accompanied by mashed potatoes and a cluster of green beans and peas. It looked just like the kind of meal she'd have made and served when she was living here with Mack.

Her chest tightened with an unexplained pang

of emptiness. She conjured a picture of him sitting right there, at the table, about to eat his dinner. His weather-beaten face most likely scowling at whatever Zoe was in trouble for at that time. His hands, calloused and lined—the etchings of age brought into stark relief by the almost permanent staining of grape juice. His gruff praise and the flash of pride in his eyes when he'd allowed her to taste a wine at dinner and she'd correctly identified its faults.

She pushed the memory away.

Patricia pulled up a chair. She took her glass of wine and held it to the light before sniffing it carefully, just like any wine aficionado.

To be polite, Zoe picked up her glass, sniffed and took a small sip. The best description she could come up with was *competent.* It was reasonably well-balanced, had some decent fruit flavors and wasn't too heavy on the oak. But it would never win any medals. It wasn't even close to being in the same league as her grandfather's wine—not that he'd ever bothered to enter any competitions.

Zoe nodded and gave Patricia a small smile. "It's good. Very drinkable." It wasn't exactly a lie. Zoe took another sip.

Patricia beamed. "I'm glad you think so. Mack always said you had a natural palate. Said you were some big-shot winemaker in California now."

"I don't know about 'big shot,'" Zoe mumbled. She swallowed a forkful of casserole and potato, grateful as the warmth spread from her stomach outward. She chastised herself for not realizing that she really did need to eat. She had a lot of hurdles still to get over, and couldn't afford to fall sick. Tomorrow she'd go to the supermarket and stock up properly. "Thank you for the meal."

"You're welcome." Patricia fiddled with the bottle, looking down at the label and smoothing away a nonexistent crinkle with her thumb.

With a prickle of awareness, Zoe realized the other woman was nervous. Why?

"I know Mack was very proud of you," Patricia continued, not quite looking at Zoe. "He was never one to blow his own trumpet, but he did like to say he'd taught you everything he knew."

Zoe nodded. "Yes, I guess he did."

Patricia's eyes finally met hers. "But I get the impression it must have been pretty lonely for you, growing up with him. He wasn't the friendliest of men."

Zoe's senses were on high alert. Something was wrong, and she was inherently suspicious of Patricia's unsubtle digging. "We did okay," Zoe hedged.

IN HIS EYES

"Still, a teenage girl with no female role models…I guess it was a blessing when he decided to send you to that girls' school in Sydney."

So Hugh had been right, and it was just as she'd thought. That was the story that everyone believed. She guessed it was better than the truth—the truth was too private to be shared. Patricia seemed lovely, and her offer of a meal was very kind, but Zoe couldn't help but think that she might have an ulterior motive. If Tangawarra still operated anywhere close to the way it used to—and Zoe was pretty sure it did—her presence back at Waterford would be pretty hot gossip. It was very nice of the woman to cook for her, but Zoe was going to be on her guard.

She swallowed her mouthful and put her fork down. "Was there something in particular you wanted to know, Patricia?"

Patricia looked up at the question, startled. Zoe could hear the threatening tone in her own voice.

Patricia's hand fluttered to her chest and she looked away again. "Oh, dear, there I go. Bert's always telling me to stop sticking my nose in other people's business. But I just didn't know how to…I wanted to talk to you…."

The older woman took in a deep breath as if gaining courage. "Bert and I were wondering… that is, we wanted to know if you'd made any decisions about Waterford. What you were planning to do. If you're going to stay, you know, or…sell. Because, well, we'd be interested…in maybe…"

Zoe tried hard to put a pleasant expression on her face, because whatever was there now was making the woman squirm. "You want to buy Waterford?" she asked, wanting to be sure she was correctly interpreting the rambling speech.

"Well, yes. Maybe. We're not sure. I'd need to talk to you about the details. The price, and so on. I'm sorry—I know it's awfully tacky to be talking about this the day after Mack's funeral. But we just weren't sure how quickly you were planning to head back to California. If that's what you're going to do."

Zoe couldn't help comparing the woman's tentative approach to Hugh's supremely confident, arrogant offer earlier in the afternoon. She'd not expected Waterford to be difficult to sell, but hadn't dreamed there'd be two offers on the table within a matter of hours.

"I know, I know, it's too soon after the funeral," Patricia babbled when Zoe stayed silent. "Mack's barely in the ground and here I am talking about financial matters. I should have known. I tried to tell Bert, but he told me to get over here and ask, because we were thinking you might want to make a decision quickly and, well, we wanted you to know we're interested."

Selling Waterford to neighbors—ones who *weren't* Lawsons—might be the perfect solution. "You're really interested in buying Waterford?"

Patricia's slightly panicked expression faded as she realized Zoe wasn't offended. "Yes!" She picked up her wine and took a long sip. "You see, Long Track Estate is still getting established, but Mack's vines—that fruit—would be such an asset to us. And we were thinking we could do up this place a little." She gestured to the dilapidated house around them. "We could rent it out as a cottage retreat."

Zoe nodded, for some reason unable to bring herself to say anything about that. The only real home she'd known as a child, her grandfather's hideaway, turned into a tourist destination? It didn't sit right, but then, once she sold Waterford, it wasn't as if she'd have any say. And it wasn't as though if she sold it to Lawson Estate anything different would happen. Although Hugh might bulldoze the place in a fit of pique.

"Thanks, Patricia. I'd be interested in knowing more about your offer. I do need to start thinking about what to do next. What exactly did you have in mind?" All Zoe needed was enough money to cover the debts and finance the bottling of the vintage. Otherwise she didn't care about the dollars.

Patricia's eyes were bright, but she pursed her lips for a moment. "Hmm, the details. We've talked to the bank. Unfortunately, we'd have to come to some kind of special arrangement, Zoe. We couldn't buy it straight away. Me and Bert, we put everything into setting up Long Track and we're still recouping our costs. The bank won't let us extend any further until we bring in the next vintage. So we'd need a long settlement—say, six months?"

Six months? Zoe needed money now. But maybe Patricia and Bert could help out, pay the bills, provide the physical assistance Zoe needed to bring in Mack's last vintage.

"Once people know that our next vintage includes Mack's Shiraz, it will race off the shelves. We'll be set. And then we'll be able to settle with you."

Zoe frowned. "Wait. You want Mack's wine, but you don't want to pay for it, or Waterford, until you've sold it?"

"Well, what else would you do with it? It would be a shame for it to go to waste." Patricia's tone was matter-of-fact. "We'll transport the wine over to our place and blend it with our current Long Track vintage. It will be a special edition!" Her eyes gleamed at the idea. "Once we get that on the market, we'll have the income to convince the bank to give us the loan."

"I…" Zoe squashed the impulse to tell the woman to get out of the house and not come back. She had been kind, after all. It wasn't her fault she was an idiot. Mix her grandfather's wine with a second-rate plonk like Long Track? Forget it!

"Thanks for the dinner." Zoe pushed the half-eaten plateful away. "I'll have to think about your offer. I'll let you know." She stood to make it perfectly clear the visit was over. Zoe knew she should tell Patricia right away that her offer wasn't acceptable. But for some reason she just couldn't bring herself to crush the woman's hopeful plans immediately.

"Of course, of course." Patricia bustled up and headed for the door, her enthusiasm undimmed.

"Good night, dear! Stay warm! I'll come over in a couple of days and we can talk again."

Zoe watched Patricia climb into the SUV, and she didn't go back inside until the taillights had disappeared down the track.

In the kitchen, she scraped the remaining food from the plate into the bin and poured the half-drunk glass of wine down the sink. She put the cork back in the bottle, though, the winemaker in her interested to find out how the wine developed. Not well, was her guess.

Then, finally, she lit the fire she'd planned an hour before and sat down on the lumpy old sofa to stare into the flames.

Was Hugh right? Was he the only one in the valley who could afford to buy Waterford outright? Patricia and Bert's offer wasn't acceptable—even though it was her only other opportunity at this stage.

Surely there were other answers.

She hadn't explored all the options yet—there were bound to be other people interested. Resolved to go into town the next day and investigate further, Zoe went to bed, knowing that she wouldn't sleep.

CHAPTER SEVEN

TWO DAYS LATER, ZOE HAD to admit that her situation had not improved. In fact, things were worse than she'd predicted.

While waiting for Stephen Carter to investigate other potential buyers for Waterford, she'd decided she might as well keep herself busy. The easiest way to do that was to sink herself in familiar wine-making tasks.

After spending a day testing and assessing the state of the wine, this morning she'd struggled with the time-consuming and labor-intensive task of racking off the oak barrels. The job involved pumping wine out of each barrel into a stainless steel vat, then painstakingly scrubbing out the sludge and crystals before returning the wine to the oak. It was an important, but thankless cleaning job, made easier at Golden Gate Estate in Napa by high-pressure cleaning equipment and many pairs of helping hands.

There was none of that at Waterford. After a full morning's hard work, Zoe had done exactly one barrel.

It was going to take days.

And there really wasn't any point to it. Stephen Carter had warned her about the tenuous state of the economy and the wine industry. Those buyers she'd thought would be lining up to take Waterford off her hands? Yeah, not so much. Australia was going through what industry insiders called a "grape glut"—too many hobbyist vintners had flooded the market and even the premium winemakers were finding it tough to make a profit. New hobbyists had been scared off, so there were few buyers of the kind Zoe had in mind. Her only option was to sell to one of the big players—like Lawson Estate—who would buy the property for the established vines and use the grapes however they pleased.

Zoe hadn't seen Patricia and Bert since Patricia's pity meal—but their offer wasn't a real possibility, anyway, regardless of what they wanted to do with Mack's wine. Zoe couldn't wait six months for a settlement when there were debtors sitting on the doorstep with grasping hands outstretched.

And as for putting out that last Waterford Shiraz as per Mack's wishes? No buyer in their right mind was interested in funding a wine that would barely turn a profit, especially when it wasn't one they could put their own name to.

Her own meager savings would cover her living expenses only through the next couple of weeks until she got back to California—certainly not enough to fund the bottling, sale and distribution of an entire vintage. The bank wasn't interested in extending the mortgage on the property. The polite but firm bank manager had left her in no doubt there.

Of course, it didn't help that her grandfather hadn't exactly made a lot of friends in his life. They'd talked big at the wake, but when it came down to it, Zoe knew no one was interested in doing such a huge posthumous favor for Mack Waters. Not many could afford to, either. Mack might have had the occasional charitable thought, might have helped a couple of people over the years, but he'd also burned bridges recklessly. When he'd considered someone a fool, he'd never had a problem saying so to that person's face. And now he wasn't even here to reap what he'd sowed.

With a heavy sigh, Zoe turned her attention to the work at hand. At least the manual labor was distracting enough to give her brain a break from the endless problems that seemed to be her life.

And then life saw fit to hand her another one as the pump at her feet began to make an ominous chugging sound.

"No! Don't you dare!" Zoe yelled at it. But

despite her warning, the pump sputtered and died, just as it had begun to feed wine from the second barrel into the stainless steel vat. Zoe let loose with a toe-curling curse. This was just what she needed after a morning of back-breaking work that seemed more pointless with each hour. If she couldn't get the wine back in the barrel and sealed away quickly, exposure to the air would ruin it. She swore again.

"You always did have a way with words."

Hugh's voice came from nowhere and Zoe spun around, startled. Her ankle connected with the edge of the pump as she did, causing yet another vicious expletive to erupt.

Hugh chuckled as he stepped from the bright sunshine of the doorway into the dimmer light of the shed.

"What are you doing here?" Zoe struggled for balance as she rubbed her ankle and tried to stand up straight and look as unwelcoming as possible. She silently ran through a few more curses at the noisy pump—it was undoubtedly the reason she hadn't heard his approach.

"Just thought I'd see how you were doing."

"I'm fine. I'd be better if the equipment would work properly." Zoe gave the pump a kick in petty vengeance.

Hugh gave another of those slow chuckles

and a rush of embarrassment went through her. She sounded like a child again, and she hated that.

"Need a hand?" He sauntered lazily over to the pump and kneeled down. Zoe couldn't help noticing he was wearing the same outfit she'd seen him in when she'd arrived: jeans, a pale blue shirt rolled up at the sleeves and that wicked cowboy-style hat. It was more casual than the suit he'd worn down at the creek, but no less threatening. His smell wafted up to her as he knelt close, the scent of a man who'd been out working in the sunshine, combining sawdust, earth and masculine sweat—the good kind—overlaid with a musky expensive fragrance.

After checking the pump, he traced the tubing and electrical cords to their destinations.

"Here's your problem." His easy, carefree tone had disappeared. Instead he sounded decidedly unimpressed. "You're lucky the pump's safety switch tripped."

Zoe muttered under her breath as she saw what he'd discovered. The electrical cord had fallen into a puddle of water that had collected from her earlier work scrubbing out the barrel. It was a stupid mistake, caused by sleepless nights and by one person trying to do the job of at least two. Zoe was physically strong and used to hard work, but there came a point in winery operations where you simply needed brute, male strength.

That point had probably come a couple of hours before.

"You most likely blew a fuse, too. Just as well—the other option would have been electrocuting yourself." He shook his head and it was once again as if he was the grown-up and she the naughty little girl. "What were you thinking?" he scolded.

Every defensive bone in her body prickled—and after a lifetime's development there were more than a few of them. "What do you care, anyway? Get out and let me get on with it."

For a moment he looked about to fight back, but he didn't speak. After frowning at her, an unreadable expression on his face, he turned away and found the fuse box.

Zoe watched as he checked the fuses, then grabbed an old towel and carefully dried the cord, rerouting it around the puddle of water. He then bent back down to the pump and restarted it. Zoe couldn't help rolling her eyes when it started first time—the bloody thing had been temperamental for her all day.

Frustration at her own helplessness bubbled over. "I don't need your help." Zoe strode forward and tore the soggy towel out of his grasp.

He let the towel go without a glance, ignoring her protest. "Why do you even have the pump running like this? You've got miles of tubing…" He frowned as he examined Zoe's setup.

"I told you, I don't need—"

"Oh, I get it." His eyes widened as he worked out what was going on. "Here. Hold this."

Before Zoe could react, he'd grabbed the tubing from the barrel and pressed it into her hand. Zoe had to hold it up high, or the precious wine would begin spilling out. She could only watch as he tilted the heavy vat and rolled it almost effortlessly over to the barrels.

Zoe swore under her breath. She'd tried dozens of times to move the thing, finally accepting that it was simply beyond her strength. She'd set up the miles of tubing as a stopgap. It had taken ages and made Zoe dirty and sweaty and angry at her own ineptitude.

Hugh Lawson strode in and did it in ten seconds.

It was a metaphor for their lives.

"Happy now?" she snapped, shoving the clear plastic piping back into the barrel where it belonged.

He took a step closer to her and propped his hands on his hips. "If it means you don't go around electrocuting yourself, then yes."

"Why do you even care?" It was a throwaway

line, a typical teenage-Zoe barb, but he seemed to actually consider the question. His eyes bored into hers, making her squirm, but she wouldn't look away, wouldn't back down.

"Because someone has to."

Her heart squeezed, but she wouldn't let his easy charm get to her these days. She was a lot older and wiser than the Zoe Waters who'd fallen for his cute smile and mesmerizing charisma. He'd say the same thing to anyone—his concern wasn't personal. "You don't even know who I am anymore, Hugh. What gives you the right to decide I need looking after?"

He paused for a moment and when he spoke, his voice was low and somehow dangerous. "I know you better than you think."

He was standing too close for comfort. Close enough for her to see the smile lines that age and weather had begun to form into creases at the corners of his eyes. To stare at his lips and remember how soft they used to be against hers. For that wildly exciting smell of his to wash over her again.

"Yeah, you know me so well, you thought I was a head case," she countered, because she never backed down from a fight.

"I was *told* you were a head case," he said reasonably. "Although that's not how I'd have put it." And then he stepped even closer. The heat of him radiated through the thin cotton of his shirt. She'd stripped down to a T-shirt, hot from her hard work, and now wished she hadn't, wished there was more of a barrier between her skin and his warmth.

She stepped back and began coiling up the lengths of tubing. "Why are you here?" she asked, her irritation clear. She wished she could sound coolly uninterested, but that was beyond her.

"I told you down at the creek—we need to talk. I want to know what happened."

"So you did." She still had no intention of going there with him. He deserved the explanation, no question—she was just in no state to be able to provide it. Admitting her reasons for that were entirely about self-preservation was also too revealing. Better to stick with the snappy comebacks. "I think I made it pretty clear what you could do with that idea."

He bent over to pick up the other end of the tubing, helping her with her tidy-up. Zoe handed the bundle to him and went to check the barrel, make sure the wine was draining into the vat properly.

"What are you doing with the wine?" he asked, surprising her with a change of topic.

"Racking it off. What does it look like?"

· He gave a patient sigh. "I know that. That's not what I meant."

Zoe knew exactly what he meant, but she didn't know the answer to his real question so it was easier to be evasive. "And here I thought you were the boss, but you must get your hands dirty sometimes if you know what's going on here." She stepped back and gave him an assessing look from top to toe, hands on her hips. "Just look at you in your shiny little Lawson Estate uniform." She shook her head, hoping she looked dismissive.

"You like it?" He plucked at his sleeve, ignoring her taunt. "I helped pick the color myself."

Zoe tried to stifle her smile, but wasn't sure she succeeded. "Very nice. That what you do over there in your fancy office? Pick out shirt colors and plan parties?"

"Pretty much."

"Sounds like fun."

"Oh, it's a blast. What about you over in Californ-I-A? You busy pouring crappy zinfandel for movie stars?"

"Absolutely. Those movie stars love themselves some crappy zin."

Hugh smiled and Zoe ducked her head to hide her answering grin. She stepped over to the next barrel, ready to prepare it for decanting. Thanks to Hugh's help she might get through more than one barrel today.

"Yeah? I heard Golden Gate's star is on the rise—because of you."

Zoe waved a hand dismissively. "I wouldn't say that. I got there at the right time—we had a great year with some fantastic fruit, I just got to take advantage of it."

"Your zin won a gold, didn't it?"

Zoe didn't want to admit to the warm glow she felt at Hugh's veiled praise. "Two, actually." She couldn't help boasting.

"Good for you."

He was behind her, doing something, she wasn't sure what. She wished she wasn't so aware of him. She swore she could feel the heat of him, even though he had to be nearly three feet away.

It was time for this silly charade to end. Zoe spun around, surprised to find Hugh was just standing there, hands in his pockets, studying her. The look on his face was hard to pinpoint, and then whatever emotion she'd seen there was quickly covered with a polite smile.

"I'm really happy that you've done so well for yourself, Zoe," he said.

Zoe wished they were still doing teasing insults. She knew how to handle those. Genuine admiration wasn't something she'd had much experience with in life.

"And you…" she began. "Well, you don't need me to tell you that Lawson Estate is…" She trailed off, remembering her accusations that he was a corporate raider. She still didn't like the Lawson-led corporatization of the valley. But it wasn't her home anymore, so she guessed she didn't really have the right to criticize.

Hugh shook his head, a knowing smile curving his mouth. "Ah, Zoe. You always were much better at fighting."

True. "I taught you a thing or two."

He nodded. "That you did."

"You might have been captain of the footy team, but you really were a wuss back then." Hugh had been able to rely on good looks and charm to get by in high school—he'd never had to use any kind of physical or verbal aggression to get his way. It was a skill Zoe had admired, even as she'd realized she'd never share it. She desperately needed her own finely honed verbal sparring skills as her main form of defense.

He tilted his head. "I guess I was. But then I also taught you a thing or two, if I recall."

He'd stepped closer and Zoe's heart sped up. Partly in fear, partly…something else. "Well, you were better at calculus than me," she said, grasping for a topic that would keep the conversation light.

"That wasn't what I had in mind."

His tone was breezy, but Zoe knew exactly what he was referring to, and she willed her cheeks not to flush.

He was close enough for her to pick out the individual stitches in that fancy embroidered Lawson Estate logo on his shirt. For a moment she wondered whether he might touch her, how she'd respond if he did. Slap him or swoon into his arms? Right now it was a toss-up....

Hugh leaned over to check the barrel that was draining, apparently ignoring her. "This one's pretty much empty." He turned off the pump and began adjusting the tubing, moving the whole set-up along, ready for the next barrel in line. "I think if we work together we can get a few barrels done this afternoon."

Zoe stared in disbelief as he continued to work.

"What the hell are you doing?" She realized too late that her anger betrayed her, showed him how much he affected her.

Hugh didn't pause, just raised one eyebrow in her direction. "Helping," he said mildly.

Gathering up every ounce of her strength, Zoe pulled herself together. She made herself unclench her fists. "What makes you think I want—or need—your help?"

She was pleased with the calmer tone of her voice when she spoke. It left him in no doubt to her displeasure, but she no longer sounded hysterical.

"I had a word with Stephen Carter this morning."

So much for staying calm. Blood pounded in her temples—a headache about to break.

She needed to leave Tangawarra soon or risk a stroke.

Hugh continued without looking around. "I understand you're finding it difficult to find a buyer who'll fund the last Shiraz vintage before taking over."

"And client confidentiality obviously has no meaning in Tangawarra," Zoe muttered between gritted teeth.

"Clearly there aren't many people who'll agree to that kind of arrangement. Why would anyone pay to produce a wine that they won't get any credit for? And with your grandfather's savings gone on medical expenses, plus the debts against this place, you've got no hope of raising the capital yourself."

He continued to busy himself with the barrel and pump, and in a far part of her mind Zoe had to admire the confident, easy way he did so. He might be the CEO of Lawson Estate, but given the familiar way he was working, Zoe would bet that he spent more than his fair share of time in the winery, taking care of some of the more menial tasks of wine-making.

He stopped and turned to her with a cool, calculating gaze. "I don't think you have many options left."

Zoe blinked.

"You know I want to buy Waterford. So here's my offer. I'll help you produce Mack's last vintage—both financially and even with some of the wine-making duties. Just to save you from electrocuting yourself," he added with a cocky grin that held no warmth at all. "I need to protect my investment, after all."

"What?"

He plowed on, ignoring her sputtered objection. "Your grandfather and my father hated each other. We managed to bridge that feud. Hell, we managed to combine their DNA," he added in a harsh mutter. The plastic piping in his hand wavered and a small gush of dark red wine splashed to the floor before he sank it inside the next barrel in line.

A surge of nausea rose in Zoe's throat. The foreboding she'd felt down at the creek returned. She knew how unlikely it was that Hugh would leave the past alone. She knew, even if she didn't want to admit it, that was the reason he was here; sooner or later—and it wasn't likely to be later—he'd demand his explanation. A little voice inside her whispered that it was an explanation he probably deserved. Another voice countered that he'd given up any right to it when he'd cut her out of his life, choosing to believe lies rather than the truth he knew of her.

"So let's take that to its natural conclusion," Hugh continued. "Waterford and Lawson Estate merging."

Zoe gave a bitter laugh. "Merging? Don't you mean Lawson Estate taking over Waterford?"

He ignored her, his focus on the wine barrel. "I think we can manage to work together for a week or so. And then we both get what we want. You get Mack's vintage out and you can go back to California. And I get Waterford. Problem solved."

He turned back to face her. His blue gaze—astonishingly bright in the dim winery—clashed with her own.

"Exactly what choice do you have, Zoe?"

She lifted her chin, determined not to be intimidated. "I can sell to Patricia and Bert. They've offered to buy Waterford."

He gave a dismissive snort. "Yeah, and I can guess exactly what their offer is. I know they can't pay you right away and I know you can't afford to wait. Besides which, as if you'd let them pour this—" he gestured to the barrels around them "—into that slop they call wine."

"People in glass houses," Zoe taunted.

If he was stung by her childish insult, it didn't show. "Zoe, I'm prepared to finance this place, to be a silent partner until the last vintage is out and sold. If you're that dubious about my honor as a businessman—and I know *trust* isn't one of your strong points—we don't even have to sign the papers until the bottles are shipped out. No commitment on your part until the work is done and the wine is finished. But then Waterford *will* become part of Lawson Estate."

"I have issues with trust?" she sputtered. It might be an accurate assessment, but that didn't give him the right to waltz in here and point out her hang-ups.

"Believe me, Zoe, this wouldn't be my first choice, either. Doing this without a watertight contract goes against my every instinct. But what do you think? Can we trust each other this one last time?"

Zoe opened her mouth to deny his accusation, but no words came out. He didn't understand. It wasn't about trust at all. It was just that she'd made a habit out of relying on no one but herself. Things were just safer that way. And now Hugh Lawson wanted her to put everything aside and let him *help* her?

If she had a list of people she'd be willing to call on for assistance, Hugh wouldn't even make the top twenty. Hell, he probably wouldn't make the list at all.

But right now, she didn't have any choice.

She couldn't come out and say it—the words would have stuck in her throat. "You can't ever use the Waterford name. My grandfather was explicit about that."

Mack had also been explicit about not selling to Hugh Lawson, but Zoe was rapidly realizing she had no choice. She never had. She'd just spent two days trying to avoid the inevitable.

Hugh's mouth softened into a hint of a smile as he recognized her capitulation. It wasn't a nice one. "Why would I want to use the Waterford name, Zoe? When Lawson Estate is known around the world?"

He'd won—he was getting exactly what he wanted—and he still couldn't resist digging at her.

"But I do have one condition."

Zoe glared at him. Now there were conditions? "You arrogant little—"

"I meant what I said about helping with the wine-making, Zoe. I want to be part of this. I

want to work by your side and watch and learn.
I want to know Mack's secrets."

"But—"

"No 'buts,' Zoe." His eyes flashed with a
determination that was almost frightening. "I
know this is your only option. I don't care about
taking credit for this wine and I definitely don't
care about using the Waterford name, but when
I buy this place, I buy Mack's legacy. I want to
know every little trick in his book."

Flabbergasted, Zoe just stood and stared at
him.

"I can see you need a little time to digest all
this. Fine." He checked the barrel he was working on, resettled the tube, then peered into the
rapidly filling vat. When he turned back to her,
his expression had relaxed into his usual laid-
back charm. She envied his ability to do that, to
seemingly turn his emotions on a dime.

"This barrel will be done shortly—you can
handle finishing it up on your own. Then we
can tackle the rest of this tomorrow morning."
He gestured to the rack of remaining barrels.
"Say eight o'clock? I'll see you then."

Taking another moment to carefully check
the pump set-up, as if to assure himself that she
wasn't going to get herself into trouble, Hugh
flashed her one of his patented hundred-watt
smiles—and then he was gone.

CHAPTER EIGHT

ZOE LOOKED AROUND THE dilapidated shed. Despite the very real chill leaching into her bones it seemed somehow unreal, insubstantial. She could still hardly believe she was back here again.

And seriously considering selling Waterford to Hugh Lawson.

Selling Waterford to Lawson Estate went against everything her grandfather had taught her. The feud between Mack and Peter Lawson went back to Zoe's childhood—she'd never known exactly how it had started. All she remembered was that long ago, they'd all been happy. She and her mother had moved to Waterford when Zoe was nine years old—yet another house in a string of houses—but this one was different.

For the first time in her life, her mother seemed settled, determined to stay somewhere for more than a few months. Her grandfather had already been a gruff, serious old man, but not quite the curmudgeon he became after her mother's death. Zoe remembered piggy-back rides, planting vegetables in the backyard and eating grapes in the sun.

Then things changed. Her mother and grandfather fought. Not in front of her, but their animosity was so strong that even a child could figure out that—like everything her grandfather disliked—it had something to do with Lawson Estate. He didn't like the way the Lawsons did business. Didn't like their wine. And, most especially, didn't like the way their estate's star was on the rise—already beginning to eclipse the Waterford Shiraz that had been the valley's pride and joy for decades. At night, when they thought she was asleep, they didn't bother keeping their voices down. Zoe remembered hiding in her bedroom, her head under the pillows to block out the noise. After one particularly vicious slanging match that had sent her mother out to the car and racing off with squealing tires, she'd fallen asleep. The next morning her grandfather told her that her mummy had died in a car crash.

All she wanted was for this whole thing to go away. Could she somehow leave and get Stephen Carter—whose bill she still couldn't pay—to work it out for her?

The sound of her mobile phone cut through

the turmoil of her thoughts, and Zoe answered it cautiously—the caller's identity was blocked.

"Zoe?"

"Who is this?"

"It's Wil. How're you doing?"

The American accent and slight delay in the line would have told Zoe instantly who it was, even if he hadn't identified himself. Wil Shepherd, CEO of Golden Gate Estate in the Napa Valley—her boss.

"Hi, Wil, I'm fine. Is everything okay?" Instantly concerned, Zoe ran through the reasons he might be calling. A problem with the vintage, an issue at the vineyard, a disaster with the about-to-be-picked crop?

Had she always been such a catastrophizer? Or was it something Tangawarra brought out in her?

"Everything's fine. I just wanted to see how you were."

Wil was a nice guy. He was one of the reasons she enjoyed working at Golden Gate so much. Perhaps also one of the reasons she enjoyed living in the Napa. Until she'd come back to Tangawarra, she hadn't realized how much of a home California had become to her—and the idea was unnerving. Zoe was careful to avoid those feelings of attachment that most people seemed to crave.

"That's sweet," she said. She could just picture Wil's white smile, ruddy face and shock of blond hair. He'd been an attractive man—twenty years and twenty pounds ago.

"Oh, and I did maybe have one tiny question about the zin while I have you on the phone."

Zoe laughed at that. It was nice to be needed for her professional abilities—and reminded that some people thought of her as a competent adult, not a petulant child with trust issues. "Shoot."

They had a brief technical discussion about the wine. Zoe only needed to close her eyes and she could recall the exact bouquet of her latest zinfandel—a handy trick when Wil was asking for her advice from half a world away.

"Thanks, Zoe," he said. "You're a miracle worker."

"Not really. If I'd left you better notes, you wouldn't have had to call."

Wil made a frustrated sound. "Why are you always so hard on yourself?"

"I'm not!" Zoe protested, surprised by such a personal comment. Maybe she was overly sensitive right now.

"Okay, sure. You just happen to be one of the hardest working, most talented winemakers I've ever had the privilege of working with. Ask anyone—except you."

Zoe rolled her eyes, but Wil's praise warmed her, a part of her that had begun to ice over since she'd arrived back in Tangawarra. "It's an Aussie thing," she said dismissively. "It's polite to be humble." She went over to the desk that was hidden in a little nook that was laughingly called the office. Mack's wine-making notebook was sitting there, still open to the page Zoe had been reading.

Speaking of humble.

She ran her finger down the broken spine. It wasn't a glamorous book—no ribbon-bound leather journal filled with illustrations and newspaper cuttings and mysterious quotations in beautifully inked script. It was just a boring, everyday notebook bound with black cardboard. Mack wrote in blue biro, mostly in all capitals and the writing got shakier as the pages went on, presumably as his health had begun to fail. Each entry started with a date and the notes below it were mostly his own shorthand jottings, sometimes a single word, sometimes just quotation marks, which Zoe took to mean "repeat of above." Much of it Zoe didn't even understand.

She tossed the book back on the desk.

"You know, maybe you need to be a little less polite on occasion," Wil said, bringing her back to the conversation at hand.

"Yeah, right," Zoe muttered. She wished Hugh and the townsfolk of Tangawarra could hear that. Zoe Waters's boss, telling her she was *too* polite. They'd laugh their asses off.

Zoe stepped outside the cold shed and made her way over to the car, which was bathed for the moment in weak sunshine. She leaned against the hood and tried to soak in the warmth.

"So *are* you really okay?" Wil pressed. "How was the funeral? You didn't say much before you left or when you called to say your grandfather had passed—I figure the news hadn't had time to sink in yet."

Or she just didn't care.

Zoe gave Wil a quick rundown of her grandfather's last days and the funeral. She mentioned needing to finalize his estate, but downplayed the seriousness of the financial woes. "He left a mess behind, Wil. It's taking a little longer than I thought to sort out."

There was a brief pause. "Do you still think you'll be home by the end of next week?"

"That's the plan." More than anything, she wanted to get away from here, even if it was just back to her plain little apartment and her plain little life. Sure, all she did was work, sleep and watch some occasional TV, but she'd choose that blandness over the emotional chaos of

Tangawarra any day of the week and twice on Sundays.

"Well, let me know if you need more time."

"We both know you can't give me any." The fruit on the estate was going to be picked very soon and Zoe had to be there for that.

"We can work something out."

Eager to change the subject, Zoe asked after a staff member who'd been ill when she left. "How's Leanne doing? Is she feeling better?"

Wil tutted. "No, she's not great, and it doesn't look like she'll be back any time soon."

She and Wil then had a long conversation about changing around the responsibilities at the winery to adjust for the loss of one of their key staff. After they'd talked it out and come to a potential solution, Wil gave a relieved sigh.

"Thanks, Zoe, that was a real help. I miss having you around to talk to—you always have such a logical, level-headed take on things."

Did she? Those weren't words she'd have used to describe herself. But then she was usually very careful about the face she presented to the world these days. Perhaps that front, that mask, *was* level-headed and logical. Whatever it was, it wasn't emotional. It wasn't the snappy, petulant child she'd somehow morphed into since she'd come back here.

"No worries, Wil," she replied, avoiding the compliment. "Anything else?"

"That's it. I'll let you get on with things and I'm going to head for bed. Although…" He paused significantly, and Zoe immediately knew why.

"We still have to talk about my contract," she said, filling in the gap.

"Exactly."

"Can't it wait until I return?"

"I guess it can. But you know I want you to sign on for more than twelve months this time. My preference would be five years."

"I never sign on anywhere for more than a year, Wil."

"I know." He sighed. "But surely it wouldn't hurt to have a bit of permanence in your life. A bit of certainty."

Zoe shook her head, even though he couldn't see her. "That's not how I do things."

"All right, all right, I give up. For now. We'll talk again when you get back."

Of course they would. But her answer wouldn't change. "Sure."

They finished the call and Zoe put the phone back into her pocket. She headed back into the winery biting her lip until it hurt.

What on earth was she still doing here? The child she'd been wanted to run away. But the adult she was now couldn't run from the responsibilities and leave the mess for someone else to clean up.

Thanks a bloody lot, Mack.

She went back to the now-empty barrel and pushed up her sleeves, preparing to hoist it down and begin the unenviable task of scrubbing it clean. At least it would be a good distraction. And an outlet for this…this…*anger* that seemed to keep washing over her since she'd stepped foot back in Tangawarra.

Maybe it was like an allergic reaction to the soil. She'd certainly been an angry young girl here. An angry young girl she'd thought she'd left far behind, but who kept jumping out at her from the shadows.

THE NEXT MORNING HUGH pulled one of the Lawson Estate utes up to their well-stocked equipment shed, selected a range of items and began carefully packing them in the back. Anything he could think of that they might need at Waterford to complete the work there. Mack's equipment was astonishingly old and much of it in poor repair—he didn't want any more accidents like yesterday's near-electrocution.

"What's up, Boss?"

Morris strolled over, hands in pockets. He seemed his usual laid-back self, but those intelligent eyes showed he knew more than he was letting on.

"Taking some equipment over to Waterford," Hugh said with a grunt as he lifted a high-pressure cleaning unit into the back of the vehicle.

Morris made no move to help. "Right." He stood, one hip against the ute, and watched Hugh go back and forth, eyes shrewd under the peak of his ever-present Lawson Estate cap.

"S'pose it's no good askin' why," he said eventually, as Hugh secured the load with a couple of ropes.

Hugh paused. Given that Morris was the operations manager, he probably deserved an explanation for why several thousand dollars worth of equipment was suddenly being transferred off the property—and to Waterford, no less.

If only he could give one that didn't sound insane.

"I'm buying Waterford."

Morris nodded—he knew it had been a part of Hugh's plan for a long time.

"Zoe's condition of sale is getting Mack's last vintage bottled before she'll sign over the winery." Yeah, it still sounded like a can of crazy. Hugh knew that any half-logical businessperson would be running in the opposite direction from a ridiculous deal like this—especially one as cautious and carefully astute as he usually was—but here he was, jumping in with both feet. And that was without all the messy *history* stuff complicating matters.

To his credit, Morris didn't so much as blink. "Ah-huh."

The other man's taciturn manner kept Hugh talking. Another one of his old tricks, but it always seemed to work. "She can't do it by herself, no matter what she thinks. Stupid girl. She'll kill herself—or break her back at the very least," he added.

"Then just as well you'll be there lookin' out for her, I'd say."

"I'm only there to make sure she doesn't burn down the place." He pulled hard on the ropes securing the load, surprised at how defensive he sounded. "Besides, someone has to look after her," he muttered, tightening the ropes on one side of the ute.

"Yep, someone does," Morris agreed. He finally moved from his lounging position and helped Hugh secure the ropes.

"Thanks." Hugh rounded up a few last-minute things and put them on the passenger seat, before climbing behind the wheel.

"Boss?" Morris held the door before Hugh could reach out to close it.

"Yeah?"

"Don't make the same mistakes your old man did."

"Like what?"

Morris shrugged one shoulder. "Just…be careful. Don't lose sight of what's really important."

Hugh gave him a disbelieving look. "You know we've been trying to acquire Waterford for years now. Strategically, it's going to add enormous value to us—the vines could become our most important asset. Even playing along with Zoe's condition of sale, it's still worth it."

"Yeah, I know. That's not quite what I meant." Morris paused a moment, as if considering his words. "Your dad—he was reckless sometimes."

Hugh sighed heavily. "I know." Once he'd fully taken over the estate and had a chance to comb back through its financial history, the volatile combination of his father's hot-headed temper and autocratic decision-making had become patently obvious. In the main, Pete Lawson's impulsive decisions had worked out—but there had also been more than a few errors of judgment that had come at a heavy cost.

"Dad made some poor choices," Hugh said diplomatically, still feeling a need to remain loyal, even though Morris probably knew better than he did the extent of Pete Lawson's mistakes. "But it's been different since I took over."

Morris nodded. "You're a...level-headed one, that's for sure. But that's not what I was gettin' at."

"What do you mean?"

"Just... Your dad didn't always get his priorities straight."

"I'm not about to make the same mistakes he did. Don't worry—I know what I'm doing. It's worth it, because of how valuable Waterford is to us. Those vines, right next door..." Hugh wondered for a moment who he was convincing. "Even with funding the vintage, it's too valuable an opportunity to pass up. Growing and strengthening Lawson Estate is what this is all about. My priorities are very clear."

"Okay, then." Morris hesitated for a moment, as if he was about to say more, but then he simply took a step back and shut the truck door with a slap that showed the topic was closed. "You'd better get going—I'm guessin' there's a stack of work to be done over there."

"You're not wrong." Hugh pictured Waterford's disheveled winery shed, so different from Lawson Estate's polished concrete and gleaming stainless steel.

"Good luck with that. With the work. And with lookin' out for that gal over there."

Hugh snorted. "Yeah. Not like she's waiting for a white knight on a stallion. If she saw one coming, she'd probably get out a shotgun." He shook his head at the mental image of a scowling Zoe standing behind the farmhouse taking aim as a white horse galloped across the vineyards.

"You know what I reckon? She's like a lion with a thorn in her paw. Her roar is pretty terrifying, but she's a pussycat on the inside. And that thorn is really hurtin' her."

Hugh's eyebrows rose. "You been out in the sun too long, Morris? That's the most philosophical thing I think I've ever heard you say." He was partly amused and partly intrigued by Morris's view of Zoe.

Morris shrugged, turning to leave. "See you 'round," he called over his shoulder.

Hugh drove the short distance to Waterford mulling over Morris's words.

Yes, the businessman in him wanted to own Waterford. He'd be stupid not to. But it was handy that there were good business reasons for it, because even if there weren't, he'd want it. He wanted Waterford with an irrational obsession that he'd harbored for years now.

Hugh pressed the accelerator harder, not necessarily a wise move on the unsurfaced, uneven road, but it helped him remember where he was. Who he was.

The CEO of Lawson Estate. An estate that was now a global empire with winery and vineyard properties across Australia, in Europe and just recently, South Africa. One of the largest producers of table wine in the country. Thanks to clever investing and shrewd acquisitions, he'd expanded quickly, making his father's vague dreams a reality faster than most people could believe. His strategy was aggressive, yet cautious. He'd never made any move that threatened the stability of the original Lawson Estate holdings—no matter what it might have looked like from the outside. His priority was expansion, yes, but not at the cost of what had already been built.

Funny, actually, now that he thought about it. It was the same damning faint praise the reviewers often leveled at Lawson Estate wines. *Familiar. Tried and true. Consistent.* There were worse things, of course, than to produce reliably good wines.

And now? The next target was next door.

He turned off the road and onto the even more shambling track that led to the Waterford farmhouse.

Would owning this place get rid of the messy feelings that were currently interfering with his peace of mind? His mind churned as he surveyed the rows of vines, and the thoughts that were never far from the surface these past few days intruded again.

His child.

Zoe had had their baby.

Hugh hadn't given much thought to family except for a vague notion that it would happen. One day. He wanted to be a father, preferably to a small brood of kids who would be able to play in the vineyard and learn to swim in the dam—just as he had.

The burning anger that had bloomed to life after Zoe had told him the truth hadn't gone away.

He needed to make her share the rest of her story. He didn't care how painful it would be— he needed some respite from this chaos and uncertainty, and he was sure that knowing what had really happened would give him that.

It wouldn't stop him wondering what *would* have happened if things had been different, though. If his father... If Mack...

Being angry at dead men was futile.

He still remembered the day his father had discovered their relationship and lied about Zoe's fate. His face had been puce with rage. Ranting about *that girl.* About Waterford trash and some high-and-mighty Lawson ideals. If

Hugh had expected sympathy as his father had broken the news of Zoe's suicide attempt, then he'd been born into the wrong family. Clearly Pete Lawson's intention had been to make Hugh feel so terrified and so guilty that he'd never dream of going against his father's orders not to contact Zoe again.

It hadn't stopped him waiting for her to contact him. He'd overheard his father intercepting her calls, and while part of him had wanted to race over and grab the phone from his father's hands, another part of him was too... *scared*. Facing Zoe after what she'd done—what he blamed himself for—scared him witless. And fear wasn't something Hugh had come up against very often in his life. Grief, yes. His mother had died after being ill for too long. But fear had been new.

So Hugh had done all the right things. He'd studied hard at school. Captained the footy team. Went to university and earned his business degree with honors.

What would have happened if he'd known the truth?

Hugh tightened his grip on the steering wheel as he pictured his father's face, blatantly lying as he told Hugh about Zoe's psychiatric care. Telling his heartbroken son that contacting her

would harm her recovery. That he should forget about her, move on with his life.

He pulled the ute up at the winery shed door
and killed the engine, looking around at the
aging buildings. The old man was dead. Hugh
would have the last laugh if for no other reason
than outliving the old coot.

"Zoe?" As he got out of the truck, Hugh noted
that the winery shed door was still padlocked,
so she couldn't be inside. His eyes ranged over
the property. Everything was still in the early
morning light. He walked over to the farmhouse, figuring that was the most likely place
she'd be.

He knocked, loudly, but got no response. He
listened for the sound of running water that
might indicate she was showering, but the house
was silent. As was the custom of neighbors in
the countryside, he didn't hesitate to open the
back door. The hinges creaked as he pulled it
open and stepped inside to call out again.

"Zoe?"

The kitchen showed only minimal signs of
habitation. A teacup and plate were sitting in
the drainer on the sink. A few pieces of fruit
were scattered in a wooden bowl on the counter. A wine magazine and a notebook were on
the table. There were some suspicious-looking
black dots on the floor beside the refrigerator

that indicated a pest problem—he wondered if there were any traps or bait put out.

Then he heard a faint rustling come from somewhere deep in the house.

"Zoe?" He tried again, taking another step inside the kitchen. "Are you here?"

He was just beginning to wonder if she was home at all when she appeared in the corridor.

The world went still as he took in the vision in front of him.

One hand was rubbing her eye. Her hair was a messy halo around her head. She wore the tiniest pink T-shirt he'd ever seen; a cartoon kitten printed across the front of it stared out with huge eyes, a cute image other than the rude finger gesture it was making. The top hugged her every curve, leaving very little to the imagination. Pink pajama pants rode low on her hips, and with her arm raised to rub her eye, revealed a strip of skin and the top of lacy black panties.

Hugh's mouth went dry and all thoughts of confronting her about the past evaporated.

"What are you doing here?" Zoe said, her voice crackling with sleep. "What time is it?"

She could have been sixteen again. All sweet and innocent with a hint of naughtiness. That was all it had ever had been. A compulsion to act out, desperate to be noticed, to prove that someone cared. Even as a teenager Hugh had wondered why he seemed to be the only one who could see that. Everyone else saw a reckless, disobedient girl, destined for a sticky end.

Hugh's body didn't recognize that any time had passed—it responded to her just as it had then. If he thought he'd learned to control his reactions in the past ten years, Zoe's mere presence blew that out of the water.

"City girl." He tried to sneer, but could feel it become a goofy smile, so he looked down and tapped his watch impatiently.

Zoe frowned at him, still sleep-befuddled. "What?"

He tried to look disdainful. "It's eight o'clock—practically afternoon. They've made you soft over in Californ-I-A. I'd have organized you a wake-up call if you'd asked."

Zoe told him what to do with that offer in no uncertain terms.

Hugh laughed at her. "I can see your vocabulary hasn't improved."

She scowled.

"Come on, up and at 'em. We've got lots of barrels to get through today."

Zoe gave a heavy sigh. "All right, all right. Make yourself useful and put the kettle on. I'll be back in a moment."

She turned on her heel and disappeared. Hugh couldn't stop a stab of disappointment that he no longer had the view to enjoy. Her quick spin at least gave him a brief glimpse of her curvy behind. And of a distinctly rude slogan printed across the back of her shirt.

He grinned as he obediently filled the kettle and began preparing tea. He had the sudden, unexpected idea that the day ahead might somehow be fun.

CHAPTER NINE

THE WORLD HAD BEEN a little out of kilter all day. Having Hugh surprise her while she was still in bed hadn't been the best beginning. Zoe was usually an early riser, but that was when she was able to get a decent night's sleep. She hadn't slept properly for a week now. She lay in bed for hours every night, and then, when she did finally manage to fall asleep, strange nightmares disturbed her.

Every morning she woke more tired than she'd been the night before and with a headache that wouldn't quit.

She put it down to being back in Tangawarra, where so many ghosts from her past waited to haunt her.

"Are you going to blend any of the leftovers from last year in with this year's vintage?" Hugh asked. He lifted a now-empty barrel from the rack and carried it over to the high-pressure cleaner he'd brought. Zoe barely stopped herself from punching the air when she saw it—the job was back-breaking enough without relying on pure elbow grease.

"Not sure yet." She was glad the conversation so far had been all business. Despite her pleasure at seeing the equipment Hugh had brought, she felt uncomfortable working in close confines with a man who could, at any moment, demand she share with him the most painful experience of her life.

As she tested the wine she fumbled with the pipette—a piece of equipment she had mastered years before—and swore quietly at herself for her skittishness. "It's a little over-oaked from being in the barrel too long," she said out loud. "But it might balance out. I'll have to see."

"We can make a blend when we rack that one off and see how it tastes."

"Good idea."

Conversation halted for a few minutes while Hugh turned on the noisy cleaner. She watched him for a moment. His crisp Lawson Estate shirt had been rumpled almost as soon as they'd begun their day's work, but that didn't in any way diminish his aura of power and control. The pale blue shirt was now spotted with wine stains, his sleeves were soaked from cleaning, and it clung to his back from perspiration. His usually neat dark hair had fallen across his forehead and that, combined with the short stubble on his jaw, somehow enhanced the commanding air he carried with him these days.

He crouched down, bending over to reach the inside corners of the barrel he was working on.

And oh, yes, those jeans fit him *very* well.

It took effort, but she managed to tear her eyes from Hugh's backside and head over to the little office area where her grandfather had kept his testing equipment. She completed the testing tasks automatically, making notations in Mack's notebook, her mind on other things.

As the morning went on, they settled into a routine that somehow worked even if she never quite lost her sense of unease. To Zoe's surprise, they were actually quite efficient. Hugh had an uncanny knack for reading her mind—he appeared at her elbow a moment before she called for him, and she seemed to know instinctively when another pair of hands was required to complete his task.

The atmosphere was friendly but brittle. All the unresolved issues between them continued to bubble away under the surface. Zoe couldn't relax—she knew that at some point Hugh would want more from her. One part of her was poised in fight-or-flight mode, awaiting the request.

And then there was the matter of the sale of Waterford, which, despite his presence and his seeming confidence that all was secure, still hadn't really been resolved in her mind.

This could only be the calm before the storm.

For now, Zoe would live with that.

There was a loud thump as Hugh returned the now-clean oak barrel to its place on the rack.

"Done." There was undeniable satisfaction in his voice.

"How many still to go?"

"We're getting close to halfway through. Should be able to get through them all today if we don't mind making it a late finish."

Zoe shook her head. "No." She was shattered. Her shoulders ached and her legs were wobbly from overexertion. She couldn't manage any more heavy lifting today. Surely he must be feeling it, too? "That's enough for now. Let's do some other cleaning this afternoon and finish the barrels tomorrow."

He gave her a challenging grin. "Wimping out on me?"

Zoe wanted to protest, but couldn't. "Yes. Yes, I am officially wimping out. I can't do any more."

Hugh let out a short laugh and collapsed in fake drama against the rack. "Thank God. I'm just about broken here."

Zoe laughed, as well.

"I am forced to admit that being a desk jockey for the past few years has taken its toll."

He didn't look it. "Wuss."

"Yeah, I guess."

"You still work in the winery, though, right?" It was obvious from today that he knew what he was doing.

"Sometimes. I help out at the peak times, like picking, and I've helped rack off a couple of times. I swore I'd never do it again, it was such a crap job." He chuckled, a low sound that made Zoe melt slightly.

"Ah, the glamorous world of wine-making." She smiled.

He returned the smile.

This was all getting a little too comfortable. Zoe slapped her hands together in a vague attempt to clean them. She deliberately turned away from that smile, busying herself with unnecessarily shifting a couple of glasses she'd been using for tasting and blending. "Okay, well, if we're done for today, I'll let you get going."

"Excuse me?" Hugh frowned.

"I'm sure you've got phone calls or emails or some such to deal with." She made her voice deliberately carefree.

His tone was clipped when he replied. "Yeah, probably."

"Right, then." Zoe gestured to the equipment spread around them. It hadn't taken long for it to become scattered through the shed, taking up residence as if it belonged there. "Do we need to pack all this up for you? Or can it wait here until we start again tomorrow?"

"We can leave it here. It's not needed right at the moment."

"Great."

There was a beat of silence. What, did the man want a medal? "Well, thanks again, Hugh."

He didn't move. Didn't say anything.

She wasn't hanging around to find out what he was waiting for. "I've got to get into town." She wiped her palms on her jeans, a nervous habit, just like babbling too much. The way she was doing now. "I know Tangawarra's shop owners are probably calling extra security now that I'm here, but you can assure them on my behalf that my fingers aren't as sticky as they used to be." She held them up as if to prove her point.

"It's not like that, Zoe."

Zoe hadn't actually been in town apart from a quick trip to the supermarket. Sure, some of the buildings and signage had changed, but had the town's heart changed all that much? Most people had been nice at the wake, but there were still those who looked at her askance, assessing her trustworthiness in exactly the same way they had ten years before. And why shouldn't they? She hadn't yet given them any reason to change those ideas.

"Yeah? What, you mean they don't pigeon-hole you into a category and keep you there for the rest of your life anymore? Zoe Waters, delinquent, unstable reprobate? Hugh Lawson, model citizen and community leader?"

Zoe caught the slight wince that crossed his face.

"Don't bother denying it. I might not have lived here for ten years, but I know just what it's like."

"Zoe, you—"

She cut him off. "Thanks again for the help, Hugh. Don't let the door hit your ass on the way out." She said "ass" with an American accent, not entirely sure why. Maybe it was a little softer that way.

She expected him to smile, or maybe complain about being pushed out the door after all the hard work he'd put in. But he just stood there, staring at her. His expression was difficult to read, but she thought she saw a flash of something close to pity.

"What?" she demanded. "Don't you dare look at me like that."

He held out a hand, as if calming a wild animal. "Zoe. I just wish you'd—"

"Wish I'd what? Behave? Settle down? Take their gossip and criticism with a smile and a wave? Forget it. I'm not going to give them the satisfaction."

"So instead you're going to show them how angry you still are? How little you've really changed?"

He was right, damn him, but no way would she let him see that. "Oh, just get over yourself. Not everyone can be as angelic a human being as Hugh Lawson." This argument felt far too familiar. She wondered how many times they'd had it when they were teens.

But grown-up Hugh didn't bite back the way teenage-Hugh used to, surprising her. "Zoe," he began patiently. "If you'd just give people a chance, you'd see that things are different here."

"Yeah? Where were you when they were making those speeches at the wake? When they were reminding everyone about my criminal past? I'm surprised they didn't start a raffle with the first prize being 'ten minutes with Zoe Waters to take out your pound of flesh.'"

Hugh sighed heavily. "The wake was about memories. It's inevitable that some of them would—"

"That's it." Zoe strode past him, their shoulders colliding as she stormed to the door. "Close the door when you leave." She patted her jeans pocket, relieved to find her keys there.

He followed her outside. "Zoe! Wait." He sounded irritated now. "You can't just walk away. We need to talk about—"

She didn't wait to hear the rest of his sentence, but headed straight for her sedan, jumped in and drove off.

As STORM-OUTS WENT, she reflected fifteen minutes later, it had been less than effective. She'd gotten only halfway down the driveway when she realized that her purse was still inside the house, making a trip into town for supplies pointless.

Unless she was going to apply the five-finger discount to her purchases, of course.

She managed a laugh at her own bleak thoughts, then pulled the car off to the side of the road.

How long would Hugh hang around before heading back to the Lawson Estate? Surely not long—there wasn't anything to keep him there.

Just to be safe, she waited another ten minutes before driving back to the house. As soon as it was clear that the Lawson Estate vehicle was gone, she breathed more easily. Then it was a simple matter of collecting her purse—only then she got a look at herself in the mirror in the hallway and shook her head.

After a shower, change of clothes and a thorough hair brushing, she was finally on her way to Tangawarra.

First stop was the supermarket. Whether it was the fresh air, the physical labor or just the influence of Patricia's homemade stew, Zoe's appetite had returned and the tins of tuna and salad leaves she'd purchased earlier weren't going to cut it. Mack's freezer was stocked with meat—likely from a neighbor—so she only needed the accompaniments to give her a pantry full of meal possibilities.

Loading the bags into the back of the car, Zoe looked around the car park. The supermarket was new—the town now big enough to attract one of the large chain stores. She wondered if the little independent grocer they'd used to shop at was still around.

Maybe Hugh was right—maybe Tangawarra had changed?

The two teens she'd noticed on the day of the funeral were nowhere to be seen. She wondered about them. They would have been little kids when she'd left Tangawarra—cute little kindergarteners, probably. Was there any way to tell at that age how kids would turn out? Had they preferred the black crayons? The books about witches instead of the ones about fairies? Or were such things all about nurture, not nature?

Or lack of nurture in her case.

Locking up the car, Zoe headed for the main street. She needed a few things from the chemist that she hadn't been able to get at the supermarket. Headache pills, for one.

Luckily there weren't too many people out and about. Those people she did pass on the street smiled or said hello. Zoe tried hard to reason with herself that this was a small town, and that was just what people did here, but it was hard to set aside her paranoia.

What were they thinking? Did they know who she was?

Or...

Was she the one trapped in a time-warp here?

It was hard to let go of her prejudices, her ideas of what Tangawarra and its townsfolk were like, but so far everyone had been, well, *pleasant.* Polite. Apart from at the wake, and maybe Hugh was right—that event was all about memories and maybe it was understandable that they'd reminisced about her wayward youth.

Was it possible that everyone had moved on—except her?

"Zoe!"

The voice came from behind her and it was

hard to resist the impulse to run away. Instead, she forced herself to stop and turn around, deliberately arranging her face in an expression she hoped didn't look as irritated as she felt.

"Hi, Patricia."

The older woman was puffing slightly as she took a few quick steps to catch up. "I thought that was you," she said.

"You thought right."

"How are you, dear?"

Patricia reached out a hand and rested it on Zoe's elbow. It made Zoe want to flinch, but she made an effort to contain it.

"I'm fine," she answered automatically.

"It's often those first days after a loss that are the worst." Patricia's mouth twisted into a sympathetic grimace.

It took Zoe a moment to realize what Patricia meant and the realization shocked her. Had she forgotten Mack already? Or did she just have too much other stuff to worry about? "Oh, yes, I guess," she replied, hoping she sounded appropriately grief-stricken.

"It just doesn't seem right that he's not with us anymore, does it?"

Zoe shrugged. "Those last few days in hospital—" Something in her throat caught and she coughed to clear it. "It's better that it's over."

"Of course, of course." Patricia tut-tutted.

"He was in pain and it's for the best, bless him." She squeezed Zoe's arm before taking a step back to survey her critically. "You're still not eating properly, are you? I told Bert I should have come over last night. We had lasagna and there was plenty left over. Tonight you must come to our place and—"

"That's so lovely of you to offer," Zoe interrupted hastily, "but I've got a lot of things to get through before I leave and I don't really have the time."

Before Patricia could insist, a deep male voice broke in. "Ah, Zoe, there you are."

Stephen Carter appeared from the doorway of his office—the building Zoe belatedly realized she and Patricia had stopped in front of. She closed her eyes for a moment, seeking out her inner supply of patience. So much for the fast, anonymous run into town.

"Mr. Carter."

"Please, call me Stephen. G'day, Patricia. How are things at Long Track?"

Patricia and Stephen took a moment to exchange pleasantries. Just as Zoe was about to make a break for it, the accountant peered at her over his glasses.

"Now, Zoe, while you're here, let's have another chat about Waterford." He gestured to his office.

The last thing Zoe wanted was to sit in that stuffy room and hear her desperate situation outlined all over again. Not to mention the urge she had to slap the accountant in the face for his completely inappropriate conversation with Hugh, revealing the private financial circumstances at Waterford. If they were alone, she wasn't sure how well she'd restrain herself. "Stephen, I don't really have time to—" she began.

"Has Zoe told you that Bert and I are interested in Waterford?" Patricia asked.

The accountant turned to her with a raised eyebrow. "Really? What sort of terms are you willing to offer?"

Patricia shot a glance at Zoe. "Well, Zoe and I had talked about making a special arrangement, with a long settlement. Bert and I would need six months to build up the capital and we'd take over the last Waterford vintage so Zoe wouldn't have to deal with it."

Stephen Carter had begun shaking his head before Patricia was halfway through her speech and she ended somewhat limply.

"Wouldn't work, I'm afraid," he declared.

"But if we came to a private arrangement with Zoe then maybe—" Patricia tried again.

"Nope. The debt situation hanging over Waterford is just untenable, Patricia."

"What do you mean?"

"Waterford's in a lot of trouble. It needs to be bailed out now. The shorter the settlement the better. Unless you and Bert have a nest egg somewhere that I don't know about, then you'd just be taking on a mountain of worry."

Patricia's shoulders slumped. "Oh. Well, I guess that's that, then."

Zoe's eyes just flicked between the two of them—shocked into momentary silence. Were they really discussing her personal finances in the street?

"It was worth looking into, though," the accountant said.

"Yes. It would have been nice," Patricia said with a wistful expression. Then she took a step closer to Stephen and lowered her voice. "What's going to happen? Bankruptcy? Or is there another buyer?"

The accountant opened his mouth to speak and Zoe held up her hands, recovering the power of speech. "Whoa!" She'd had just about enough of this. "Stephen, this is a private matter. I don't want it discussed out on the street!" Her voice had the slightly hysterical edge that she hadn't been able to get rid of since coming back to Tangawarra.

He looked momentarily chastised, but then turned to frown at Patricia. "Exactly what I was going to say. Sorry, Patricia, but I can't discuss that with you."

Patricia looked hurt and Zoe was annoyed with herself for feeling guilty about that. It was none of the other woman's business and she deserved to have her wrist slapped for prying. But then she remembered the beef casserole and the other kindnesses Patricia had shown her and she tried her best to smooth over her irritation.

"Sorry, Patricia," Zoe began. "It's just we're out here on the street where anyone could overhear. You know how private Mack was. He wouldn't want his business discussed like this."

"Of course, you're right. Mack would be looking down on us with that frown of his!" Patricia's hurt faded and she seemed almost gleeful now. "He was so good at playing the grumpy old man card."

That's because he was a grumpy old man, Zoe felt like saying.

"Zoe, when can we catch up?" Stephen asked.

Zoe was still furious with the accountant for his conversation with Hugh—regardless of whether or not that was the only viable option for Waterford. By all rights, she should march the man into his office and give him a lecture about confidentiality and appropriateness. But that would take energy she didn't have to spare.

And Stephen was, as far as she knew, the only accountant in town. She needed him on her side.

"Sometime tomorrow," Zoe said, settling for a vague answer. "I'm busy for the rest of today."

"Okay, well, give me a call and we'll make a time. We can't sit too long on this," he added in a warning tone.

Zoe nodded. The vague niggle at the back of her neck that had required this walk to the chemist had begun to bloom into a full-blown headache. She needed peace and quiet to gather herself again without the threat of Hugh's demanding presence, Patricia's well-meaning kindness or Stephen Carter's solemn pessimism. About a month of it, if possible, but a few hours was all she was likely to get.

"I'll call you," she promised. "And thanks again, Patricia. I'll see you around."

CHAPTER TEN

THAT NIGHT ZOE SET THE alarm clock, determined not to be caught sleeping in again.

It probably wasn't really necessary, though, because she slept fitfully, plagued by unsettling dreams. Then there were the periods of wakefulness when she could only lie there and stare at the cracks in the ceiling and worry. What to do with Waterford. What to do about her life. What to do about Hugh.

If she'd never met him before and had seen him walk past her on the street, he'd have turned her head. If she'd seen him in a bar, she'd have made eye contact, let him buy her a drink, seen where things went…

But he wasn't just a man she'd met in a bar. He was the man who wanted to buy Waterford against her grandfather's wishes. Against *her* wishes—sort of. But he was also the man who could offer her the only reasonable way out of her dire financial circumstances.

And then there was their personal history…

She'd forgotten how quiet it was out here at

night. No traffic noise, no background hum of a city going about its nightly business. Just the crickets to keep her company, their continuous drone a fitting soundtrack for her whirling thoughts.

She'd already made a deal with the devil. Every day that Hugh Lawson spent in the winery helping with the vintage was another tie binding Zoe to his contract of sale. He hadn't made her sign anything yet—she could still back out, take his help with the wine and sell to someone else.

But she wouldn't.

And at some level, Hugh had to know that.

It went against her every instinct to trust him the way she was. Trusting him to keep his word. To trust him to do the right thing. If he was anyone else in the world there would be no way…

Zoe liked to think she'd changed in the years she'd spent away from Tangawarra. But her basic principles, the fundamental core of what made her who she was—had that altered dramatically? Probably not.

And neither had Hugh. He had always been the knight in shining armor. Even as a teenager, he'd been a hero. He'd been so popular that his friendships with geeks and misfits—like her—didn't affect his reputation. Dating the school's delinquent had only enhanced his aura and had made Zoe cool by association—for a while at least. It had never been a position she'd been comfortable with.

She had no doubt it would be the same now. Dating adult Hugh would be like a grown-up version of going out with high-school Hugh. Just like back then, she was sure his girlfriend would be under the spotlight, her behavior, dress, language, all scrutinized for appropriateness and suitability. Hugh was important to the town—always had been—and they wanted only what was best for him.

A night bird called out, a species she couldn't identify. It shattered the crickets' concentration and their whine halted for a moment before starting up again.

Then there was Hugh himself. He'd become a carbon copy of his father—only more successful. His confidence, his self-assurance, the whole package that made up adult Hugh Lawson was more than a little intimidating.

All it did was serve to reinforce the disparity between them—the vastly different outcomes their teenage split had wrought. Hugh had been told lies and gone on to build himself a prosperous future, surrounded by a community that adored him. She'd had no choice but to deal with the truth, and had had to make her own way in the world.

The idea there could be anything between them now, after everything, was laughable.

"Stop it!" Zoe growled at herself, punched the pillow and stared at the old-fashioned alarm clock beside the bed. It would be morning soon, thankfully. For now the chill in the air was enough to keep her in bed, but soon she'd get up and dress and get to work.

JUST BEFORE SUNRISE ZOE gave up trying to sleep. It was a cool morning, windy with patchy rain that hurled itself against the windows as if trying to get inside. She fixed herself some breakfast—porridge heated up in Mack's ancient microwave to help stave off the cold.

By the time Hugh arrived, she'd already been in the winery for almost an hour and had made good progress on draining another barrel.

"Good morning," she called out as she heard his footsteps approaching.

"You're an early bird today," he said.

"You sound disappointed," Zoe said, without lifting her head from the work she was doing. "What, did you want to catch me in my pajamas again?"

He gave a low chuckle. "I refuse to answer that question on the grounds I may incriminate myself."

Zoe's cheeks heated and she bent over to hide

her face. It had been a joke. She'd expected vigorous denial, not flirting. She wished he'd stop doing that—it made things unnecessarily confusing.

Worn and muddied boots appeared in her sightline.

"So, Boss, what's on for today? Where do you want me?"

It took a moment for Zoe to think about the question and answer it in a way that was not at all suggestive.

"I want to continue with racking off—see if we can finish it today. I'd also like to make a start on the office when we run out of steam. There's a whole bunch of stuff in there that needs to be sorted out." She straightened and faced him, determined to be all business.

"Okay."

"I know the admin stuff wasn't exactly what you had in mind, but if you want to know all of Mack's secrets, then you'd better be prepared to deal with the dust and dirt as well as the grape juice."

"Zoe, I said okay." He had a gentle smile on his face, as if indulging a petulant child. It was just the sort of thing that would usually make Zoe feel chastised, but her lack of sleep had left her short-tempered and irritable.

Don't bite.

Zoe gritted her teeth. "You can start with cleaning. Over there." She pointed to a barrel that was already empty and ready to be scrubbed.

"Yes, ma'am." Hugh gave a cowboy-style touch to the brim of his hat.

Don't smile.

He walked over to the barrel, his hands already busy unbuttoning his shirt cuffs and rolling up the sleeves.

And don't look.

HUGH WAS SURPRISED BY how much he was enjoying the physical labor of working at Waterford. It wasn't that he didn't do any hands-on work at Lawson Estate, but generally speaking his time was better spent in the office. He'd built a solid, qualified team who ran things for him on the ground and although he checked in with them regularly, he didn't need to be out there working alongside them.

Having been raised on a vineyard, though, Hugh was used to the "all hands on deck" seasonality of the business. He'd grown up picking grapes, pruning vines, sweeping and mopping out the winery.

He hadn't realized that he kind of missed it.

It helped that he and Zoe seemed to work so well together. Apart from her occasional snarky remarks—she was clearly in a bad mood today—they'd managed to find an effective and efficient working style. All day they'd worked smoothly with each other, stopping only for a quick bite at lunchtime, and they'd made impressive progress.

Sometimes he'd been able to get her talking. She'd forget, for just a few minutes, about all the implications of their past and what they were doing now. And when she did, he got a glimpse of who Zoe Waters was today. And... he liked her.

"So, tell me about Golden Gate," he prompted after they'd been working in silence for a while. He took off his hat and rested it on the barrel rack, taking a moment to lean back and rest.

She started and a little of the wine she'd been siphoning into a tasting glass spilled on the concrete floor leaving a bright purple splotch. "What? Why?"

Hugh stopped himself from sighing in frustration. Today's Zoe still had all the old personal barriers. Cautious about giving out personal information—anything that someone might be able to use against her. He should have eased her into it. "Competitive analysis," he bluffed. "Always good to keep your ear to the ground, I've found."

Zoe gave an unladylike snort.

"What?" he asked.

"Industrial espionage, Hugh? I didn't think you'd stoop that low."

The fact that she thought so little of his business practices rankled. She'd insulted Lawson Estate several times now, and her barbs hurt. Perhaps because they'd once been so close, he hadn't expected that from her. But they were virtually strangers now, and all he was asking for was a chance to change that.

"I wasn't asking for state secrets, Zoe," he said, trying to maintain a cool tone. "I was just asking about the winery. Give me the tourist spiel if you want. Or not." He busied himself with a task so that it didn't look like he was putting pressure on her by standing and waiting for an answer.

Zoe was silent for a moment. Then perhaps she realized how snappy she'd been, because when she spoke her voice was softer. She was the grown-up Zoe again.

"It's a nice place. Quite large. About twenty-five acres of vines, mostly on the property in Napa but they've also got another property in Sonoma. They make an estate zinfandel, chardonnay and a sparkling wine. They buy in grapes to make a pinot noir and a cabernet. They grow some pinot on the estate, but it's not good enough to stand on its own, which is why they buy in. There, that's a secret for you."

He ignored her provocation. "Do they have a cellar door?"

"Yes. With the requisite tasting room and gourmet grocery." She paused, as if wondering whether to continue with the conversation. To Hugh's surprise, she did, by asking him a question. "Have you ever been to the region?"

"Once, years ago."

She nodded. "Then you know that there's really no such thing as a small place there. Golden Gate isn't huge, but it would be at least the size of Lawson Estate—one of the medium-size players."

"Do you like the wines?"

Zoe stopped what she was doing to study him with a frown. "What a strange question."

"Not really. I don't like all of Lawson Estate's wines. I love our premium Shiraz and our cabernet. I think our chardonnay is excellent, but I don't enjoy the sauvignon blanc. Then again, that's one of our biggest sellers, so goes to show what I know."

"I think Lawson Estate's Shiraz is very good."

Hugh couldn't help smiling. "Ah, damned by faint praise."

"That's not what I meant."

"It doesn't matter." Hugh shrugged it off. "You're not saying anything I don't read in the wine reviews. We make good wine. It's not great wine, but we make a lot and sell a lot, and I'm proud of what we put our label on."

"You should be."

"Again with the faint praise."

"Why are you reading into everything I say?"

"Am I?"

They stared at each other for a moment. What was going on in that head of hers? She looked faintly annoyed. *Frustrated.* Zoe had never been good at talking about anything that really mattered. Like her feelings. She'd always been much faster with a sarcastic quip than at expressing what was in her heart. Maybe she'd learned it from Mack—the man hadn't exactly been forthcoming himself.

There was so much Hugh wished he could change about the past—quite apart from the obvious. Report Mack Waters to child services for neglect, for a start. No child deserved to grow up the way Zoe had. So much of what she said and did had seemed extreme and bizarre to him back then. Now, with ten years of perspective, he could see where it had come from.

Where it was still coming from.

"Get back to work," Zoe said finally, returning her attention to the barrel she was working on. She leaned over to suck up a measure of wine into the pipette, putting a thumb over the tip to hold it, and then releasing it into a glass. She sniffed and tasted, walking to the door to spit her mouthful onto the grass outside.

"Needs some acid," she muttered to herself.

"Is it any good, do you think?" Hugh asked.

"It's…great." She sighed. "It's…it's one of the best. He'll go out on a high."

Hugh couldn't muster much enthusiasm for that thought. Neither, it seemed from her flat tone, could Zoe.

"Waterford will go out on a high," Hugh said, correcting her.

Zoe rewarded him with a tiny smile. "Yeah. Waterford will."

She looked as if she was going to say more, so Hugh stayed silent, hoping that would encourage her.

His patience paid off.

"Funny, I don't really feel any great connection to the Waters family. But Waterford, the actual land here—" She broke off, busying herself with writing in a black-bound notebook.

Hugh bit his tongue once again.

After a long pause, Zoe continued. "When I was little, my mum would talk about Waterford. About what it was like to grow up here. She and Mack never got along, but as much as she wanted to get away from here, I know she missed it. We would come here in summer sometimes, when I was on school holidays, and I remember having fun. Mack was always telling me not to touch things, but he also let me sip the wine and pick and eat the grapes. Nanna would be baking and I'd play with Lucky and…" She trailed off.

"I remember Lucky," Hugh said. "A fat blue heeler, right?"

Zoe smiled. "Yeah, that's right. He died just after Mum and I moved here. Mack never got another dog—I don't know why."

"Maybe he couldn't replace Lucky."

"Maybe." She shrugged. "I think Lucky was Nanna's dog. Maybe that's why he didn't want to get another one."

"When did your grandmother pass away?"

"Um, when I was six or seven, I think. We came to live here when I was nine, so, yeah, that'd be about right."

"And your mum died two years later—a year before mine."

"Mm-hmm." Zoe nodded.

All this talk about family. About mothers and children.

Would this finally prompt the conversation he was desperate to have?

He held his breath, watching as Zoe continued testing the wine.

He had to know.

He cleared his throat to be sure his voice wouldn't crack. "Were you scared about being a mother?" *Idiot.* Could there be a more obviously stupid question? "I mean, in Sydney, did you have help? Someone who showed you what to do?" He didn't even know how long their baby had lived. Days? Weeks? Months?

Zoe was silent so long, he wondered if she was going to reply. Then, finally, she said, "I stayed with my great-aunt."

It wasn't really an answer.

Hugh tried to work out his next question, but before he could, Zoe shook herself as if clearing away dust or cobwebs.

"God, here we are doing all this reminiscing when there's work to be done. Mack would not be impressed!" She gave a quick, bleak laugh that betrayed the pain behind it.

Hugh wanted to scream. Instead, he fisted his hands and willed himself to be patient. He knew how Zoe worked—well, how she *had* worked, and from what he'd seen so far, he guessed she hadn't changed that much. She was like a door with a rusty hinge. If you wanted it to open, forceful pulling would only break it and make the job more difficult. It needed a gentle touch to make any kind of progress.

"Zoe, Mack's not here anymore."

"I know."

"So it's okay. You can do what you want. He's not going to criticize. Not ever again."

Her shoulders sagged. "Yeah, I know."

"You can miss him and still hate him." Hugh was familiar with that feeling. It was one that he experienced regularly when he thought about his father. Hate was a strong word, but it definitely hadn't always been *love* between them, either.

She looked up, surprised, as if he'd read her mind. "Really?"

He nodded.

"Hugh, I..." she began. The pipette twisted in her fingers and her eyes flicked away from his to look down at it, as if fidgeting with it took all her concentration. "I'm sad, but I'm not sad. Does that make sense?"

"Perfectly."

"Well, I'm glad it makes sense to you, because it sure as hell doesn't to me."

"It doesn't have to."

"But it's nicer if it does."

"It is easier, yeah." Hugh leaned his hip against the barrel rack and tucked one hand into his jeans pocket. "But it doesn't always work that way."

She looked so lost and lonely, Hugh had to restrain himself from hugging her. He honestly had no idea how she'd react if he did.

"I was sorry to hear about your dad," she said, surprising him.

Hugh swallowed, recognizing the lump of grief that stuck in his throat. He hadn't thought much about his parents, his losses, in a very long time, but the past few days had brought it all back again. "Thanks. It was…tough to lose him."

"He always seemed so invincible. So strong and powerful."

"Yeah, I thought so, too."

"I wonder what the world would be like if no one died," Zoe said, her voice wistful.

"Overcrowded," Hugh replied dryly.

She managed a little laugh. "Yeah, I guess."

"At least…" Hugh began, wondering if he was really going to say this. "At least with Dad and with Mum, I had time to prepare. Mum was sick for nearly two years, and when the end came it was a relief as much as anything. I was young and I didn't really understand, but she was so open about talking about it, that made it easier. And with Dad…well, we knew it was only a matter of time with him, too. I didn't want him to go, but he wouldn't have wanted to linger. After watching Mum…"

Zoe was listening to him with a sad smile on her face. "Sometimes it sucks being the ones left behind," she said, her voice barely a whisper.

"True, but what's the alternative?"

Zoe shrugged. A careless gesture, so incompatible with the weight of their conversation. Hugh couldn't help dropping his gaze to her wrists. She wore a long-sleeved sweater and her scars weren't visible. He believed her, believed she hadn't tried to kill herself since that desperate cry for attention when she was thirteen. But Hugh had no doubt she'd found other ways of punishing herself. Punishments that didn't show on the outside.

THERE WAS A MOMENT OF stillness while Zoe waited for Hugh to continue. He was standing several feet away, but Zoe could almost feel him touching her. Or perhaps it was wishful thinking.

"You don't want to be dead, do you?" he asked.

Zoe shook her head. "No, but…" It wasn't that simple.

"You wish things were different."

Of course she did. "Don't you?"

He shrugged. "I don't know. I don't really believe in fate, but I guess I do think that things happen for a reason."

"You wouldn't say that if you'd seen her." *Damn.* Her stomach dropped as if she'd stepped out onto a ledge. Hugh had always had a way of getting past her defenses. They'd get cozy like this and then suddenly she'd find herself saying the very things she was doing her best to avoid. Wasn't that why she'd wanted to keep away from him when she'd first come back to Tangawarra?

Hugh swallowed, making his Adam's apple bob. "Yeah, you're probably right."

Change the subject. "It doesn't matter how hard you wish, though, life just keeps going. The world keeps turning. That's the way it is." She fought to sound philosophical, not devastated. To keep her rolling stomach under control.

"That it does."

Deep and meaningful conversations like this one were usually reserved for down at the creek. "D and Ms," they used to call them. And they usually happened when they were lying together, touching, as close together as they could get.

Now, even though they weren't physically

touching, Zoe felt that same sense of connection. They were breathing in unison, and even their postures—leaning against the rack of barrels—mirrored each other. He was the man around whom she needed to be most on guard, and yet here she was, letting him close again—physically *and* emotionally.

Suddenly, he was standing a lot closer. She could pick out the individual spots of wine on his shirt.

He brushed a tendril of hair from her face with his finger and then rested his hand against her neck. She put her own hand against his chest, half to steady herself, half because she wanted to be prepared to push him away. His shirt was hot and damp; his heart thudded reassuringly against her palm.

"I'm so sorry, Zoe," he said.

She shook her head. "Don't." Her throat ached suddenly, as if trying to close down her ability to speak.

He looked about to continue and she shook her head more forcefully. "Really. Don't."

"Enough D and M for you?" he said, as if he'd picked the words from her thoughts.

She smiled at that. "Enough D and M," she said. *Please let him drop it,* she pleaded internally.

"Okay."

"You're never going to get this shirt clean," she said, searching for something else to talk about. She left her hand where it was, unwilling to move away just yet.

"Yep. You're working me hard. I'm all sweaty, too," he said, his voice low and quiet.

And he smelled divine. *Get a grip.* She deliberately stepped away, dropping her hand. "I suppose you should go," she said.

"Still a lot of daylight left." He gestured to the window. The earlier sunshine had clouded over and the heavy threat of rain was back. "And we've still got plenty of work to do."

He was right. But her arms and shoulders were tired, and that headachy feeling had returned. "I don't think I can handle any more barrel cleaning."

"Fair enough."

Could they keep this up? Continue to work together without Zoe letting down her guard? It was exhausting maintaining this front.

But if they stopped working, it would only delay everything by another day. And the last thing Zoe needed was *more* time in Tangawarra. That thought strengthened her resolve.

"If we're not going to do any more barrels today, maybe we could clean out the office," she suggested.

"Fine." He gave her a clipped nod, and then he was gone, crossing behind the barrels to the shelved alcove that had been her grandfather's office. Unconsciously, Zoe breathed deeply as he brushed past her, taking in his masculine, spicy smell. Clearly, coming back to Tangawarra had made her lose some of her grip on sanity.

By the time Zoe had taken the few steps to the desk, Hugh had already begun lifting boxes of papers down from one of the shelves.

"I think it'd be best if you went through these things—you'll have to decide what to keep and what to throw away." He was all business again and Zoe internally cursed his ability to switch gears in an instant. Her stomach still felt queasy, as if she'd just stepped off a roller coaster ride. But she took his lead and tried to keep her voice steady.

"There won't be much to hang on to—most of this is destined for the tip."

"If there are wine-making notes, though, or personal papers, you'll want those. Or I will."

Zoe shrugged. She couldn't imagine there'd be anything of her grandfather's she'd want to take back to California with her or that would ultimately be of much use to Hugh.

She turned to an elderly metal filing cabinet

and struggled to open the top drawer. Finally, with a nerve-grating screech, she dragged it free.

"Geez." Zoe sighed. It was filled with a mess of papers—any filing system her grandfather might have employed was impossible to discern. Bank statements sat next to invoices for winery supplies, some of which were yellowed with age. It would all have to be pulled out and dumped.

Then she saw a bill from the tax office, dated two months earlier. Had it been paid?

She groaned. It wasn't going to be as simple as throwing everything in the trash—she'd have to go through it all, page by page.

The next piece of paper she pulled out only confirmed that—a recent bill from a winery equipment supplier for almost four hundred dollars. No receipt or other record of payment. She'd have to cross-check every invoice against Mack's bank statements and those she couldn't track, she'd have to call and find out if they were still owed money. *Oh, joy.*

Pulling out a sheaf of paper, Zoe settled cross-legged on the floor, mentally preparing herself for a more tedious, draining task than scrubbing out barrels.

"Um, Zoe—have you seen these?" Hugh had

been stacking boxes near the door. He was currently staring into one of them.

"What?" Irritated, Zoe pushed back a sweaty lock of hair from her forehead.

"I think you'd better…just come and have a look."

CHAPTER ELEVEN

THERE WAS A STRANGE tone in Hugh's voice, so Zoe gave up her struggle with the filing cabinet contents and stood. She looked at the dirty white cardboard boxes he'd lined up—there were three so far. "Where did they come from?"

"Over there—behind those shelves."

Zoe frowned. There was a small space behind the bookshelves that lined one side of the office. She'd never thought to look there.

"What's in them?" she asked when Hugh bent over a box.

"See for yourself." He straightened and took a step back, giving her space to inspect his discovery.

The first box held half a dozen bottles of wine and they looked familiar. Zoe picked one out. The gold seal over the cork, the white-and-gold label… "What?" she said in utter disbelief.

Golden Gate Estate zinfandel.

"Why would he…?" Puzzled, Zoe pulled the wine out of the box and checked the vintages. There were three bottles of each vintage of each year since she'd begun working there. The wines she'd been part of creating. Only those years—no others.

"Look at the box," Hugh prompted gently.

On the side of the cardboard, in shaky, old man's handwriting were the words "Zoe's wine" and the years of the vintages inside.

A sick sensation grew in Zoe's stomach.

"There's more."

Between the two of them, they excavated four additional boxes from the gap. Eventually they were sitting on the cold concrete floor, surrounded by the cartons they'd discovered. Each box had "Zoe's wine" written on it, with years next to them. Not all of them were full, and the contents hadn't been particularly carefully packed—snails had feasted on the labels of more than a few. In total, there were about thirty bottles from most of the wineries Zoe had worked at over the past ten years—even ones where she'd just been picking grapes.

Zoe shook her head as she held a bottle from a winery she'd worked in for a short time in France. She couldn't even remember telling her grandfather she'd been there. Another box even contained a few bottles from when she'd worked with the unbearable Pierre Renault.

But the most astonishing box was the one filled with unlabeled bottles. The dates on the

front went right back to when Zoe was fourteen and still living at Waterford. She pulled
one out and held it up to the light. The year
was scrawled in white marker pen on the side.

"What is it?" Hugh asked, frowning.

"A joke. It must be." Zoe felt her stomach
clench again. "It couldn't be..."

"Couldn't be what?"

Zoe hesitated before answering. Were her
eyes deceiving her? Surely this wasn't real.

"After my mother died, when it was just me
and Mack here—" She broke off, disgusted by
the quaver in her voice.

"He started me working in the winery and
vineyard. He'd said he was a child when he'd
started working for his father, so it shouldn't be
any different for me."

Hugh nodded for her to continue.

"Mostly I just did chores—cleaning things
up, helping the pickers, pruning the vines, that
kind of thing. When I was fourteen, he let me
start work with him on the wine-making side
of things."

"Fourteen's kind of young for that."

Zoe gave him a rueful smile. "Yeah, I guess.
Although I never did any binge drinking—
you know, even as a teenager I hardly ever got
drunk. I did plenty of other bad stuff." She shot
Hugh a sideways glance, but he was just sitting

there, an encouraging expression on his face. "But I think I respected alcohol too much." She laughed at herself. "That sounds so stupid."

Hugh didn't laugh. "No, it doesn't. Go on." He reached over and took her hand in his, giving it a gentle squeeze. Surprisingly, his touch comforted her. Despite the risk inherent in allowing him so close, she couldn't bring herself to let go.

Zoe stared at the bottle of wine in front of her, memories welling inside her like objects bobbing up in the ocean from a shipwreck. There was danger in letting them surface, she knew, but she couldn't stop.

"When he started letting me help with the wine-making, he gave me a small barrel to make my own wine. At first I just copied him—I was too scared to do anything different. He'd drummed into me how important the wine was—and I thought I'd get into trouble if I ruined it. But then as I learned more, I started to experiment, to do things slightly differently. If it turned out okay, he would sometimes drink it with dinner. And every now and then, I'd be allowed a glass. If it didn't work out, well, it got thrown away. I never knew he'd kept any of it."

She returned the bottle she was holding to its box and pulled out another. Again, it had no label, just a date.

Hugh picked up the bottle she'd put down. "So this is a fourteen-year-old vintage Zoe," he said.

Zoe gave a small laugh. "Yeah, I guess it is. Probably bloody awful, too." She shook her head and put the bottle back in the box. "Why would he keep this? Why would he buy the wine I made overseas?"

"You really don't know?"

Zoe grabbed a Golden Gate bottle and examined the label. She'd always liked the winery's elegant branding. "I guess he just wanted to know if his teaching had rubbed off."

"I think it's more than that."

Zoe snorted. "I doubt it."

Hugh took the bottle from her and turned it in his hands so he could see the label. "Winemaker: Zoe Waters," he murmured as he read. He looked up at her. "I think it's like a parent keeping finger paintings on the refrigerator. He might have been a cold bastard, but he was proud of you, Zoe."

No. The idea went against every notion Zoe held about her grandfather. She backed away from the boxes. If she was wrong about that—the foundation she'd built her life on—then what else had she been wrong about?

She paced, twisting her fingers together. "Mack and I barely spoke, unless he was telling me how to prune a vine or test the acidity of a barrel."

"He was a stubborn old man." Hugh's voice held more than a touch of bitterness. "And he wasn't a good parent to you, Zoe. He treated you more like an apprentice than a child he was raising. But I think he cared for you. In his own way."

"He cared that I was around to help him run things."

Hugh stood up and grasped Zoe's shoulders, stopping her from pacing. "It was more than that, Zoe. Don't you see? If you needed proof, then this is it."

"It doesn't prove anything." Zoe turned away. If she accepted this new version of her grandfather, as a man who cared for her, was proud of her—well, that would mean she'd have to mourn him. The sadness she felt, not just at his loss, but at the fact that the only family she'd really known was gone, would be something she'd have to face.

It was much easier to ignore it and pretend that she and Mack had meant nothing to each other. Admitting otherwise might release something she didn't want to let out. Because if she did, what else would come out with it? She'd spent a lifetime ignoring anything that contradicted her view of the world. It was easier—

safer—to believe the worst of people, because then they couldn't disappoint you.

Then it wouldn't hurt so much when they left you.

Her life had been filled with loss—her grandmother, her mother, Hugh, their daughter and now her grandfather. All that sorrow was stored up inside her, and if she let just a tiny bit of it escape she feared it would be like a crack in a dam. A crack that would widen and then, instead of a tiny trickle, there'd be a flood. And if that happened…

Zoe didn't know if she'd survive.

Hugh was frowning as if he was trying to work out a puzzle. "I'm not trying to make excuses for him, Zoe, but I think I might be beginning to understand him. He was a sad, lonely man. I don't think he knew how to take care of you—of anyone. He'd lost his wife and then your mum—his only child." He paused for a moment and sucked in a deep breath before his eyes met hers. "I've started to understand what that's like, and I didn't even know our baby."

Zoe's stomach revolted. She ran outside, terrified she was going to vomit, but after dragging in a few deep breaths of icy air, the feeling abated. She leaned over, hands on her knees, and heard the inevitable footsteps behind her.

"You okay?" Hugh rubbed her back.

"Not really." She straightened up and stared unseeingly at the empty vines. The sun had dipped in the sky—the days were short at this time of year, and when the sun dropped low the hills to the west made dusk come even faster. The gloom suited the turmoil inside her.

The time had come.

"Zoe." Hugh voice was gentle, but there was a steely thread that told her he would not be put off again. "I need to know. You have to tell me."

She'd known this would happen eventually, but the build-up didn't make the reality any easier to bear. And yet there was also a strange sense of relief she hadn't expected—like going to the dentist with a nasty toothache, knowing the procedure would be unpleasant, but that it wouldn't hurt as much afterward. Zoe couldn't imagine the pain from that time ever dimming, but at least the dread, the foreboding, would be over.

She gave a short nod. "I know." Zoe looked behind her into the messy shed—papers strewn everywhere, boxes piled up and puddles of water on the floor from the day's work. Even outside she could still sense the pungent aroma of dust, oak and wine—smells she'd always found reassuring, part of her normal world. Right now they overpowered her.

"Let's go into the house," she said eventually. "I'm sick of this place."

HUGH FOLLOWED ZOE INTO the kitchen, every muscle tense, every nerve on high alert. The day had been a roller coaster, beginning with the surprisingly smooth ride of working together, then the sudden highs and lows when their conversation had veered into personal territory. Now the ride had taken a very different turn and they were in a dark tunnel, spiraling downward, faster and deeper—toward what, he wasn't sure.

He'd wondered if pushing Zoe to reveal the truth would be a kind of revenge. When he'd thought about this moment, he'd expected to get satisfaction from making her relive it—retribution for his own pain and the memory of it he'd carried around for the past decade.

But now that the moment had arrived, he was aware of a strange emptiness and a clawing curiosity. More than anything, he wanted to *know*.

Zoe went through the motions of making tea. She moved haltingly, as if having to remind her body what to do. He wanted to hurry her up, to shake her and make the story come faster, but he knew that wouldn't work. Instead he took a seat at the table, willing himself to be patient.

The story had waited ten years to be told, after all—what were a few more minutes?

After long moments of silence, Zoe placed two mugs of milky tea on the table and took a seat across from him. She clasped her hands around her cup and stared down at it.

"Zoe?" Hugh prompted.

"I fainted at school because I hadn't eaten anything," she said.

Hugh was momentarily shocked that she'd simply launched into it without any further prompting, but he leaned forward to let her know he was listening.

"I had morning sickness. I wasn't throwing up—just too nauseous to eat much." She took a sip of her tea, her hand shaking as she set the cup back down on the table. "Mack was furious when the school nurse told him. He went white with rage. He'd never hit me—despite everything—but I really wondered if he was going to then. I sort of wanted him to. As punishment. I knew I'd always disappointed him, but this was on an entirely new level. I knew he'd never forgive me and everything would be changed, forever."

Hugh hadn't stopped to think about that. Zoe's mother, Margie, had moved them around a lot when Zoe was a kid, Hugh knew. When they'd come to live with Mack, Zoe's life had settled a little. Zoe had never had a stable family life, but Mack sending her away was the end of the only real home she'd ever known.

"Mack locked me in my room and called your father. Pete came over and they talked for about an hour and then he drove off."

"He came home and yelled at me." Hugh tried for a smile, but wasn't sure he succeeded. The memory was still too painful.

Zoe looked up from where she'd been staring at the table. "Yeah?"

"He was so angry. I'd never seen him like that before." For a moment, Hugh was transported back to that night, to the overwhelming fury of his father, cursing and spitting his accusations. "He trashed my room, turned everything over. He yelled at me for being involved with you, for…risking his reputation." Hugh winced as he recalled that part of his father's rage. And the insulting things he'd said about Zoe, her mother and the Waters family.

She nodded sadly at his revelation, as if she'd expected nothing less, then stared down at the table again, scratching at a dint in the surface with a broken fingernail.

Just as Hugh wondered if he'd offended her, she began speaking, her voice quiet and lifeless.

"Mack sent me to live with some distant aunt I'd never heard of, Maureen. She lived in Sydney, alone, in a big cold house. She made no secret of the fact that I was an imposition, that she'd taken me in only as a favor to Mack, because what was an old man going to do with a pregnant teenager?"

"Oh, Zoe."

"I wouldn't say she neglected me, exactly. I got fed, went to a school nearby. She let me go to the library to get books to read, and she bought me maternity clothes as I needed them. But we didn't talk much and she went out a lot." She fiddled with her tea, lifting the cup and then returning it to the table without taking a sip. "I was alone when the labor started—it was nearly a month early. When Maureen finally came home, I was sitting in the hallway, waiting for her. I was...hysterical. She called me a stupid girl and asked why I hadn't called an ambulance."

Zoe flashed the table a wobbly smile. "Of course she was right. That's exactly what I should have done."

Hugh spluttered. "You were alone, frightened and in pain! It wasn't stupid, it was perfectly understandable that you panicked. What a bitch."

Zoe looked up, genuinely surprised. As if it hadn't occurred to her that the woman who had been supposed to care for her was a heartless cow.

His fists tightened under the table. "You had every right to be scared."

Zoe's shoulders lifted in a little shrug. It was such a typical gesture—dismissing yet another person who had treated her badly.

Her eyes returned to the table as she continued her story. "As soon as I got to the hospital I knew something was wrong. The nurses and doctors were everywhere, whispering, and there wasn't any heartbeat on the monitor."

A cold sweat broke out on Hugh's forehead as he pictured the scene. He'd wanted to know this story and yet now... The reality of it was more shocking than he'd imagined. What would it have been like if he'd been there? If he'd witnessed those moments of panic? He wasn't sure how he'd handle it even now, but as a seventeen-year-old? He could barely comprehend the terror Zoe must have experienced.

"Eventually they told me the baby had probably died a few days before. But I had to go through the labor and delivery. That was... pretty hard." Zoe's breath was coming faster, even though she spoke in a monotone.

Her eyes were unfocussed and her voice fell to a whisper so that even as she tried to downplay the trauma she'd been through, the gravity of it struck Hugh like a cement block, freezing him to his chair.

"It was a girl. She was beautiful. She was perfect. I named her Sara Rachel. Sara was Mum's middle name and Rachel was Nanna's name."

Her voice was flat, robotic, but also clearly close to sobs.

"She was cremated. I have a picture of her. But it's back in California. I can send it to you, if you want."

The sight of her colorless face was enough to unfreeze him. "Christ, Zoe, breathe. You'll pass out." Hugh leaned across the table to grab her hands and squeeze them hard, trying to bring her back to the present. Eventually she took a longer, shaky breath and her eyes lost their glazed look. She shook off his grasp and gulped the hot tea in front of her.

He didn't know what to do next. Her story had left him reeling. He had no idea how to process this new reality, so what could he possibly say to her? How on earth could anyone make what she'd been through okay?

He was surprised when she continued with the same flat, emotionless tone—as if she was telling a story that had happened to someone else.

"I stayed with Maureen for a few weeks, but as soon as I was physically healthy again, I left—I ran away. I was eighteen by then and Mack had given me some money. I took it all, bought a ticket to London and that was it. I ended up in France pretty quickly, then went to Italy. Then Spain. I worked in wineries, I picked fruit, I ran cellar doors. When I couldn't speak the language, that was pretty challenging." She gave a small laugh at the memories.

"Then Napa the last few years—I kind of stuck around there. Golden Gate is a lovely place. A bit like here—they even have gum trees on the property. That was the first place to put my name on the label as winemaker."

She looked up at him, chin raised even as her lip trembled. The face he remembered so well: proud, bold, ready to face the world, deliberately pushing all her uncertainty and fear away so no one could see how vulnerable she really was. The prickly, angry, rebellious Zoe that hid the fragile woman inside.

A woman who'd paid a terrible price for the love they'd shared.

A *daughter*. They'd had a little girl.

A painful, nagging grief welled up inside him. For Zoe and what she'd had to go through alone. For himself, for what he'd lost. For both of them and the future they'd been denied because of two old men and their ridiculous feud over who made the best wine. A feud that should have been about boasting down at the pub over who had the most trophies, not been blown out into a tragedy of Montague/Capulet proportions.

Since Zoe had told him the truth about why she'd left, Hugh had been feeling all kinds of emotions. Anger. Frustration. Annoyance. He'd been lied to, and—almost worse—he'd swallowed the story and built his life on falsehoods. What he hadn't felt was the reality of what had happened.

Zoe had been through one of the most traumatic experiences anyone could imagine. He'd thought she'd broken her promise to him and tried to kill herself. And his grief about that had been mixed in with so much anger and hurt, he couldn't pull it all apart. Now he knew she'd just been a scared kid in an impossible situation. She'd done as she was told, just as he had in ignoring her attempts to contact him.

But most fundamentally, most stunning and distressing of all, was how affected he was by the knowledge that they'd had a daughter and that she'd died. It echoed inside him, making him feel hollowed out.

"Zoe, I'm so sorry." The words seemed pathetically inadequate.

Her bottom lip quivered. "I know it was selfish, but I wished so many times that you'd come and rescue me."

Oh, God, if only he could turn back the clock.

"I would have. If I'd known—" His fists tightened in frustration. "I'd have been there before you could blink. I promise you. If I'd only...if I'd known..." With a frustrated growl, Hugh stopped himself as his voice rose with renewed hurt.

Zoe shrugged.

She didn't believe him, he could see that. The spark of anger inside him grew brighter. He could see it clearly now. Even once she'd been free from her aunt, she hadn't tried to come back to him because she couldn't trust him again. Those few phone calls, the ones his father had intercepted, had only strengthened her conviction. Zoe Waters had never been able to believe that anyone could love her. Not even him.

And he couldn't blame her. That realization, the utter wretchedness of that fact, doused his anger.

He stood up in a rush, ignoring the chair when it tipped and fell to the floor with a crash. Zoe was in his arms a moment later, and he wasn't sure if it was because he'd grabbed her or she'd leaped there herself. It didn't matter.

All that mattered was holding her.

She shivered against him, and he tucked her head under his chin, pulling her closer, again desperately wishing he had the power to change the past.

They stood like that for a long time, his arms around her, her head against his chest. She wasn't crying, still hadn't shed a tear. Zoe was motionless except for the trembling that every now and then built to a shudder. When that happened she'd push herself closer to him, as if she were hiding. Hugh pressed occasional kisses to the top of her head, but didn't speak.

What was there to say? How could any words make up for what she'd been through? For what they'd both lost?

Her arms were trapped between them and she moved, pushing herself away a little, her hands rising to his neck. But it wasn't until the cool air hit his chest that he realized she was undoing the buttons of his shirt.

"Zoe?"

She pressed a kiss against his chest as she pulled his shirt open. "Mmm?"

Her little tongue darted out to lick him before her hands moved lower and undid the next button in line.

"Zoe, what are you doing?" Even as his brain puzzled over her moves, his body responded. Her touch, her mouth, the tickle of her fingers against his skin as she popped each button... His body strained toward her even as every rational sense told him to pull away.

"I should think that was obvious," she mumbled against his skin, trailing kisses down his torso, moistening his skin with her attention. One hand skated down his body and she trailed cool fingertips over the front of his rapidly tightening jeans.

"Wait." Hugh grasped her wrists and took a step back. Her flushed face looked up at him and it was such a contrast from the pale, wan woman he'd just been speaking to he was almost shocked. "Are you seducing me?"

She tried for a sexy smile, but it communicated more desperation than desire. "Do you have a problem with that?"

"Zoe…" His tone was a warning. He'd never before felt such powerfully confused lust. Was making love now, after the conversation they'd just had, the right thing to do? Was it even vaguely appropriate?

But he didn't want to leave, didn't want to walk out of here and have to deal with the ramifications of all he'd just heard. Didn't want to think about it—any of it.

Zoe's expression turned pleading. "Please, Hugh. I need this. You…" She swallowed. "You made me remember it. Now you have to make me forget, make it go away again. You got what you wanted. Help me, please, I need this."

Perhaps she wasn't the only one.

Despite the gravity of the situation, the raw

emotion swirling through him, Hugh's body was hard. He wanted nothing more than to lose himself inside Zoe—just as he had all those years ago.

Her wide brown eyes looked up at him, pleading with him, and they were impossible to resist.

There was a sense of inevitability about it all. Zoe Waters had come back to Tangawarra. Hugh was going to make love to her. The second fact somehow seemed an inescapable outcome of the first.

He hesitated one last moment. "Are you sure?"

Zoe's answer was to surge toward him, surprisingly strong, breaking free of his grip. She reached up on tiptoe so her mouth hovered in front his. "Kiss me," she whispered, her sweet, tea-scented breath brushing over his face. "I want this. I need this."

Yes, and so did he.

With a low growl he took her mouth as she offered it, open and eager, her tongue meeting his, ready and willing. There was no tentativeness, no holding back as they learned each other. Despite the years that had passed, this was a kiss of reunion, of lovers who knew each other well, who understood each other.

He ran his hands down her back, measuring her curves, coming to rest on her bottom. He cupped it and lifted her slightly, fitting her to him.

They both groaned.

Zoe began to scrabble at the hem of her sweater at the same time as she tried to toe off her shoes.

No.

Hugh managed to tame his lust long enough to think clearly.

If they were doing this, they were going to do it properly. It wasn't going to be a hurried assignation on the kitchen floor.

He let her go, and grabbed her hands when she started to lift her sweater over her head.

"No, Zoe. The bedroom."

Zoe frowned. "What? Can't we just…"

"No." He scooped her up and she squeaked a protest, but her arms went around his neck. "Bedroom," he said again.

Hugh headed down the corridor to the room that held so many memories. He forced himself to focus on the present, on his goal: the old-fashioned brass bed covered neatly with a patchwork quilt. He carefully lowered Zoe, snaring her mouth for another kiss as he did so, bending over her, their lips connected. When he pulled back, Zoe fell away with a sigh, her head landing on the pillow.

A grey dusk had fallen while they'd talked, and the room was shadowy and dim. But there was enough light to make out Zoe's expression. She stared up at him with all the cheek and wonder that she'd had when she was sixteen.

Was this another mistake?

His face must have betrayed his thoughts, because Zoe's eyes darkened.

"Hugh, don't. Please. Just don't think about it." She sat up and cupped his face in her hands. "Please."

Her pleading broke whatever fragile strings were holding him back. Was this a good idea? He didn't know. Was it something he'd regret? He also didn't know. All that mattered was being close—close enough to chase away the shadows of the past. The irony that Zoe Waters would banish those shadows wasn't lost on him.

"Ah, Zoe." He climbed on the bed and leaned over to claim her mouth again. She responded, her lips opening under his, welcoming his tongue into her mouth, stroking it with her own.

He was sixteen again, when kissing wasn't just the beginning, it was the whole point. He and Zoe had taken a long time before they'd made love, and along the way, they'd become good at kissing. World-record good.

Zoe licked at him, catlike flicks of her tongue against his before she grasped his bottom lip between hers and sucked. Hugh repeated her moves back to her. He stroked her tongue with his, plunging in and out of her mouth until they both groaned.

Hugh was desperate, every inch of his body demanding hard and fast and forever. But he was equally determined not to waste this opportunity by behaving like a teenager. He and Zoe had always loved each other passionately—now he wanted to do it skillfully, as well.

Hugh wrenched his mouth from Zoe's, leaving both of them panting. Her fingers clutched at his chest as if to bring him back to her, but he sat on the edge of the bed, grabbed her hands and kissed each palm in turn.

"There's no hurry, sweetheart. I'm going to make this last."

She frowned at him. "No, don't, I can't..."

He shook his head and smiled at her. "Trust me."

She sat up to face him. Instead of responding, she bent her head and kissed his neck, nibbling on the sensitive skin where it met his shoulder before making her way to his ear and biting gently on his earlobe and soothing the hurt with her tongue.

Hugh shuddered even as he noted her lack of an answer. Did Zoe Waters trust anyone? Would she ever?

He pulled away from her to reach down and remove his boots. Zoe did the same to her own. He'd said he'd take his time and he meant it, but the jeans had to go. And Zoe had undone his shirt, anyway, so he shrugged out of that, too.

He was left with only his white cotton boxer briefs.

Zoe's eyes raked him from head to foot, devouring him.

"You've changed a lot," she said, licking her lips nervously.

"Yeah?"

Her fingers rested on his shoulder and circled the muscle there, her eyes tracing their path. "Yes."

Her cheeks were already pink, so it was hard to tell, but Hugh was sure she blushed.

"Your body, I mean," she said, sounding almost shy. "You're—" She broke off as her fingers reached the swell of his biceps. Her fingertip traced the colored lines of ink in his skin. Her eyes flashed to his, wide with surprise. "Really?"

Hugh shrugged. "It's an ankh."

"The Egyptian symbol for life," she murmured as her finger continued to follow the outline.

"Yep." Hugh's stomach muscles clenched at her delicate touch.

"I went to Egypt. Years ago. It's amazing."

"I've never been. I just...liked the design," he lied. It had been back in his university days. He'd been drunk, out with friends and they'd dared each other to get a tattoo. The parlor had a book of names with meanings attached and in his inebriated state, the name he'd found himself looking up had been *Zoe*. It meant life. He'd asked the tattoo artist for an image with the same meaning—and then been the only one of his friends to actually get something done. Strangely, although he'd spent a long time trying to rid himself of his memories of Zoe, he didn't regret the permanent reminder of her in his skin. For a long time it had been a symbol of all the things he was striving to achieve: life and light and permanence instead of death and darkness and uncertainty.

"You know, some people say that the symbol represents male and female," she said. "The female, *here*." She traced the loop at the top. "And the male, *here*." She stroked the straight line that ran down from the loop.

Hugh groaned.

She grinned. "You're such a good boy! I never thought you'd get a tattoo."

"Meanwhile, where are yours?"

She gave him a sly look. "You'll just have to find out."

"You always were a tease."

She swallowed and paused before answering. "I always gave in." A shadow flickered through her eyes and Hugh cursed himself.

"Bet you can't guess," Zoe said brightly, clearly pushing away anything remotely attached to their previous discussion.

"No, but I'm going to love finding out."

Hugh bracketed her with his arms and lowered his torso over her. Zoe leaned slowly back, keeping her mouth about an inch from his, until her head touched the pillow.

She sighed, and for a moment all Hugh could read in her eyes was desire and happiness. He felt strangely gratified that he was the cause, that he'd been able to erase the heavy burden Zoe bore—even just for a few moments.

He leaned down to kiss her gently. Their lips touched in a whisper of a kiss, and Hugh did it again, over and over, while her hands ranged over his back.

Her skin smelled of roses and wine and he knew they both smelled of the physical work they'd done that day. But somehow that only enhanced her femininity; the fact that he'd watched her lift and carry and work as hard as any male employee at Lawson Estate made her more irresistible, not less. Zoe Waters might always have been a broken, fragile girl, but she knew how to work and how to look after herself.

Zoe's fingers left his back and wiggled between their bodies. He realized she was undoing her jeans, so he pulled away to help.

While he stripped the heavy denim from her legs, Zoe rid herself of her sweater and T-shirt, and then she was lying there, laid out in front of him. Hugh stroked a finger across the soft skin of her belly, smiling as it quivered under his touch. Her underwear was plain, no lace, but oh-so-Zoe—black panties and a black-and-white pin-striped bra, each decorated with a little red satin bow.

While he watched, Zoe arched her back to reach behind and undo the clasp of her bra letting it trail down her arms until she tossed it over the side of the bed.

Zoe had always had amazing breasts.

Now, though?

Hugh felt as if the girl he'd made love to back then had simply been the caterpillar, because now she was the butterfly. A lush, woman's body lay before him. She'd grown into her curves, and oh, my, but they were nice curves.

"If you keep staring, a girl could get a complex," Zoe teased, her finger tapping on his chin as if to bring him back to reality.

Hugh dragged his gaze from her breasts to

meet her smiling, if uncertain, eyes. "Beautiful," he muttered.

Her smile widened, but to erase any trace of uncertainty, Hugh lowered his mouth to her breasts. Zoe groaned and her eyes fluttered closed. Hugh trailed his mouth down to one ripe pink nipple and fastened his mouth around it. She arched when his teeth bit down gently.

His fingers traced his mouth's path, kneading and rolling one nipple between his fingers while his mouth kissed the other. He alternated between them, enjoying listening to the little noises of pleasure she made.

While he loved her breasts, Zoe's hands ranged over him. One moved lower until she reached inside his boxers to encircle him, her fist tracing up and down his length.

He hissed out a breath.

"Ah, God, Zoe." He groaned as her fingers tightened around him.

Following some unspoken agreement, she let go of him so she could pull her panties down. Hugh helped her push them away before doing the same to his briefs.

For a moment, they lay pressed together, skin to skin. They breathed in unison, and Hugh wasn't even sure if he could feel his own heart beating—all his focus was on Zoe, her heat, her skin, her beautiful body, the scent of her arousal.

Zoe tugged on his arm and her legs parted in blatant encouragement.

"I told you, we're going to take our time." Hugh smiled against her hair.

"You can take as long as you want, but stop torturing me!"

Hugh chuckled and he felt Zoe's strangled laugh as her breasts brushed against his chest.

He continued to make love to her breasts and his hand slid between her legs. For a moment he paused, remembering what their previous love-making had created. He wondered if she was thinking the same thing, because she stiffened as he stroked her.

"Shh, it's okay," he whispered reassuringly, kissing her collarbone, then rising to her throat and kissing her pulse.

He continued to touch her, exploring her body, relearning her secrets with the knowledge of a man instead of the eagerness of a boy. He smiled when she breathed, "Yes, there," into his ear.

He kept up his intimate stroking, kissing her neck, propping himself up on an elbow to kiss her mouth when he felt her body begin to tense under his hand. He stole her cry of pleasure, his mouth covering hers as she shuddered beneath him. Her lips clung to his, her gasps of climax turning into whimpers as her body's release rippled away.

God, she was beautiful, with her eyes still shut and her face flushed.

Hugh was surprised when her hand grasped him again, almost too tight, rolling up from root to tip in a way that made his back arch.

"Oh, Zoe," he groaned. Whatever restraint he'd possessed had shattered watching her orgasm. "Now, I need you now."

"Yes, yes," she murmured in agreement.

He searched out his jeans, finding his wallet and the condom he kept stashed there. In a moment he was sheathed and he fell back on the bed. Zoe was lying half on top of him, so he shifted, inserting his legs between hers until she was kneeling astride him, her eyes shining in the dim light. A sudden stillness fell between them, filled with the tangled weight of the past. For a moment he wondered if she was going to run away.

"Zoe," he said, pleading, desperate.

"Shh." She leaned down and kissed him, their tongues meeting. He felt her hips moving, fitting herself to him. Then she positioned him and pushed down, slowly, slowly, until he was buried to the hilt and she let out a breath against his lips.

"Are you okay?" he asked, unable to help himself.

"I'm perfect."

"Yes, you are."

She smiled and Hugh smiled back.

She raised herself, using her thighs to control how deep she took him. Hugh clenched his hands into fists, restraining the urge to grab her hips and slam her down on top of him. Instead, he waited, and was rewarded when she began to move, her body adjusting, her breathing shallow gasps.

It only took a minute before she was rocking against him, every downward stroke accompanied by a moan of pleasure, and Hugh was once again almost at the edge, urging her to continue.

"Yes, Zoe, oh, yeah."

He pressed his thumb against her for added pleasure and delighted in the keening cry of near-agony it immediately provoked, her body clutching and shuddering around him. He tried to focus on maintaining the pressure and thrusting through her spasms until he couldn't manage to hold off any longer. His peak took him in waves that made him feel as though he might black out.

CHAPTER TWELVE

ZOE COULDN'T REMEMBER the last time she had felt this *right*.

And that made her nervous as hell.

Lying with her head on Hugh's shoulder, their naked limbs entwined and his heart thudding rhythmically against her palm, it was too easy to pretend the world no longer mattered.

He'd fallen asleep—just as he always had after sex. It usually wasn't for long, just a quick nap—as if making love to her had taken everything his body had to give.

It was powerful, this moment afterward, knowing she'd made this strong man surrender everything to her. He lay there, as vulnerable as it was possible to be, letting her watch over him.

Down at the creek, moments like this had been her favorite. Lying on a blanket, the dappled sunlight warming their bodies, her beautiful boy sleeping next to her.

Then he had been a boy. He'd taken exquisite care with her. Been gentle and loving and sweet.

Now he was a man. All that he had been then, and more. And Zoe had never had a better lover.

Her body still tingled with the pleasure they'd shared. Most annoyingly, though, instead of being satisfied, Zoe's hunger for him seemed only to have intensified—and that was the real reason for her anxiety.

Her original purpose for their lovemaking was to push away the memories of the past. That had worked—momentarily. But it had also awakened a new need in her. A need she'd never felt with any of the men she'd been with since she'd left Australia.

How on earth was she going to work with him without stopping every few minutes to kiss him? Without stripping him naked and making love to him?

Worse, how was it going to feel when she signed Waterford over to him and went back to California?

Zoe's head bobbed as a deep breath made Hugh's chest rise. His body stirred. He smacked his lips and swallowed. "I could use a drink," he said, his voice scratchy and rough. Giving her gave her a quick squeeze, he untangled himself and climbed out of bed.

Zoe turned to her side and curled up in the warmth he'd left behind.

"You want something? A glass of wine?" He peered down at her.

What do *I want?* Zoe forced herself to smile back. "Thanks, that'd be nice." *Wine will do for now.*

Hugh jumped out of bed, not pausing for clothes. He switched on lights as he went and she could hear him rattling around in the kitchen. When she heard his footsteps returning to the bedroom, Zoe propped herself up against the pillows and tucked the quilt under her armpits. He appeared holding a beer and a glass of red, wearing a smile and nothing else.

She'd felt those hard planes of muscle under his skin; she'd seen his physique under a layer of clothing. But nothing prepared her for the magnificence of Hugh naked. The unadorned light bulb in the room cast no shadows and Zoe looked her fill.

Lines of definition were visible on his legs through the light dusting of dark hair. Narrow hips widened to a powerful chest, topped by strong shoulders.

She'd already noticed that time had been kind to Hugh Lawson. Dark hair fanned across his chest—he'd had that even when he was seventeen—and trailed down his body, converging at the juncture of his legs. As she watched, he hardened, prompting an answering surge that swarmed low in her belly. Her eyes rose to his. He was grinning at her.

"Had a good look?" he asked cheekily.

Zoe opened her mouth to protest but closed it again, knowing she'd been caught out. Her cheeks heated and she pulled the sheet tighter around her, feeling a sudden, unexpected shyness.

He climbed into bed, carefully handing her the wine. Zoe jumped when his toes connected with her legs, making it splash on the sheets, anyway.

"Hey! You're freezing!"

"It's cold out there."

He took a long drink of beer, tilting the brown bottle up to his lips. Zoe watched, suppressing a sudden urge to kiss his stubbled throat.

"Drink up," he said when he finished.

"I'm not swallowing a glass of wine in one gulp!"

"You'd better, if you want any. Because you've got about ten seconds before I take it away from you and make you use your hands and mouth for something else."

His eyes glittered with the teasing threat, playfulness and something darker around the edges.

With a certainty that gave her a physical ache, Zoe knew she'd made a mistake. Even though it had been at her urging, making love to Hugh had made her vulnerable to him in so many ways. Instead of easing the pain, she'd opened herself up to a whole new world of hurt.

She gripped the wine glass tightly and drank almost all of it.

"That's the way," Hugh encouraged.

The wine settled uneasily in her stomach, swirling around to mirror her troubled thoughts. But then Hugh lifted the glass from her hand, his mouth nibbling her ear as he stripped the sheet away.

"Hey, it's cold," Zoe protested.

"My turn to look."

He grasped her wrists so she couldn't cover herself and took his time raking his eyes over her body. When they reached her hips, his eyebrows rose in surprise. "Ah, there it is."

Zoe shivered as he let go of her hands to trail his fingers over her hip, urging her to twist slightly. His fingers followed the grapevine etched onto her skin.

"I thought it was appropriate," she said, her voice weak as his fingers followed the trailing vine to where it ended in a bunch of plump grapes on her butt cheek.

His eyes rose to hers again. "I guess it is. It's pretty."

"Thanks."

Smiling at her, he held her gaze right up until he kissed her. The kiss was still deep, but this time slow and sweet, making something hidden and dark in Zoe's chest flip over.

It was too late for regrets.

Tonight they were together. Like Scarlett O'Hara, she'd deal with it tomorrow. Because tonight she was going to take everything Hugh Lawson had to offer.

ZOE SLEPT PATCHILY. Her usual nightmares haunted her, but this time, instead of waking up shaking and alone, Hugh had woken her, comforted her and stroked her hair until she was calm and they'd made love again. It had almost been worth it.

In the morning light, Zoe put her hand in the indent in the pillow beside her and sighed. At some point in the night he'd disappeared.

Last night had been…a mistake. A very sensual, physically gratifying mistake, but still a mistake.

Hugh's absence told her that he clearly agreed.

The only thing to focus on now was the wine. Unfortunately, she still needed his help, but that was all. He'd gotten what he wanted from her and now Zoe had to concentrate on finishing the job and putting this behind her. And Hugh was getting Waterford in the bargain. He should be pleased with his week's work—all it had cost him was a few days' labor and a night in her bed.

Shivering, Zoe threw back the covers and headed for the bathroom, ready to get through another day that took her closer to going home. Wherever that was. Suddenly, Golden Gate, her little apartment, California, seemed barren and lonely. She pushed the thoughts away.

She showered, dressed and headed for the winery, suppressing the strange hungover feeling in her head. If she'd thought that sharing her story with Hugh might have lightened its burden, she was wrong. The base of her skull ached again, threatening a migraine. Her stomach fluttered, as if something important was about to happen and she'd forgotten to prepare for it.

Inside the winery, Zoe breathed in the familiar smells, trying to settle her nerves. She deliberately avoided looking at the boxes of wine they'd uncovered the day before.

The place was in a shambles—her grandfather would have been appalled at the mess. The papers she'd begun to go through were still dumped in an untidy pile, the drawers of the filing cabinet open, spilling their contents. The desk was practically invisible under notebooks, testing equipment and yet more paper. The scent of wine was pervasive over everything, testament to the hard work of the past couple of days and the stunning bouquet of her grandfather's vintage.

They were almost there.

Once all the barrels were racked off, the wine would be ready to be bottled—and there were only a few left. Zoe didn't know what arrangements Hugh had in place for bottling, and she made a mental note to ask. There were a couple of tweaks she wanted to make to the wine— perhaps add a little acid—but otherwise she planned to let her grandfather's wine stand on its own merits.

It was going to be magnificent.

If only he'd gotten the recognition he deserved.

As much as she was trying to ignore them, she couldn't stop her gaze drifting to the boxes of "Zoe's wine." To the bottle of Golden Gate Estate that had "Zoe Waters" on the label as winemaker.

Zoe had given a great deal of thought to her grandfather's approach to wine-making over the years she'd spent in Europe and the U.S. She'd been exposed to other methods, other approaches. Mack had been more or less a recluse. He'd never wanted to open a cellar door to bring customers into the winery to taste and buy directly, despite the money it might have brought in, because he hadn't wanted to deal with people.

He'd never made an effort to do any proper marketing, to enter shows or competitions or advertise his wine. When his competition had begun to outshine him, the only action he'd taken had been to criticize their methods and denigrate their product.

Waterford's Shiraz succeeded not because of him, but in spite of him.

If he'd needed a concrete example of how to be successful, all he'd needed to do was look over the fence.

She'd never thought that much about why Mack and Hugh's father had shared such antipathy. Now she was beginning to wonder if she understood.

Lawson Estate was the more successful business—both men could see that. But Waterford produced the better wine. And, no doubt, both men were aware of that, too.

So why hadn't Mack made it big like Lawson Estate?

Fear.

It was the only explanation Zoe could come up with. If you tried to be successful, if you reached for the stars, you might fail. But if you didn't try at all, you never ran the risk of failure. That was the advantage the Lawson family had over hers: Pete Lawson—and then, later, Hugh—had been prepared to take a risk.

Mack Waters never wanted to.

And Zoe was beginning to wonder if that aversion might just be genetic. After all, Hugh was out there risking everything to make Lawson Estate a global player in the wine market. And what was she doing?

Her mind went to the conversation she'd had with Wil Lambert. He wanted her to sign a five-year contract with Golden Gate. *Five years!* For her entire adult life, Zoe never thought much beyond the next vintage.

Five years was asking her to put down roots. Become part of a place, a community.

Just like Hugh in Tangawarra.

The very idea was terrifying—up there with skydiving and bungee jumping.

Even at her wildest, Zoe wasn't a risk-taker. Yes, she'd sprayed graffiti on the hardware store. And she'd gotten caught. But that had been the plan all along—even if she would never have admitted it at the time. There was no point to it if she didn't get caught.

The biggest risk she'd taken in her life had been falling in love with Hugh Lawson when she was sixteen. And the second biggest risk was going to bed with him last night.

A flush wormed its way through her body and heated her face as the events of the night flooded back.

She shook herself. She couldn't afford to waste time daydreaming. And she still hadn't decided how to behave when Hugh arrived, as he inevitably would.

NINE O'CLOCK CAME AND WENT with no sign of Hugh. Zoe didn't need any further anxiety in her life, but still she found herself watching the clock, wondering why he hadn't appeared at the crack of dawn, the way he had the past couple of days, and what would happen when he did turn up. How would they behave now? Would it go back to the way things had been? Or would it be different?

Idiot. Of course it's different. Everything is different now.

When she found herself sitting at Mack's desk twirling a pen and staring aimlessly into the distance she gave herself a good scolding. There were plenty of tasks still to be done— plenty of things that she didn't need Hugh's help for. The filing cabinet for one.

Her heart sank. Record keeping wasn't her strong suit and luckily, at Golden Gate, she had a cellar administrator who took care of most of that sort of stuff. The idea of sitting with reams of paper and trying to sort them out made her twitch.

But they did need more sulfur dioxide. A quick trip into town would solve that, and if Hugh happened to turn up while she was gone, he could spend a little time wondering and worrying about where *she* might be.

As she drove past the supermarket she couldn't help noticing that the two black-clad, wild-haired teens she'd noticed on the day of the funeral were once again standing outside the supermarket.

What day was it? Thursday. They should be in school, surely.

The purchase of sulfur dioxide was quick and painless at the winery supply store in town. The fact that Tangawarra had a winery supply store had been a nice surprise—and that the owners were new and not especially curious was even nicer.

As she was driving back past the supermarket, she decided to fill in some more time with one last grocery shop. She estimated it would only be another two or three days before the wine would be done and she could think about heading back to the U.S. Assuming all the other details were taken care of by then. Assuming the deal with Lawson Estate went ahead without any hitches.

She watched the emo-goth kids as she pulled into the car park. Couldn't seem to drag her eyes away from them. An old lady walked past and the kids called out to her—Zoe was too far away to hear what they said, but she didn't miss the expression on the old woman's face. Disgust and fear. It was an expression she had been more than familiar with when she was their age.

The trio exchanged a few more words—Zoe was too far away to make out what. The old woman shook her head and then kept walking. The two kids huddled back around a light pole, one of them reaching into his backpack and pulling out a book.

Satisfied that they were okay, Zoe headed into the supermarket and made her purchases. It was difficult to choose what to buy—she didn't want to end up throwing out food, but she also didn't know exactly how long she'd be around. She figured she could give leftovers to Patricia—she'd no doubt be able to make something of them.

Zoe was putting her purchases in the car when a police car stopped next to the teens. It pulled over on the wrong side of the road, so the officer in the driver's seat could lean out the window to talk to them. The lights weren't flashing, but she didn't miss the arm gesture as he called the teens over to talk to him. The kids shared a look before reluctantly slouching their backpacks over their shoulders and ambling across to the car.

The old lady must have reported them. The same thing had had happened to Zoe more than once when she'd been a kid. All she'd wanted was to put off going home to her grandfather—but then some old busybody would say she was "loitering."

These kids had only tried to talk to the old biddy. Yes, they probably should be in school, but other than that they weren't breaking the law, for goodness' sake.

Before she realized it, Zoe found herself striding over to the scene.

"They weren't doing anything wrong," Zoe called out as soon as she was close enough.

All four people—the teens and the two cops—turned to look at her.

"What?" the older cop asked.

"They weren't doing anything wrong. I saw the whole thing."

The cop frowned. "And you are?"

"Zoe Waters," she said without hesitation. "And these kids were just talking to her, nothing else."

"Zoe?" The young cop in the passenger seat craned his neck to see past his partner. "Zoe Waters from Waterford?"

Suddenly unsure of herself, Zoe halted a couple of steps from the car. "Uh, yeah."

"I'm Neil Swindon. We went to school together."

Now that she was closer, his face did look vaguely familiar. He'd been one of Hugh's gang, she thought. It was insanely weird to see him in a police uniform. "Oh, yeah. Hi, Neil."

"I heard you were back. Sorry to hear about your grandfather."

"Um, thanks." Having inserted herself into this situation without thinking, now she was at a loss. What exactly had she hoped to achieve by stepping in here? And why exactly had she jumped to the teens' defense? She had no idea what they might have done.

All she could think was that when she had been in this situation, she'd often wished some fairy godmother would appear at her side and make it all go away. Was she just trying to protect the old Zoe? A Zoe who no longer existed?

The older cop turned his frown back to the two teens. "And just what should I be worried about that you *weren't* doing?"

"Nothing, Dad," the boy answered, eyes wide. "We just asked Mrs. Stuart to do our survey, but she said she didn't have time." He held up a clipboard and turned to Zoe. "Do you wanna do our survey? It's for social studies. We're asking people if they think Tangawarra needs a second supermarket—for competition—to keep prices fair."

The young girl studied Zoe with faint boredom. Her kohl-ringed eyes blinked slowly under her long, shocking-pink fringe, as if she didn't have a care in the world. Zoe knew that meant the exact opposite, because she'd been behind that mask.

Still was, in many ways.

"S-sorry, I think…I misunderstood what was going on," Zoe stammered. Now she felt, perversely, as if she were letting them down.

"How's the survey going, Tim?" Neil Swindon asked. Zoe was grateful for the rescue, but the older cop was still looking at her suspiciously.

The kid held up his clipboard. "We still need another ten responses to have a statistically representative sample."

Neil laughed. "Whatever that means. Social studies wasn't my thing at school at all." He looked at Zoe as if for verification. She gave a one-shouldered shrug and a smile, hoping that would convey whatever it was he was looking for. She barely remembered him from back then—let alone what subjects he'd liked.

"We need to ask a few demographic questions first." The girl finally spoke up, taking the clipboard from Tim and holding her pen ready to take Zoe's answers.

"Okay, I'll leave you guys to it," the older cop said, pulling back into the car. "Tim, call me on the mobile when two you need a lift back to school."

"Sure, Dad."

"See you later, Zoe," Neil called. He held up a hand in a wave as the car drove off.

"How long have you lived in Tangawarra?" the girl asked Zoe.

"Um…" This had to be one of the most bizarre interactions of her life.

"Over ten years," Tim said, leaning in to point to the appropriate box on the form. "Didn't you hear Neil? They went to school together—that means she's lived here forever."

"Actually, I don't live here anymore." The words sounded strange coming from her mouth.

"Okay. So where do you live?"

"In California. Just outside San Francisco."

"Really? Cool." The girl's indifferent stare warmed for a moment. "So you got out of this place."

"Yeah, I did." *But I still came back.*

The kids ran through the rest of their questions and Zoe answered as accurately as she could.

"Thanks, that's it," Tim said when they were

done. They gathered their stuff and slumped off back to the light pole that was obviously their waiting place.

Zoe wanted to tell them that they'd have more luck getting people like Mrs. Stuart to complete their survey if they stood straight, washed off some of their eyeliner and removed some of the leather bracelets. But then she'd just sound like every other adult they came into contact with, so she bit her tongue. Didn't stop her reflecting on how unfair it would be if they were to fail their assignment because they didn't get enough responses. Because what they did to get attention, to express themselves, was exactly what made people want to ignore them.

As Zoe got into her car and drove away, she watched the two teens in her rearview mirror. They were still standing at the light pole, examining their clipboard with furrowed brows. Their hands, by their sides, were linked by their little fingers.

CHAPTER THIRTEEN

"There's the sound of a man who didn't spend last night in his own bed."

Hugh hadn't even realized he'd been whistling. He stopped immediately and turned to face his foreman in the corridor of the estate building. "Checking up on me, Morris?"

The older man grunted and shoved a piece of paper at him. "Need your autograph."

Hugh studied the delivery receipt for a moment as he tried to gather his thoughts. He regretted that his mood was so transparent. But, in a way, it was lucky Morris had caught him on the upswing of the emotional seesaw he was riding this morning.

What he and Zoe had shared last night had been both exquisite and excruciating—listening to her tell her story had shredded his heart and he still hadn't recovered. The sex had been great, but this morning's afterglow kept being punctured by the memory of Zoe's hollow eyes and his own sorrow.

Swinging between the two extremes was exhausting.

He'd do anything to change the past. Even if it meant staying away from Zoe in the first place—although he didn't know if that was actually possible. Even now, when he had absolutely no reason to be with her—and was old enough to know better—he hadn't been able to tear himself away.

Hugh didn't do temporary. Everything in his life was about achieving certainty, security, solidity. A one-night stand with Zoe Waters didn't fit that strategy in any way. But once she'd been in his arms there'd been an inevitability about it all that he'd been powerless to resist.

"It's for the new deck chairs," Morris prompted, referring to the invoice in Hugh's hand. He realized he'd been staring at it blankly. "We won't put them out till summer, but we got a good deal, so it doesn't hurt for us to buy 'em now and put 'em in storage."

Hugh shook his head and focused on the numbers on the bottom of the page. "Fine." He found a pen and scrawled his signature across the bottom of the page.

Morris took the signed paper and folded it, slipping it into his shirt pocket. He lifted the brim of his cap and studied Hugh carefully.

"What?" Hugh asked. He looked around—

another Lawson Estate employee was mopping floors, but too far away to overhear their conversation. Hugh had been in meetings all morning—since slipping away from Zoe before dawn he'd barely had time to shower and change before he'd been needed on the phone for a teleconference. He'd been back on the property early, so he hadn't thought his overnight absence would be noted, but he should have known nothing would escape Morris.

"Do you know what you're doing?" Morris asked after a moment's silence.

Hugh paused. "Authorizing the purchase of a couple of dozen deck chairs?"

There was a beat of silence. "Fine." The older man's one gruff syllable conveyed an acre of meaning.

"What?" Hugh folded his arms as he leaned against the wall, any trace of his good mood suddenly gone. "Something you want to tell me, Morris?"

"Nope, not a thing."

"Obviously something's on your mind."

Morris folded his arms, too, and gave Hugh the imperious stare the man used on recalcitrant employees or drunken visitors. "That equipment—you going to return it any time soon?"

"Yes. Tomorrow. Or the day after. As soon as we're finished with racking off at Waterford."

If Morris wanted to discuss any other details of what was happening over at Waterford, he was out of luck. Hugh didn't know how he felt himself—certainly not well enough to try to explain what was happening to someone else.

Morris gave a short nod. "Fine."

"Fine." Hugh felt like a teenager being scolded for staying out too late. He reached for something to restore the balance between them. Giving orders was a good start. "I'll need you to arrange bottling for the Waterford Shiraz. Should only take a day. We'll be done tomorrow, so we could get the guys in the day after." He hadn't discussed that with Zoe, but he figured it was probably his decision to make, anyway.

"I'll give them a call, see what their schedule is."

"Good. Thanks."

They stood in the corridor a moment longer, arms folded, staring at each other. "Boss?"

"Yeah?"

"I just…"

Hugh could have sworn his foreman looked uncomfortable. Morris shifted on his feet and his eyes left Hugh's to aim somewhere at the wall behind him. Well, there was a first time for everything.

"What is it, Morris?" Hugh asked, suddenly

worried about whatever could be making this seemingly unshakable man nervous.

Morris's eyes met his again, full of concern. "Just be careful, okay? Don't want history repeating itself. There's been enough tears and blood spilled between the Waters and Lawsons to last…well, a very long time."

Tears and blood was a bit extreme, but Hugh could only agree. "And this is where it ends." Soon, Waterford would be his. Swallowed up by Lawson Estate as if it had never existed. Zoe Waters would be on the other side of the world; the entire Waters family wiped from Tangawarra as if they had never existed.

Hugh wasn't sure why that idea unsettled him so much.

Morris nodded slowly. "Okay. Good."

"After the wine's finished and Zoe signs the papers, there is no more Waterford. It's all over." *Damn.* His own words echoed inside him. Sleeping with Zoe had been a really stupid move. As inevitable as it had felt last night, it could only cause complications now. Exactly what those complications were, and how he would handle them, he didn't know.

Morris thinned his lips before speaking. "I…I hope that's true. And I hope…that's *right*. You know, the right thing to do."

"Of course it's right." Hugh wished he felt as

certain as he sounded. He stood straighter and dropped his arms, making an instant decision. "I'm going back over there now."

Morris raised an eyebrow. "Not coming to the operations meeting?"

Crap. Hugh had completely forgotten about it. It was only a meeting they had every week at the same time. When he was on-site, Hugh always attended, just like his father had.

He shrugged, hoping his expression didn't betray him. "You can handle it, can't you?" He needed to get back to Waterford. To see how things were.

Morris nodded. "Sure."

"Call me if you need anything."

"Will do. Catch you later."

ZOE TURNED ON THE PUMP and began emptying one of the last barrels remaining to be cleaned. She siphoned off a glassful and had a quick taste, making a few notes in her grandfather's notebook about balance and acid, out of habit more than anything.

The swirl of the wine in her mouth brought back thoughts of Hugh's kiss, his body, those arms—his surprising tattoo—and the previous night's activities began to replay on her inner movie screen despite her best intentions. They were just such lovely memories. And they

would have to last. Because once the vintage
was bottled and Waterford was signed over to
Hugh, that was it. She was out of here and would
never have any reason to come back again. Even
if Napa wasn't forever, there was nothing left
for her here. There were still wine regions in
Chile and South Africa that she hadn't explored.
When she got back to Golden Gate she'd see
how long she could avoid talking to Wil about
that contract he wanted her to sign.

Maybe it was time to move on.

Zoe watched the wine slowly drain from the
oak barrel and empty into the stainless steel
vat, the swirling liquid a dark, velvety red. It
was almost hypnotic, and Zoe let her mind go
blank. When the pump had done its job, Zoe
switched it off and stared at the empty barrel.
Empty, but still very heavy. Her back began to
ache in anticipation of lifting it.

"Hi." Hugh's voice was quiet, but it still startled her.

"Oh!" Zoe spun around, brushing her hair
away from her face with a wine-stained hand.
"You're back." She winced as she blurted out
the words, making her surprise and relief obvious. So much for the carefree attitude she'd
been planning. Or for making him worry by
not being here when he turned up. Of course he

was back. Hugh still wanted to own Waterford. That, if nothing else, guaranteed his presence.

"I am. I had meetings—sorry. I wanted to let you know, but I realized I don't have a mobile number for you. I tried the house number, but that wouldn't have done any good if you were out here." He was babbling nervously— most un-Hugh-like. He flicked a glance at the oak barrel she'd been about to lift. "I knew I couldn't trust you not to go doing things you shouldn't. Barrels are expensive, you know. Don't want you dropping and breaking any— they're practically mine, now."

His words were a cool reminder of the situation they were in, but his tone was gentle. His eyes were a warm blue in the morning light.

She waved his concern away with one hand. "I know. But that's ridiculous. It's got to be done."

"Zoe, Zoe, Zoe." He shook his head, but it wasn't the rebuke it had been when he'd turned up a few days ago and discovered the electrical cord in the puddle. He stepped forward, close enough for her to feel his heat, to take in his fresh, clean scent. "What am I going to do with you?" One side of his mouth kicked up in a smile and his nervousness fell away. "I'd take you over my knee and spank you, but I'm afraid you'd enjoy it."

Zoe's mouth dropped open, first in shock and then in protest. Then she closed again. *Maybe she would.* "Oh," was all she said.

"Yes, 'oh.'" He took a final step that closed the gap between them, pressing her between his body and the barrel rack.

This wasn't what she'd expected and she wasn't in the least prepared. Zoe looked up at him and only had time to swallow before he gathered her into his arms. Their lips met and it was as if no time had passed since they'd been in bed together. Her legs trembled and her body responded to his touch with a rush of liquid heat.

The fact that she was making another big mistake seemed suddenly irrelevant.

Zoe returned his kiss with all the passion she could muster.

"Hugh," she murmured as his mouth traced a path from her lips to her ear, sucking on her earlobe before blazing a hot, wet trail down her neck. His fingers tangled in her hair, pulling out her ponytail as his lips returned to hers, urging her to open for him.

This was the problem, she thought. When Hugh did this, her brain ceased to function.

Then she didn't think anymore, just kissed, pressed her body against his, threaded her fingers into his hair, wound one leg around his hips. He pushed up the hem of her sweater until his palm grazed the lower curve of her breast as she tried to tug his shirt free from his pants.

"I think the wine tastes great," he whispered, pulling back an inch and licking his lips slowly.

"Hmm?" Zoe asked, dazed.

"At least, I'm guessing the wine tastes like you. If it does then I'll need to buy a few cases of it myself."

Before she could think—or say—anything in reply, a voice rang out and they both froze.

"Yoo-hoo! Is anyone home? Zoe?"

The look she and Hugh shared would have been comical if she'd been watching it on television, Zoe figured. Instead, she was too busy untangling herself from Hugh's embrace and fixing up her hair. A chill went through her at Hugh's sudden absence and she was glad for the support of the barrel rack behind her as she struggled to pull herself together.

"Patricia, I haven't seen you in ages!" Hugh's voice dipped as he stepped outside, giving Zoe valuable moments to retie her ponytail and adjust her sweater. She hoped her no-doubt flushed face could be explained by the work she was doing.

"Hey, Patricia," Zoe said, blinking as she stepped out into the sun a moment later to join them.

"There you are," Patricia said, her smile broad. "I just thought I'd stop in to see how you were doing."

Zoe didn't miss the way Patricia's eyes flicked between her and Hugh, clearly trying to work up some gossip. She'd have to try hard, Zoe thought, because although she couldn't vouch for her own, Hugh's demeanor and expression gave nothing away. He looked just as he had when he'd walked in—although his shirt was a little rumpled from where Zoe had fisted it in her hands.

"I'm fine," Zoe said, shaking the thoughts away. "Hugh's been helping me with racking off—we're nearly done."

"I should have guessed Hugh would be here lending a helping hand where it's needed," Patricia said with an almost sickly sweet smile. She reached over to squeeze Hugh's arm.

"How's Bert doing?" Hugh asked. "Taking it easy now? No more issues with the ticker?" He put a hand to his chest in illustration, smoothly releasing himself from Patricia's hold at the same time.

Patricia's smile dropped, but didn't vanish. "He's still got to be careful, but he's doing much better. Doctor Carroll says he'll be fine as long as he doesn't push it for a while."

"Good to hear."

"Sorry, Patricia, I didn't know Bert hadn't been well," Zoe said, figuring she should at least make an effort at polite conversation. Even if her head was still scrambled.

"That's okay, love, you've had enough of your own things to deal with, that's for sure." Patricia took a step closer to Zoe. "And, I was just wondering, how is all that going? Do you know what you're doing? Made any decisions?"

"I, uh—" Zoe began.

Patricia turned to Hugh, leaning in close again, as if sharing a confidence. "Hugh, I don't know if you'd heard, but poor Zoe is in it up to her neck here. Mack left things in a right state. The place is practically bankrupt."

Zoe couldn't help the impatient sigh that made Hugh look at her sharply.

"Bert and I wanted to help out," Patricia continued, "but, of course, as much as we wanted to do the right thing, we can't take on bad debts. Not at our stage of life."

Zoe suppressed a smile. Patricia's plan had suddenly become a charitable offer instead of a business one? Well, it was probably a better story to put about town.

"Lawson Estate will be purchasing Waterford," Hugh said from beside her.

Zoe shot him a look. Great. And now the whole world would know in a matter of hours.

"It's not something we're making public yet," she rushed in to say. "So I'd appreciate you keeping it confidential." Why exactly she didn't want everyone to know was something Zoe wasn't entirely sure of herself. Perhaps it would just make everything so *final*.

"Of course, of course," Patricia said. "My lips are sealed." And she looked utterly thrilled about it.

"We appreciate it."

Hugh frowned at her. "I guess the paperwork isn't signed, so it's better to keep it quiet for now, but the deal *is* done."

There was that steely thread in his voice again. It made Zoe want to argue, just for the hell of it, but she stifled the impulse.

"I'm so glad you've sorted things out, Zoe."

"Thanks."

"You must come over for tea with me and Bert. What are you doing tonight?" Her eyes lit up and flicked between Hugh and Zoe once again. "Maybe you could both come?"

"No, we—" Zoe began, but Hugh interrupted smoothly.

"That's a lovely offer, Patricia, but I'm afraid we've got a lot of work to do here. As you so rightly pointed out, Mack left the place in a mess. There's not only the wine to take care of, but acres of paperwork, too."

Patricia tutted sympathetically. "Oh, you poor things. Of course, it must be a complete disaster. But if you get hungry, you just give me a call, okay? You're welcome anytime, or I can drop something around."

"Thanks, Patricia." He put on that saintly smile again. The one that made Zoe want to kick him in the shins.

"Yes, thank you," she echoed instead.

"Well, I'd best be off. Take care. Let me know if there's anything I can do."

Hugh walked with Patricia over to her car. She'd parked by the side of the house—probably why they hadn't heard her approach. Ha! Who was she kidding? When Hugh was kissing her, a marching band could come up the drive and she wouldn't notice until the trombone knocked her in the head.

Zoe watched Hugh farewell Patricia—noticed her get in a peck on Hugh's cheek before she climbed into her car—and waited until she'd driven off before stepping back inside the winery.

Lord knew what kind of gossip would have circulated if Patricia had walked in and put two and two together. She couldn't bear to think about what might have happened if the woman had turned up a few minutes earlier. Walked into the shed without calling out. What she might have seen...

She loathed the idea of the Tangawarra townspeople talking about her. Maybe it was just that she hated the idea that nothing had changed. *Poor girl—no money, no chances. Poor girl—stuck with her grandfather's mess. Poor girl—thinks she has a chance with Hugh Lawson.*

Hugh's motivations wouldn't come into question, she was sure.

It was a sobering thought. Just the kind of thought to break the strange, drugging spell Hugh seemed to have cast over her. How could she have ended up in his arms *again?*

The object of her thoughts reappeared, smacking his hands together as if wiping them of their visitor.

"We have to finish racking off soon," Zoe said, switching to business mode as best she could. She reached for the tasting glass and the notes she'd been making earlier so she didn't have to look at him while she spoke. "The wine's on the verge of being over-oaked—it's pretty much ready for bottling. We need to get through the remaining barrels as quickly as possible without any more...distractions." It was hard to sound brisk and efficient after what she'd just allowed to happen, but Zoe did her best.

There was a moment's silence and then he just said, "Right." His voice had turned to ice. Zoe watched out of the corner of her eye as he adjusted his shirt, tucked in hastily earlier, smoothing out the back and fixing the front where it disappeared behind his belt buckle.

A shudder went through her as she watched, half a ripple of pleasure and half a shiver of disgust at her own lack of self-control.

He gave her a measuring glance. "But, Zoe, we need—"

She didn't let him finish. "We need to finish this as soon as possible." She lifted her chin. "Golden Gate called me. I have to be back in California by the end of next week. So we have to get everything done by then."

Hugh stood rock still for a moment, his jaw clenched. Then he gave her a short nod. "Fine. Let's get to work, then, shall we?"

His clipped words echoed in the shed before he spun on his heel and headed for the empty barrel, hoisting it easily onto his shoulder and over to where the high-pressure cleaner was set up.

Hugh sounded hurt. But his face had shuttered down into that cool mask of composure that she'd noticed he wore easily now. It gave nothing away. And there wasn't anything Zoe could do about it, anyway.

HUGH WAS QUITE SURE Waterford's barrels had never been cleaner. Scrubbing them had left him sweaty, soaked and uncomfortable. But it was better than grabbing Zoe Waters and trying to shake some sense into her the way he wanted to.

She'd turned running away into an art form. Whether it was physically or emotionally, Zoe was better than anyone he'd ever known at putting distance between herself and anyone who might even try to get close to her.

It was lucky for her he understood what was going on. He wondered what other men had made of her prickly nature. Or did she save that for him? Maybe she'd had plenty of successful relationships, letting people close, comfortable with the intimacy of it. He couldn't imagine it. But then, he realized, he didn't want to, either. Thinking about Zoe with other men made his gut twist.

He started to scrub out a barrel. A juvenile kind of silence had reigned inside the winery shed since Patricia's ill-timed visit. They were pretending to ignore each other, like warring kids who'd been forced by a well-meaning but misguided teacher to work together on a school project.

He didn't mind it—for now. It provided a precious opportunity to work through his thoughts. He needed a little time inside his own head, trying to figure out what was going on in there.

Zoe, mostly.

His head was full of her. And of the fact that she was heading back to California in a few days.

Of course she was. That had always been the plan.

At first, she'd been a challenge. When someone caused the kind of disruption in your life that Zoe had in his, even if it had been ten years ago, it was only reasonable to expect to examine that, wasn't it? Funny though, when he'd first seen her—standing on the grass at Waterford, hair whipping in the wind, skin prickled with goose bumps from the weather she wasn't dressed for—that hadn't been the first thought he'd had. Mostly he'd thought, *Zoe Waters grew up into a babe.*

Then she'd revealed her secret and things had changed. Would he have pushed her to tell him if he'd known how tragic it was? How much it would hurt her to relive it? How much it would hurt him to *watch* her relive it?

Yes.

Despite the pain retelling the story had brought, Hugh was glad that he knew the truth.

He scrubbed the barrel in front of him harder, relishing the ache in his arms and shoulders—so much more bearable than the pain he and Zoe had faced last night. And so much easier to understand than the pleasure they'd shared.

He looked up from his work to find Zoe frowning as she sorted through a pile of paper on Mack's desk. Deliberately not looking at him. Deliberately not talking to him.

Was this it? Were they just going to ignore each other and what happened last night until she left?

He turned back to his cleaning task.

He'd skipped an important operations meeting to get back here. And though his initial motivation had been to sort everything out with her, clear the air, work out where they stood with each other, when he'd seen her his only thought had been how quickly he could get her naked.

That wasn't supposed to be how it worked. Not part of the plan.

This—this work that was going to result in him owning Waterford—this *was* part of the plan. Part of building Lawson Estate into a rock-solid operation that could weather any storm. And to get Waterford he was helping Zoe with the vintage. It wasn't necessarily the smartest business decision—it certainly wasn't a profitable one—but it was the only way.

Once the vintage was done, and Waterford was signed over, Zoe would disappear back to California. She'd never pretended anything else, and she'd just made it perfectly clear that her plans hadn't changed.

Would things go back to normal then?

"Hugh? I think that one's done," Zoe called out, a touch of teasing in her voice.

Hugh looked at the barrel he'd been working on—it was so clean it almost gleamed. Ridiculous.

"Yeah."

At least she'd broken the silence.

He gave the barrel a final rinse and then pushed himself to his feet. He returned it to the rack and collected the next one in line.

"Only a few left," she said. Her tone was polite, friendly. As if she'd hit a reset button that took them back to the first couple of days they'd worked together.

"Yep. It'll be into bottles soon. You should buy your plane ticket home. Although I suppose you already have." He couldn't hide his accusing tone.

She nodded and, to his surprise, answered calmly. "I have an open-ended return ticket.

I can go back whenever I want—just have to book it."

"You always did make sure you had an escape route planned." It sounded like an attack. He meant it to.

She just shrugged. "I guess so."

"I hope Golden Gate's management isn't counting on you hanging around for long."

Zoe made a noncommittal noise and looked down at the papers in front of her.

It was a reversal of their usual dynamic. Hugh needling, Zoe not rising to the bait. It was almost as if the real Zoe had retreated somewhere, leaving an automaton behind to go through the motions.

Not good enough. Not after everything.

"You're really going to do this?" He dumped the barrel on the floor with a loud thump that rattled the whole shed.

A heavy, tired-sounding sigh and then she finally looked up. "Do what, Hugh?"

"Let's have it out."

"Have *what* out?"

His fists tightened. Her insistence on playing dumb was infuriating. "Whatever it is that's going on here. Let's get it all out in the open. This time when you leave, let's have a clean slate."

"We already do. As far as I'm concerned, the slate was cleared last night."

The one-shouldered shrug of defeat that had inspired his compassion the previous evening only irritated him this morning.

She was lying. He could see it.

"I was quite happy to let it go," she continued. "Make last night water under our particular bridge. But clearly you can't."

"Why would I want to forget it?"

"Because that would be easier for the both of us."

"Why?" He realized it was a question he actually wanted the answer to.

Zoe fiddled with a page in front of her before her shoulders slumped and she leaned both elbows on the desk. "Because that's how we do things. It's how we did things before. It's…it's what I do."

"It's not what *I* do."

"Really?"

Really? The question echoed around the shed. Hugh had never intended to pretend their lovemaking hadn't happened. But he hadn't been entirely sure what he'd do when he saw her, either. Kissing her again hadn't been deliberate. It had just been an instinct, as hard to resist as breathing.

"I…don't know," he said honestly.

The only thing he did know was that before Zoe Waters had reappeared, he'd been sure of things. Sure of what he wanted, his plan, his future. But now, now he wasn't. He'd spent his life striving to achieve security—to build an empire so solid that he'd be protected from all the uncertainties of life.

A pipe dream, he realized now.

All it had taken to bring his foundations tumbling down was for Zoe to walk back into his life.

The fight drained out of him. "I'm sorry," he said, not entirely sure why he was saying it and knowing it didn't come close to expressing what he really felt.

"Yeah, me, too. But that's life."

Was it really so easy for her to dismiss what they'd shared? Was he the one blowing things out of proportion?

Zoe's expression softened. "Can we call a truce? We still have a lot of work to get through. Let's just agree to let all of this be part of our history—leave it in the past—and move on."

That was probably the best idea. He should have been relieved.

He wasn't.

"Truce," he said.

Zoe nodded and smiled. "Good."

Hugh turned away and busied himself with

the barrel, taking it as far away from her as he could get.

Suddenly the shed seemed far too small.

CHAPTER FOURTEEN

BY LUNCHTIME THE NEXT DAY, all the barrels were done and Zoe heaved a sigh of relief. It was past time to get out of here. Away from Tangawarra and Waterford and Hugh. And the ghosts that haunted her.

They had managed to keep up their carefully contrived "truce," working together in the winery. In fact, Hugh had been completely businesslike, almost cold. Zoe wanted to feel pleased that he'd agreed to her "water under the bridge" solution, but the feeling didn't come.

She told herself that it didn't matter, anyway. In a matter of days he and this place would be behind her. Again.

Her future lay elsewhere. California. Or anywhere, really. She probably was getting a little too attached to Golden Gate and the people there. That meant it was time to move on. She was happiest when she had no ties binding her. That was why Tangawarra belonged in the past.

Only, the sense of peace she'd expected as her

opportunity to escape got closer was missing. Instead, there was a strange, gnawing anxiety. As if something was nibbling away inside her. The odd feeling had begun to grow over the past two days, ever since she'd told Hugh the story of her—their—past. She couldn't eat, her fingers trembled when she tried to work and her breathing came too rapidly unless she forced herself to focus. If she didn't know better, she would have called it panic. But it was probably just her eagerness to get away, to leave all this messy stuff behind her.

"I have to get the equipment back to Lawson Estate," Hugh announced, cutting into her thoughts. He stood in the middle of the winery, surveying the space. "Morris is already practically having a heart attack because he can't see what we're doing with it."

Zoe looked around the shed. The equipment he'd brought over was spread throughout, integrated, as if it belonged there. And it did. It was Lawson Estate equipment; this would soon be a Lawson Estate shed. Zoe was the interloper. A strange feeling to have in what had once been her home.

"No problem. Shouldn't take long," she said, forcing a relaxed smile onto her face to accompany her deliberately breezy tone.

For some reason, that didn't seem to please him. Then again, nothing she'd done in the past twenty-four hours had pleased him. He'd kept the truce, but she could tell he wasn't happy about it. But what was the point of another painful D and M when everything would be over soon, anyway?

"I'll get Morris to come over and help you pack up. There's things I need to do back at Lawson Estate." His tone was as clipped and fake-professional as hers had been fake-carefree.

Was this it? Their final goodbye?

She wanted him to leave, and yet at the same time she didn't.

Would she see him again? They'd have to meet to sign paperwork, at least, wouldn't they? But that would be in Stephen Carter's office—they wouldn't be alone.

Funny how she'd thought she couldn't wait for this to be over, and yet now here the end was in sight, and that strange panic was increasing, not waning.

Her eyes lit on the pile of papers she'd excavated from the filing cabinet—they still hadn't been touched. Maybe Hugh would hang around to help. Or now that the wine was done, perhaps he felt his obligations were at an end. Would he leave her alone to finish things? Send in his lieutenant to mop things up?

She brushed her hair back with shaking fingers.

"I don't think we need Morris's help, do we?" she found herself asking. The longer they took to pack up, the more time she had to...*to what?* "We'll be okay to pack everything up, if we—"

But Hugh was already dialing his mobile phone and he turned his back on her to talk into it.

Could he really not stand to be alone with her for a minute longer?

She'd told him she had to return to California. He was accepting that. Letting her go. She should be thrilled he wasn't pushing her for more explanations, more conversations, more dissections of their past.

"He's on his way over," Hugh said in those clipped tones.

"Fine."

Zoe packed up the high-pressure cleaning unit and then grabbed a broom and began sweeping out the shed while Hugh stacked all the borrowed equipment near the door. No further words were spoken.

Her sweeping was pointless. She kept going over the same stretch of concrete in much the same way as her mind kept looping through the same thoughts. She wanted him to leave. She didn't want him to leave. She wanted to talk more. She didn't want to talk ever again. *Which is it, Zoe?* The contradictions were wearing her out—both mentally and physically. Her body seemed to have been leached of its strength and she couldn't manage to apply enough force to sweep properly.

So she just kept up her futile cleaning, hoping Hugh was too wrapped up in his own tasks to notice.

A few minutes later a vehicle approached, and with the slam of a door, the craggy, cap-wearing Lawson Estate foreman walked through the door.

He nodded to Hugh and called out a greeting to Zoe.

"Hi, Morris." Zoe swallowed hard. It was a definitive reminder—if she needed one—that things had changed. Having Hugh in her grandfather's winery was unusual, but because of their history it hadn't felt so strange. Morris's presence—especially in his full Lawson Estate uniform—was incongruous and a reminder that she was now the stranger here.

Soon she'd be gone, back soaking in the sunshine of California, and all this would be behind her. She would seal off her past—as she'd done once before—and get on with her life. Everything here would be neatly put away and tied up in a box. Never to bother her again.

She just needed to get enough distance.

About half the world would have do.

"How'd ya go?" Morris asked. He'd already carted most of the equipment out to his ute, only a few small things remained.

"It's all good," Hugh answered before Zoe had a chance to speak. "The barrels are racked off. They're ready for the mobile bottling service."

Morris gave a short nod. "No worries. I talked to the guys last night and they're all lined up. We'll have it here tomorrow."

Zoe raised an eyebrow in annoyance. Hugh hadn't told her any of that. "I didn't know you were organizing bottling tomorrow," she said, unable to keep the edge out of her voice. She dropped the broom to the floor, where it clattered against the bare concrete.

"You said the wine was ready," Hugh said mildly.

"It *is* ready, but if I'd known the bottling was happening tomorrow I might have made a few adjustments to the acid levels." She didn't really need to do anything further to the wine, but she was annoyed that he'd made the decision without consulting her.

Hugh stopped what he was doing and turned

to face her. "You said you didn't want to change it too much from what your grandfather had done."

Zoe put her hands on her hips. "That's not the point. *I'm* the winemaker. I should know when *my* wine is going to be bottled."

Hugh narrowed his eyes and his hands clasped into fists by his side. "*Whose* wine, Zoe?"

Zoe's mouth dropped open in surprise. She sputtered for a moment, almost relieved to feel her old anger flaring to life. Getting angry wouldn't solve anything, but it had to be better than this weirdly paralyzing anxiety.

"I know financially it's your wine, Hugh." She put her hands on her hips to stop them shaking. "But it will still have the Waterford name on it and so it's *my* family's reputation we're talking about here."

She was working herself up to a full head of steam. But before she could continue, Morris interrupted.

"You two remember when I caught yas in the tractor shed at Lawson Estate?" His low voice rumbled through the echoing space.

Both she and Hugh turned to face him. Her anger took a sideline when the older man met her eyes, his gaze knowing and a little cheeky. Her face heated with a blush as the memory washed over her. She could have sworn Hugh's did the same.

Tractor shed. Only a couple of months after they'd first gotten together. Hugh's hand on her breast, but over her bra. Her fingers against his bare chest, exploring the lines of hard muscle. The bang of the door and sudden sunlight that had blinded them. The way they'd leaped apart as if burned. The way they'd giggled about it afterward.

Morris gave a raspy laugh. "You sure were more careful after that."

"Morris." Hugh's voice had a very adult warning tone in it that Zoe hadn't heard before.

Morris ignored it. "I sure never understood how your dad never noticed you two sneaking off together," he continued. He leaned against the doorway, casually picking dirt out from under one of his fingernails as he spoke. "I mean, old Mack wasn't gonna work it out. So wrapped up in his wine, he wouldn't have known if war broke out until the soldiers were on his property."

"We used to go down to the creek after you caught us," Zoe said, not entirely sure why she was offering that piece of information.

Morris nodded as if he already knew. He pinned Hugh with a purposeful stare. His next words were precise. "I reckon Pete did know.

He just didn't want to admit that it was a case of like father, like son."

Zoe could see the puzzled look on Hugh's face. She didn't know what Morris meant, either.

"What are you talking about?" Hugh said.

"Your dad." He inclined his head towards Zoe. "And Margie, Zoe's mum."

"What?" Hugh and Zoe spoke in unison.

The concrete floor under her feet seemed to tilt and Zoe put a hand against the barrel rack to keep her balance. She was light-headed with nausea.

"Gonna run away together, they were. Never quite forgave your dad for that, I have to say, Hugh, even if he did come to regret it. Your mum was sick and she needed him. Maybe he'd had enough of that—enough of the responsibility. But for a man like him to give up everything—his wife, his son, his business—he must have been do-lally for that gal. She must have had him wrapped around her little finger."

"He was...*what?*" Hugh spluttered.

Morris made a "don't ask me" gesture with his hands. "From what I know, they were gonna take Zoe with 'em—Margie insisted on that. But when Margie told Mack, he went ballistic. Told her he wouldn't let her take Zoe. Said he'd take her to court, prove she was an unfit mother, get custody." He glanced at Zoe. "Bad habit of hers, running off with blokes and draggin' you around with her, from what I'm told."

Zoe wanted to argue, but her bottom lip trembled so violently she knew she couldn't speak.

"After she fought with Mack over Zoe, Margie jumped in the car. She was driving to Lawson Estate to see Pete when she was killed. She swerved to miss a kangaroo and the car went into a tree."

Zoe was still struggling to make sense of everything. She saw Hugh run a hand through his hair. "Oh, crap," he muttered.

"Your dad blamed Mack." Morris nodded to Hugh. "Said that if they hadn't fought, Margie wouldn't have been out driving in the middle of the night. Mack blamed Pete. Said if they hadn't been carryin' on in the first place, it would never have happened."

"Why didn't anyone tell me this?" Hugh said.

Morris shrugged. "Reckon I'm the only one in town who knows about it. And your dad told me not to tell you—both Pete and Mack didn't want it getting about as gossip in town. Although given what happened with you two, I wish now…" Morris broke off and scratched his head under his cap for a moment before pinning Zoe with a sympathetic look.

"Pete never told me why you was sent to Sydney, Zoe, but I can guess. Didn't work it out at the time. If I had… Well… Truthfully, I dunno what I would've done, but it woulda been different."

"So why are you telling us now?" Zoe asked, her voice weak. She'd definitely exceeded her upper limit for personal revelations and family crises. She wasn't sure she even fully comprehended the story Morris had just told.

"Well, I just figure… If those two old fogies weren't still hung up on what had happened between them with Margie, maybe they'd have seen that things could be different for you two, maybe they'd have let you have a chance. But by the time I figured that out, it was too late."

A brief silence fell, punctuated only by a muttered expletive from Hugh.

Morris cleared his throat before continuing. "In answer to your question, Zoe, I'm tellin' you all this because maybe it'll make a difference to what happens between you two now. If Mack and Pete hadn't let the past rule them, hadn't been stuck fighting each other over something neither of them could do anythin' to change, they might have made a different decision back then—a better one. I think, just maybe, there's somethin' you two can learn from that."

He looked at them both in turn, his mouth a straight line. "I've got everythin' packed up,

Boss. See you back at the ranch." With a short, salutelike wave to Hugh, he was gone.

Zoe's knees felt weak, so she let herself slide down the steel strut of the barrel rack until her bottom hit the cold concrete. She rested her forehead on her knees, her head suddenly too heavy for her neck to hold up.

Hugh's reaction was the opposite. He began to pace back and forward, angry, heavy steps that echoed off the tin walls.

He swore viciously. "Bloody Mack. And my father. If they weren't already dead, I'd strangle them both myself."

Zoe raised her face to Hugh. His blue eyes were bright with anger. "What?"

He shook his head and his hands were tight fists by his side. "All these secrets. What good has it done? Any of it?"

Zoe scrambled to her feet, feeling suddenly vulnerable. Crouching in the corner was no defense against an enraged, pacing tiger. "What good would honesty have done?"

"My mother—she was so sick and they were going to…" He trailed off. "I hope she never knew about this."

Zoe's tarnished image of her mother dulled a little further. Taking another woman's husband, a woman fighting cancer who needed her family, her husband… "Margie never thought of anyone but herself," Zoe said quietly.

Hugh spun on his heel to face her. "They were all so selfish."

"And so were we, I guess."

"How do you mean?"

"We wanted our own lives, we wanted to pretend that nothing else existed. We were reckless…we…" Zoe tried in vain to calm her shattered nerves.

"Well, there is one good thing to come from this," Hugh said after a moment.

"What's that?"

"If the wine in the boxes wasn't enough, this proves it. You have to admit it now, Zoe. Mack really did love you."

Zoe's anxiety grew until she thought she might faint. She told herself it was all a reaction to Morris's news, but in all honesty she'd never felt so strange.

She took a staggering step back and reached for the barrel rack to steady herself as she shook her head. "Mack was angry with my mother for taking up with his business rival. It had nothing to do with me."

Hugh frowned. He sucked in a deep breath and then let it out slowly. Some of his anger seemed to go with it. His hands relaxed and he moved closer to her. "Zoe, you're a clever

woman. You always have been. But about some things in life, you're really, really dumb."

Zoe reached for her usual ally, anger, but it slipped through her trembling fingers. "What are you talking about?" She hated that her voice sounded thready instead of defiant.

"Your mother loved you as best she could. She knew she wasn't doing a good job as a parent, so she brought you to Waterford to try to get more settled. Then she ended up with my father...." His eyes unfocused for a moment, but then they flashed with an anger Zoe dearly wished she could borrow. "I guess we'll never know. But she was going to take you with her. Uproot you again, take you from the only stable home you'd ever had. Mack fought her for you. He wanted what was best for you."

She shrugged. "He just wanted another pair of hands around the place."

Hugh shot her an exasperated look. "Yeah, 'cause it's so much simpler to take custody of a ten-year-old girl than to hire an employee. Face it, he loved you."

The crack that had opened in Zoe's emotional fortress the night she'd told Hugh about Sara began to widen. A rushing sound filled her ears.

She held up a hand, but Hugh kept talking. "What is it that makes you think you're so unlovable? Why do you push everyone away?"

"Don't," Zoe warned, not exactly sure what she meant.

"It's fear, isn't it?" He cocked his head to one side, studying her as if she were an interesting museum piece.

Zoe shuddered. "Hugh, don't. Please. I can't…"

Hugh's eyebrows went up as insight dawned. "No, it's worse than that," he breathed. "Oh, Zoe. If they didn't love you, you don't have to love them back. You don't have to mourn everyone you've lost."

How dare he! Zoe finally felt her anger stirring. The relief was short-lived. The anger was a tidal wave, an overwhelming, all-consuming rush. It was going to wash through her in a flood and leave nothing behind.

Hugh's hand cupped her cheek. "Oh, sweetheart. I'm so sorry."

Zoe was blinded as tears filled her eyes and her heart boiled with rage. A knot somewhere deep inside her pulled tighter, ratcheting up her blood pressure, speeding up her pulse. Every bitter moment, from her mother's death to her miserable and lonely abandonment in Sydney welled up inside her chest. And, suddenly, it was all Hugh's fault. If he'd never made her tell him about Sara…if he'd never made her feel again…if only she'd never met him in the first place….

"I hate you!"

He flinched. "Zoe, don't…"

It was too much to keep locked up inside. A volcano erupted within, spewing hot tears, bitter loneliness and pointless, futile anger.

A primal growl tore from her throat. "I hate you!" she screamed again.

The first punch landed in his stomach and she heard a quickly stifled "oomph" before the next punch connected somewhere near his rib cage.

"Zoe! Don't do this, I…"

Hot, hated tears—ten years' worth—began to flood from her eyes and pour down her cheeks. The dam had broken.

Her arms flailed, hitting Hugh's arms, stomach and chest, until he caught her wrists and held tight. She struggled against his restraint, her foot flying out and connecting with his shin.

"Zoe!" His hands tightened on her wrists, even as he took a step back to avoid her kicking him again.

"I hate you, I hate you," she repeated, now not even sure what the words meant. Howling sobs wracked her body as she was filled with pain, gut-wrenching and brutal. She wondered if it was possible to feel this way and survive.

"I hate you," she managed to yell one more time. She wrenched one wrist from his grasp and lashed out to hit him, not caring where it landed. She heard him swear and then everything happened in a rush. He deflected her fist by pushing her arm away from him. At the same time he stepped forward, bringing their bodies close. He wrapped his arms around her, pressing her to him, restraining her, holding her so tightly that it was impossible for her to raise her arms.

"No-o-o," she wailed. Something dark and poisonous had awoken inside her, and Zoe had never been more afraid.

CHAPTER FIFTEEN

EVERY INCH OF ZOE'S body trembled against him. She struggled awhile longer, twisting and fighting to escape his grip, and she was strong— but he was stronger. Then the fight went out of her, turning her limp in his arms. Her muscles wilted, but her rapid, hysterical breathing continued, and he worried that she might pass out.

"Zoe, you need to calm down." Hugh did his best to sound authoritative, like a doctor might, but he could hear the tremor in his own voice.

He wondered if his words even penetrated the storm that raged within her. The look in her eyes terrified him—he'd never seen anyone so...*broken.*

Realizing that words would have little impact in Zoe's current state, he went for a more basic approach. He carefully maneuvered them both to the floor, Zoe following him bonelessly. He propped himself against the wall and surrounded her with his body, his arms around her—still restraining her hands just in case—

and wrapped his legs around her hips. Her head was buried against his chest.

Once they were settled, Hugh rocked gently back and forth, his lips pressed against the top of her head. He murmured to her, stupid, silly words like "everything'll be okay," reassuring platitudes that sounded hollow even to him.

Zoe's breaths became gasping, hiccuping sobs that broke his heart.

"Zoe, please sweetheart," he pleaded, unsure what exactly he was asking for.

She shuddered and cried. He wondered how—*if*—a human body could withstand such an outpouring of grief.

"Sweetheart, you need to breathe. Calm down. Please." The front of his shirt was soaked through with tears, and he could feel the wet press of her face there. His ribs and stomach ached from the punches she'd landed—he knew there'd be bruises later. But his own physical pain was nothing compared to the agony of the shattered woman in his arms.

Later—it seemed like hours but had to have only been minutes—his words finally penetrated—either that, or her energy simply ran out—and Zoe's hysteria finally began to wane. Her breathing was still ragged but it had slowed, and her body had lost its almost lifeless limpness. He could feel that her heart was still beating a mile a minute, and she was fluttery and weak in his arms.

Hugh continued to mutter soft, mindless nonsense. When she stiffened and sniffed and tried to push away from him, he tightened his grip, refusing to let her go.

"No," he said, still rocking them gently.

"But I…" Her voice was hoarse from screaming. "I'm okay now."

Her broken voice and the continued trembling of her body revealed that for the lie it was.

"You really are the most stubborn woman in the world." Hugh managed a wry chuckle. It came out strangled, betraying the tears stuck in his own throat.

"You don't have to…" She tried again.

He couldn't help the anger rising inside him. "Yes. I do. For God's sake, let me comfort you. Stop struggling against the world. Just for a minute."

He could sense her inner argument. Her independence—something she'd honed to a fine point simply because life had forced her to—battled with her weariness and grief, her bone-deep need to share those overwhelming emotions with someone and be cared for in return.

Finally she sagged against him. Whether he'd

won the battle to let him take care of her or she just gave in through pure exhaustion, he didn't know.

He stroked her hair, kept one hand moving in slow circles on her back.

They sat that way for a long time. Hugh watched the shadows grow longer and knew when the sun dipped behind the mountains in the west. Zoe's breathing slowly became more normal and even, and for a moment he wondered if she'd fallen asleep. But then she shifted ever so slightly and he knew she was awake. She was just letting this happen, and he was grateful for that.

His own mind was strangely blank. When he tried to think about Morris's revelation, about what it meant for the memories he held of his parents, it was like encountering an empty desert. Sure, there were things there that could kill you, but at first glance it just appeared to be a barren expanse of sand. Hugh wasn't sure when—or if—he would want to examine it more closely.

Finally Zoe's head lifted slightly. Her voice was muffled against his chest. "Hugh, I…I don't hate you."

Her brittle confession sent a chill through him. He strived for a joking tone, but wasn't entirely sure he succeeded. "I'm glad to hear it."

"I…don't even think I hate Mack."

He tightened his arms around her in a quick squeeze of acknowledgment. "No, I don't think you do, either."

"He did his best. He got saddled with a ten-year-old girl to raise when the only thing he should have been thinking about was Waterford and getting on with his own life. And Hugh…I wasn't an easy child."

She was talking into his chest, her head bowed so he couldn't see her face. He loosened his grip on her now that the danger seemed to have passed, and stroked a lock of silky hair back from her shoulder.

"Zoe, you'd lost your mother. And she'd not really been a stable influence in your life." He remembered Zoe's occasionally confessed stories of her childhood: moving from house to house, school to school, never settling anywhere for long. Leaving as soon as her mother ran out of money or met a new guy.

"Yeah, but I…"

"It wasn't your fault."

"It was…a bit."

"You were the child, he was the adult. He held the responsibility in the situation."

She sighed. "Yeah, I guess."

She wasn't going to be convinced, Hugh knew. Not today. It would take time. Time they didn't have—she was leaving soon and they'd each be left picking up the pieces on their own. Perhaps that was for the best. Together they didn't seem to be able to achieve much in the way of peace of mind.

Zoe shuffled away from him, burying her head in her hands. "I must look a fright."

Hugh looked down at his shirt. He wasn't sure if there was ten years' worth of tears soaked there, but it had to be close. He stretched and his ribs twinged. He let out a muffled grunt and rubbed his side. "You've got a solid right hook there."

Zoe looked up at that, meeting his eyes for the first time. They no longer held the wild grief, the borderline madness he'd seen there before. Now they were just sad. And bloodshot. Her face was blotchy and tear-stained, her eye-lids puffy. And he had the strange thought that she was the most beautiful woman in the world.

"I'm really sorry, Hugh." Her eyes widened in horror as they went to the hand clasping his ribs.

"I'll live," he said gruffly.

Zoe ran trembling hands through her hair and her eyes dropped back to the floor. "I'm so tired."

"I'm not surprised. That was the emotional equivalent to running a marathon." Hugh stood and offered Zoe his hand. She took it and got shakily to her feet. "I think you should lie down for a while."

Zoe just nodded. He tried to let go of her hand so he could put his arm around her shoulders, but she squeezed it tightly and wouldn't let go. "I'm okay," she said, not looking at him.

Hugh gave a short nod, even thought he didn't believe her in the slightest.

They set off for the farmhouse in silence. The wind had picked up again, and heavy dark clouds gathered on the horizon. Another storm. In this part of the country, rain was almost always a good thing. The air smelled of dust and dirt and the approaching squall. Hugh thought wryly that the weather had gotten it wrong. The storm was over now. There should be sunlight peeking through retreating clouds, blue sky visible as the dark clouds scattered away.

Zoe dropped Hugh's hand once they were inside the farmhouse. She walked straight to her bedroom and sat down on the old, squeaky bed to remove her boots.

Hugh stood in the doorway, not quite sure what to do. He stepped into the room and Zoe's head snapped up.

The expression on her face immediately told him something was wrong. She looked… *scared.* No, not just scared. *Terrified.*

She blinked and did her best to conceal her feelings, plastering a weak smile on her face. But Hugh knew what he'd seen.

"What's the matter, Zoe? Sweetheart? What's wrong?" He took another step toward her, intent on pulling her into his arms again, but she held up a shaking hand to stop him.

"Nothing's wrong," she lied. "I'm fine." Another lie. "I just need some rest. Please. There's no point you being here. You've got plenty to do back at Lawson Estate. Why don't you head back over there?"

Hugh frowned. She still needed comfort, but it was the last thing she would ask. He had no doubt she'd asked many things from people over the years—jobs, money, favors, sex—but he was quite sure she'd never, *ever,* asked for someone to take care of her. "I don't think you should be alone—"

"That's exactly what I need." She swallowed hard. "Please, Hugh. I just need some time to myself. To…think. To…sleep. To…" She waved a hand in the air as if searching for the words. "To *process* everything. *Please.*"

Hugh shook his head. "Always so stubborn, Zoe," he said under his breath. He reached down and took off his boots, then unbuttoned his tear-soaked shirt and shrugged it off.

"No, Hugh, don't." Her tone was less sure now.

Hugh padded over and leaned down to finish taking off her boots. He then climbed onto the bed and pulled her with him. It didn't take much effort—either she wasn't really interested in resisting, or she had no energy left. Perhaps it was both.

"Come here." He nestled her in beside him, pulling up the crocheted blanket from the end of the bed to cover them both. He rested his chin on the top of her head, one finger stroking her hair back behind her ear.

Zoe sighed, but it wasn't a contented, satisfied sigh. He wanted to ask what was wrong again, but then realized what a stupid question it was.

Finally Zoe's hand went to his chest and her head lolled more comfortably against his shoulder. Her fingers were clasped into a fist, but for now he was just grateful that she'd decided to accept his comfort. To trust him with herself, even just for a little while.

"Hugh?" Her voice was still croaky. "This is a really bad idea."

Was it? Yes, Hugh had to admit it probably was. The last thing they needed—just as everything was about to be finalized, Zoe about to return home, his world to return to what passed for normal—was to become even further entwined with one another. So what was he doing here?

Zoe needed him. That was why.

But that wasn't the whole story.

Something in the empty desert of his brain became clearer. Like, perhaps, this wasn't all about Zoe.

"I...I need this, Zoe," he admitted hesitantly, the thought only becoming concrete as the words left his mouth.

Her head nodded against him. "I know."

Slowly, her fingers began to uncurl from their fist until her hand lay flat against his skin. Her thumb stroked him softly.

Without warning, Hugh's throat tightened and his eyes burned. He blinked, then squeezed them shut, hard. His teeth bit the inside of his lips, but it wasn't enough, and as hard as he tried, he couldn't help it when his next breath caught in his chest.

"Oh, baby," Zoe crooned.

"You were right, this was a really bad idea." He tried to joke, but his voice was too thick to even come close to the levity he was trying for.

Zoe shifted, pushing herself up on the pillows, snaking her arm under his neck until their positions were reversed: Hugh's head now rested against her breast and her lips pressed against his forehead.

"I'm so sorry, baby," she whispered.

This wasn't the way this was supposed to go. How could Zoe possibly comfort him when *she* was the broken one?

Tears stung, hot and painful. They leaked out, betraying him, tracing down his cheek. Zoe kissed them away.

"I wish…" he began.

"Shh." Zoe's lips were a whisper on his, not so much a kiss as a seal. He understood. There was too much that had been left unsaid for too long.

He fought to pull himself together. There were too many things he didn't want to feel. "This sucks," he managed to say with a dark chuckle.

Zoe echoed his humorless laugh. "Welcome to my world."

"I know, sweetheart, I know." He sighed.

He shifted them in the bed, so they lay side by side. It was no longer one comforting the other but a shared grief and a shared solace. Too much for two people to handle—and certainly too much for one person alone.

What was going to happen when they had to?

"What are we going to do about this?" He couldn't stop himself from asking. He wasn't entirely sure what he meant by "this," but Zoe seemed to be on the same wavelength.

"What we've always done," she replied, her voice surprisingly firm.

"And what's that?"

"Pretend it never happened."

He snorted. "Sounds healthy."

"I don't know about healthy, but it works."

"Does it really?"

"I…" Zoe's words trailed off and she was silent for a moment. "It's the only way I know of coping."

"Yeah. I guess." His voice betrayed his doubt. Whatever Zoe had been doing to cope was clearly not very effective given the past couple of hours. Was that what was in store for him? Some kind of unpredictable emotional breakdown when he least expected it? He hoped not. He hadn't suffered in quite the same way as Zoe. He'd had a stable family life—well, mostly, anyway. He'd lost his parents, but their deaths had been expected, and they'd had time to prepare, to say their goodbyes. He also had the community of Tangawarra around him—all rallying to his support when he needed it.

Zoe had been alone for so long. He wondered if she'd ever be able to cope with a "normal" life—a relationship, home, *children*. Had what happened to her—to them—robbed her of any possibility of a happy future?

"Hugh…it is what it is," Zoe said, shrugging against him.

He turned on his side and she twisted to face him. Lying like this, back in her teenage bed, threatened to swamp him with memory. She looked vulnerable, almost childlike again, but Hugh knew now, more than ever, that Zoe was a grown woman with more than a lifetime's worth of pain inside.

"But we—"

"Shh."

Zoe pressed a finger to his lips. "Enough. It's enough for one day. Don't you think?"

The pleading expression in her eyes was sufficient to overcome his need to get to the bottom of things, to find a real solution to what was going on.

"Okay," he said, even though he felt they'd only begun to scratch the surface.

Zoe looked exhausted, as if she'd gone ten rounds with the heavyweight champion of the world. The least he could do was to give her a break. Even if it was only temporary.

"Get some sleep," he said. He reached for her hand and interlaced their fingers. Zoe gave his a little squeeze and closed her eyes with a grateful smile.

Hugh lay in bed, watching her. She was fast asleep in minutes, her face relaxed, her body slack. She rolled onto her back, and Hugh let her hand go so she could settle more comfortably. If there was one thing Zoe deserved, it was a moment's peace.

Peace he was finding impossible to achieve himself. He stared at the ceiling, listening to her breathing, his brain in a never-ending loop of *what ifs* and *if onlys*. He tried to focus on the future—on what he could do to solve this situation, to help Zoe and himself, but he honestly couldn't think of anything that might work.

Whenever he tossed and turned, Zoe stirred, and he realized he was disturbing her. It was still early—it had been just past dusk when they'd crawled into bed, but he wanted to let her sleep as long as she could.

Eventually he realized that neither he, nor Zoe, was going to get any kind of rest if he stayed there.

Moving gently so as not to wake her, he climbed out of bed and found his shirt. It was creased and messy, but he pulled it on and did up a few buttons. He grabbed his boots and tiptoed into the kitchen before stopping to put them on.

Hugh climbed into his ute and started the engine, hoping the noise wouldn't carry into the house. He headed back toward Lawson Estate, his thoughts going to Morris's story, to the night almost twenty years ago that Zoe's mother had made this same trip. It was pitch-dark and Hugh was vigilant as he drove, watching the shadows, putting his headlights on high to illuminate the road. Where the moon managed to find a gap in the clouds it showed a sky that had taken on a sickly color, a strange greenish-gray, forewarning of a nasty storm to come.

The color echoed the churning thoughts inside of him.

What to do about it? That was the question now.

CHAPTER SIXTEEN

ZOE SLEPT HEAVILY, as if she'd been drugged. She woke when it was still dark. The crocheted blanket had been enough of a covering when Hugh had been lying next to her, his warmth seeping into her and making the bed cozy. But he was no longer there and she was shivering with the chill.

She called his name, not expecting an answer. The cold and silent house told her she was alone.

She slipped under the covers and pulled them around her, but the shivering didn't stop. She shook as if she were battling a raging fever, and eventually the tears came again. She'd thought she'd cried them all out, that it surely wasn't possible for her body to hold any more, but somehow she still managed to soak the pillow under her cheek.

She cried, but it wasn't the hot, painful crying that she'd done back in the shed. She didn't know if crying could be called *peaceful,* but this was different from before. Calmer.

It was *relief.*

She'd cried and stopped—something she'd feared might not happen if she let herself give in to sorrow. That meant she could stop again. The walls holding back all that hurt and grief and loss had crumbled and let everything out.

And she'd survived.

As her tears began to subside she became aware of noises outside. Wind howled around the farmhouse, whistling through the many cracks and gaps in the weatherboards. A perfect soundtrack for a horror movie, she thought distractedly, but she had enough to worry about without adding monsters under the bed.

A furious storm broke outside. Rain pelted down, deafeningly loud on the tin roof, while the wind continued to whip and moan, one minute hurling rain against the bedroom window, the next torturing the branches of the trees and scraping them against the house.

Funny, it was as if she'd transfered her inner turmoil to the weather outside. This storm had been brewing inside her for ten years and now it had broken.

She'd survived.

She wasn't sure how long she lay in bed, listening to the storm outside, lost in her own thoughts. By the time she got up, the brief but intense storm was over. Tendrils of morning sunshine peeked through the retreating clouds and tried their best to warm the house.

A faint headache, scratchy eyes and a dry mouth were the only physical symptoms of her breakdown the day before.

After she washed, her stomach growled loudly and Zoe realized she was honestly hungry—for the first time since she'd arrived in Tangawarra. She quickly cooked up some eggs, smiling to herself as she pictured her new, million-selling diet book: lose five kilos in a week by returning to your hated childhood home, burying the only family you have left, facing bankruptcy, sleeping with your childhood sweetheart and then pouring out ten years' worth of grief in a couple of hours. No sweat.

She chuckled grimly at her scrambled eggs and toast. They disappeared quickly and Zoe realized her diet wasn't exactly sustainable.

A new lightness filled her. It wasn't exactly pleasant, more an unnervingly untethered sensation. She pulled on her heavy boots as a kind of anchor and grabbed her warmest fleecy pullover. It was automatic, getting dressed to go outside, except today there wasn't any real reason to. The wine was finished. The truck was coming today to bottle it.

Completing the job of sorting out her grandfather's papers seemed futile. But still, she tensed against the cold and pulled open the door.

"Oh, geez." Zoe froze as she stepped outside, right into the middle of a giant puddle. She couldn't help a gasp of horror. She'd known the storm had been severe, but hadn't realized it had been anything like this.

It looked like a tornado had touched down.

Broken tree branches were scattered everywhere. The shed door with the broken hinge lay on the ground, ripped off by the wind. Waterford's solid, precious grapevines were fine, but over the fence line some of Lawson Estate's younger vines looked less than intact, and the rosebushes planted at the end of each row had been decimated.

For a moment, Zoe thought Mack's collection of rusted car bodies at the back of the sheds had been covered in a layer of lumpy snow, but then she realized it was paper—and that the door to the winery stood open.

That last fact finally made her feet move.

She rushed over, every nerve on high alert.

With one hand on her chest as if to hold her rapidly beating heart inside her ribs, Zoe didn't take a calm breath until she'd touched each of the twenty barrels and was reassured the wine was okay.

There was a huge mess—the papers she'd set

out a couple of days ago had been tossed everywhere. It seemed as if half of them had ended
up outside; the rest were scattered throughout
the shed.

Zoe gave a mental shrug. Funny, as long as
the wine was okay, she couldn't bring herself
to care about the rest of it. If there were unpaid
bills in there, the creditors would no doubt be
in touch. Everything else…didn't matter.

She wandered outside again and lifted her
face to the sun, closing her eyes for a moment
and enjoying the first real warmth she'd felt
since she'd arrived.

As if embarrassed by her impetuousness,
Mother Nature was doing her best to pretend
nothing had happened. It was a perfect day: a
satin-blue sky with just a smattering of white
fluffy clouds, warm sun, the slightest breeze.
The air smelled impeccably clean, of eucalyptus, earth and fresh rain. Kookaburras laughed
in the distance as if they were in on the joke.

Zoe walked through the sunshine, stepping
carefully over broken branches. Before she'd
even thought about her destination she found
herself down by the creek.

It was swollen and running fast. No longer
the calm, trickling stream of a few days ago, it
rushed and eddied and foamed, throwing the
occasional piece of detritus onto the bank.

Branches were broken down here, as well. A heavy old tree had fallen over and one of its long limbs had claimed the cupboard she and Hugh had built.

Zoe carefully stepped closer to view the damage.

A testament to the hardiness of the structure they'd built, it hadn't collapsed under the weight, but it was certainly beyond repair. The top and back panels were broken almost in two and the doors hung open at crooked angles. There was nothing inside, and the shelf that had been there had disappeared, probably collapsed to the bottom.

The symbolism wasn't lost on Zoe.

She'd been closed up tight, in danger of self-destructing, when she'd first arrived. And all those ghosts she'd had to face, the reckoning she'd had to do of her past, the grieving she'd finally been forced to confront, had cracked her open. But unlike the destroyed cupboard, the breaking open had been her salvation.

She knew now that the way she'd been living had never been healthy or sustainable. The breakdown would have happened, whether she'd returned to Tangawarra or not. Her mind, body and spirit would have cracked at some point, because she'd stressed herself to the point of shattering. As much as she'd tried to bury her feelings, the question of facing them had always been *when,* not *if.*

The only thing she could do now was keep going.

Zoe wandered over to the old log on which Hugh had perched when they'd met here—a conversation that felt like a long time ago now—and took a seat. She closed her eyes again for a moment, and the sun and dappled shadows of the leaves above painted pink-and-gray pictures on the insides of her eyelids.

She had to go back to California.

Leave all this behind.

Not because she wasn't prepared to deal with it, but because she had begun to confront it, and it no longer had the same hold over her.

Maybe Mack had loved her, as Hugh insisted. Maybe he had his own history, his own reasons for the way he'd treated her. Zoe couldn't forget the misery she'd experienced at his hands, but maybe she could begin to forgive it.

She grimaced.

Forgiveness was a big word.

If not forgive, then at least understand. And that might just be enough, might bring with it a measure of peace.

Mack's last-ever wine would be going out for sale in a matter of weeks. It was a magnificent product. Absolutely worthy of the Waterford label. The people who drank that wine would—for a brief moment—savor Mack's hard work, Mack's legacy, and Zoe knew that would have been enough for him. Besides, regardless of the name of the property, the vines would continue. Year after year, they'd grow leaves, bear fruit, hibernate for winter. In another fifty years someone else would be tending their branches and only the vines would remember all the people that had cared for them over their long years of life—including a sad old man and a bratty teenager.

Selling Waterford to Lawson Estate would set Mack's teeth on edge beyond the grave, she knew that. But now that she knew the history of that feud, she wondered if other ghosts might be smiling at the idea. Perhaps her mother and Hugh's father would be happy to see the estates finally united.

It certainly would make Hugh happy. It was what he'd wanted all along.

Something inside her twisted at the thought of Hugh. She could picture him so clearly, from his boyhood grin, nothing of himself held back in the slightest, all the way through to the powerful, confident and carefully guarded man he'd grown into. She'd seen him in passion, in pain, in joy and in sorrow.

And she knew that what was best for him

now was to allow him to get on with his life. To move forward, as she was going to.

Hugh needed to start a new life with someone who wouldn't constantly remind him of the difficulties of the past. He'd grieved with Zoe, knew exactly how messed up she was.

The thought gave her a little shiver. She'd taken such care to make sure that no one ever saw that side of her. The idea of someone seeing through her act, knowing that all her bluster was just a mask for the deep, pervasive vulnerability she hid from the world, made her feel sick.

It was another reason she needed to get away from him. Hugh didn't let her hide behind her walls. He saw through them.

It was time to go back to California and work out where she went next.

THE CALM RATIONALITY ZOE had gained down at the creek faded when she returned to the farmhouse and saw the truck turning onto Waterford's track. The mobile bottling service. She knew Hugh wouldn't be far behind.

The truck driver pulled up behind the farmhouse and leapt down from the cab. "G'day."

"Hi," Zoe replied.

"I'm Matt. Morris organized us to come do your bottling," he said, gesturing to the other guys emerging from the truck.

"Yes, of course. You might want to pull over closer to the shed." Zoe pointed out the winery.

"Sure." Matt began to climb back into the truck.

"Um, do you know…" Zoe said, halting him. "Is Morris or, uh, anyone else from Lawson Estate planning to come over?"

"Morris was gonna come, but apparently something's going on and he said they're all caught up over there, so he asked me to handle it myself. It's not a problem." He gestured to the two other guys sitting in the truck's cabin. "We've got enough manpower, so we don't need help with lifting or anything."

Zoe smiled. "Good. That's…good." It wasn't the lifting she was worried about.

So Morris wasn't coming to help with the bottling, and from the sounds of it, neither was Hugh.

But eventually, he would be back.

The thought of what would happen when he returned made Zoe's belly flip over.

Because now that the wine was complete, the only reason she and Hugh had to get together again was to sign those papers and…say goodbye. Except she knew he wouldn't leave it at that. He'd want to continue the conversation they'd begun last night—he'd want to talk more, fix things, wouldn't admit that he was trying to solve the unsolvable. It was just the way he was.

The panic that had dogged her for the first few days she'd been back in Tangawarra returned in a wave.

Why, exactly, she wasn't sure, but it wasn't something she wanted to hang around debating.

The thought of being with Hugh—of spending more time with him—scared her to her very marrow. Zoe had never been one to back down from a fight, never let anyone see her fear, but this time she was going to let her cowardice win. When it came down to it, it was a matter of what scared her least—never seeing him and dealing with the aftermath and pain of that, or facing him again and continuing the journey and work that had begun last night.

It was a no-brainer. She had to get out of here.

She helped the chatty and cheerful Matt and his team get organized to begin the bottling process, but then left him to it, telling him she had things to organize in the house.

It took barely a few minutes to pack her bag. She'd kept everything neat and confined to her bedroom—almost as if in fear that Mack would criticize her messiness.

Organizing the house took a little longer. She threw out any remaining food, donned her rubber gloves and gave the kitchen and bathroom a thorough going-over. She cleaned out the refrigerator and freezer, unplugged them and left the doors ajar. There was so much left to do. Mack's clothes hung in the wardrobe in his bedroom, the hall cupboards were packed full of God-knew-what and the lounge still featured the wall of ancestors—the disapproving, mildewed photos of scowling Waters family members.

But Zoe didn't have time to deal with that. Nothing here meant anything to her, anyway, so she didn't especially care if it got donated or went in the trash. The only thing she hesitated over was one of the tattered band posters in her bedroom, but she rolled her eyes at herself for being silly and left it with its yellowing tape up on the wall.

By the time she got back outside and threw her bag in the back of her rental car, Matt and the gang had the bottling up and running and the machinery was working at full speed.

"That was quick," she said as she walked over to him, surprised.

"No mucking around when it comes to wine—actually, no mucking around when it comes to Lawson Estate jobs," he joked. "Morris would have my head."

"Or Hugh Lawson would."

Matt seemed to consider that. "Nah. Morris is definitely scarier. Hugh's too nice."

Zoe shrugged. He was probably right, but personally she'd face Morris over Hugh any day.

"Can you give Morris a message for me?" she asked.

"Sure. I'll be calling him when we're done—he'll want to know it's all under control."

"Can you ask him if someone could take care of the rubbish here? I don't know what the council collection days are, or if they still have them, but there's a lot of trash to get taken away. Food waste and stuff—I emptied out all the cupboards and the fridge. Not good to leave that sitting around. There's already a mouse problem in the house—don't want it getting worse." Zoe didn't want to think about the contents of the freezer sitting outside for too long—she was leaving enough of a mess behind as it was.

Matt gave a curt nod. "Yeah, sure. No problems, I'll pass it on. Have a great day."

"Thanks, you, too." The reply was automatic. Zoe didn't quite yet know how her day was going to turn out, but she doubted it was going to be great. "I…uh, have to go out. If you guys finish before I get back, can you lock up and leave the key under the rock by the back door?"

"You bet."

She watched Matt walk back into the winery and heard the cheerful sound of clinking glass and men joking with each other as they worked.

Time to go.

A quick wave to Matt and the guys and she was in Tangawarra before she knew it. Zoe glanced at the supermarket car park as she drove past, almost disappointed to find that goth Tim and his black-clad, pink-haired girlfriend were nowhere to be seen. Back in school, no doubt. Good for them.

It was even more surprising how quickly Stephen Carter was able to produce the required documents when she turned up unannounced. Her hand shook, but her signature was legible. She left him with the power to make all the decisions regarding the estate and clear instructions to sell everything to Hugh Lawson. She asked him to pass on her regret at leaving Hugh with the unpleasant task of sorting out her grandfather's belongings, but asked him to make it clear that she was happy for those to be donated to charity or thrown away.

There was a long wait at the airport—she unfortunately hadn't timed her escape well with the airline schedule. But after dozens of laps of the duty-free stores because she was too fidgety to sit still, finally she was on her way.

"Chicken curry or beef casserole?" the flight attendant asked.

Zoe had been so caught up in her own whirling thoughts that the take-off and first hour of the flight had disappeared without her noticing. She straightened up in her seat and flipped down her tray table.

"Uh, the beef, thanks."

"Red or white wine?"

"Red."

"Here you go, love."

An unappetizing buff-colored tray was dumped in front of her holding a foil-covered dish, a plastic bowl full of what might have been salad, a bread roll and a miniature bottle of wine. If her appetite had been tentative before, it fled completely as a bump of turbulence made the wine roll over on the tray, turning up its white label with the elegant black script and flowing red ribbon.

Shaking her head at the irony, Zoe picked up the bottle and peered at the label.

Lawson Estate Cabernet Merlot.

On the back, the blurb extolled the virtues of the wine and ended with a scrawled signature.

Hugh Lawson.

Without thinking, Zoe cracked the twist-top and poured the wine into the plastic goblet. She sipped it.

Not too bad. Not great, but not awful, either. Better than Long Track's.

She stared at Hugh's signature until it blurred. Two fat tears surprised her as they rolled down her cheeks. She wiped them away, sur-reptitiously looking around to see if anyone no-ticed. Thankfully, her seat companions were all too busy with their meals and the tiny TV screens in front of them to be bothered with a fellow passenger's tears.

Zoe sat back with the wine and stared down the aisle to the business-class section at the front that was closed off with a curtain. That was what she had to do. Pull a curtain across everything that had happened and move for-ward. She'd done it before and she'd do it again.

She took another long sip of the wine.

Drinking it might at least help her sleep.

"HEY, BOSS." MORRIS STUCK his head into Hugh's office. He looked dirty, sweaty, hassled and tired—and Hugh knew he was no better.

Lawson Estate had had quite a morning.

Both he and Morris had been up at dawn, working with some of the other staff who lived onsite to try to rectify damage from the storm.

For now, it looked as though the vines and the winery operations were relatively unscathed. A leak in the tasting room had caused minor flooding, but that was mostly a clean-up job and a relatively easy repair to the roof.

The restaurant, however, hadn't fared so well. A piece of stray debris had smashed one of the massive—and expensive—panes of the feature picture window. As a result the interior had suffered significant water damage and there was a hell of a mess.

It was painful to look at—he felt the damage to the estate as if it were a physical hurt.

The next job was to contact the insurance company, but when he'd gotten back to his desk, he'd collapsed into his chair and just stared at the wall for a while. His exhaustion didn't allow for the kind of focus that sort of conversation needed.

Some kind angel had brought a pot of coffee to his office and Hugh had his hands wrapped around a cup to warm his fingers as he sipped.

"Hey, Morris," he replied. "Come and sit and grab a coffee. You deserve it. We both do."

"Thanks, Boss, but I can't just yet. Gotta get over to the tasting room—the roofer's arrived."

Hugh nodded. "You need me to come?" It was the right thing to ask, but Hugh hoped more than anything that he didn't have to move for at least another hour.

Morris shook his head. "Nope. Once I get them set, I can come back and join you for that cuppa."

"Sounds good." Hugh gave Morris a grateful smile, feeling honestly indebted for all the hard work his foreman had put in. The two men hadn't had time to discuss anything related to Morris's revelations yesterday—the practical matters in front of them had demanded their entire attention. But Hugh had no doubt that, when they had a moment, that can of worms was going to be opened right back up.

"Just wanted to let you know I heard from Matt. He's bottling the wine over at Waterford as we speak—so far it's all going without a hitch."

"That's good."

"Um…" Morris scratched his beard thoughtfully. "He had a strange message for me, though. Thought I'd pass it on. Zoe asked him to ask me to take care of the rubbish over there. Said there was food and stuff, and she didn't want to attract pests."

"Yeah?" Hugh frowned. "Well, we can do that, can't we?"

"Sure we can. It's just…I thought it was a little odd."

"Why?"

"Well, why would she be throwing out all the food? Still, none of my business, I guess. I'll be getting over to the tasting room. I'll give you a hoy when I get back." He disappeared out of the office.

Sheer exhaustion meant it took a little while

for Morris's words to sink in, and even longer before the meaning of them became clear.

Zoe had thrown out the food because she was leaving.

Well, what had he expected? The wine was done. There wasn't anything else holding her here. Was there?

He needed to get over there. He'd make her talk. Drag her down to the creek, if that's what it took.

He'd thought he didn't have any energy left, but a moment later he'd changed into a clean Lawson Estate sweatshirt and was reaching for his hat and car keys. The phone rang just as he curled his fingers around them and he hesitated. He decided he needed to take the call—it could be the glaziers about the new restaurant window.

"Hugh Lawson," he said in clipped tones into the phone. He sank back into the desk chair, groaning as his aching body protested. Some of the ache was caused by the morning's activities, but more of it was due to Zoe's bruising punches. He covered his still-tender ribs with one hand as he yawned.

"Hugh? It's Stephen Carter." The accountant sounded vaguely excited about something.

"Hi, Stephen. How'd you fare in the storm?"

"Oh, fine, fine. Bit of water got into the bathrooms at the office, but a quick mop and it was all good again. How 'bout you?"

Hugh gave a quick rundown of the state of affairs at Lawson Estate.

"Sorry to hear that, really sorry,"

"Thanks. Look, Stephen, if it's not urgent, I've got a lot of things to do—"

"Sure, understand, but this is important."

"Okay, shoot." Hugh shook himself and took a gulp of now-lukewarm coffee to try to help his concentration.

"Waterford's yours," Stephen Carter said with a distinctly proud crow in his voice. "Zoe came in and finalized the instructions with me and her solicitor this morning. I need you to come in and sign the contracts—or I can bring them out to you." The man sounded simperingly happy, no doubt imagining the nice fat bill he'd be making out to Hugh.

It took a moment for the meaning of the accountant's words to sink in.

Waterford was his.

Finally.

Another goal set and achieved. Another element added to the Lawson Estate corporation, strengthening and helping it grow. Another plank shoring up the future against uncertain possibilities.

He should be excited. But all he felt was tired.

It was distinctly unsettling.

Hugh shifted in his chair. "The papers are ready?" he asked. His unease turned to puzzlement as he thought it through. With their truce in place, he'd figured that he'd have at least one more conversation with Zoe to iron out the details before they sat down to the contracts.

This news, on top of what Morris had just told him about the rubbish, made it clear. It seemed like Zoe was moving quickly to get things sorted out. There were still at least a couple of days' work at Waterford to clear out Mack's belongings and get the place ready for handover, but clearly she wanted to get away immediately. Still, he was surprised she hadn't talked to him before signing anything.

But maybe yesterday had been a catharsis of sorts. Maybe she'd woken with a new perspective on the world and she needed to take action.

He knew it wasn't as simple as it might seem on the surface—after everything Zoe had gone through, it wasn't as if one good cry had solved everything. She still had a long way to go— perhaps they both did. But admitting to those feelings was the first important step.

He wished, suddenly, that he hadn't left her last night. He wished he'd been there when she'd woken up, to see if she looked or felt any different. To continue their conversation from the night before.

"Yes," Stephen continued. "Everything is in order. Once I have your signature, it's yours."

Hugh leaned back in his chair and propped his feet on the desk, crossing one ankle over the other. Through the window he could see across to the fence that divided Lawson Estate from Waterford.

Finally. After all these years.

Again, he reached for the sense of achievement he expected.

It wasn't there.

All he felt was a strange, gnawing ache to get back to Zoe. He bizarrely wanted her to celebrate with him. Something that was at best unlikely, and at worst bordered on the ridiculous.

"She's signed it over lock, stock and barrel—literally," Carter continued with a laugh at his own weak joke. "So you'll have a clean-up job ahead of you. I did think it was a little irresponsible leaving you with all that, but then this is Zoe Waters, I guess. Some people never change."

Hugh bristled at the accountant's assumption and felt a new stab of sympathy for Zoe. She wasn't completely imagining the fixed ideas of a small town.

"I'm sure she'll help with that," Hugh said, his voice tight.

"Um, well…" The accountant paused. "Not unless she worked a small miracle between leaving my office and catching that plane."

"Huh?" Hugh thought for a moment he must have heard wrong.

"She was heading for the airport from here. She told me she'd left everything pretty much as it was. Now, what time is it? Yep…would have just left. She's gone. No time to do any kind of cleaning, I'm afraid."

Hugh leaped to his feet. "What?" he yelled into the phone.

What an idiot!

But he wasn't angry with Stephen. How on earth had he not seen that this was exactly what Zoe would do? The minute Morris had mentioned the rubbish, he should have known.

Zoe was a stray cat. Any attempt to domesticate her was going to terrify her, and send her running away.

Last night had to be as close as Zoe had let anyone get to her—possibly ever. It was just like her to run and hide as soon as she had the chance.

Hugh swore viciously under his breath.

"Uh, she went back to California. Napa Valley, isn't it? That's where she lives now?" There was no mistaking the confused and slightly fearful tone of Stephen's voice. "Don't worry, I've got power of attorney. If you need anything we shouldn't have a problem—everything can be sorted out without her here," he offered quickly in reassurance.

Hugh ran a hand through his hair.

He should have known.

Zoe Waters had made a career out of running away. Why hadn't he seen this coming? And why was he so upset by it?

He curled his hand into a fist and slammed it down on the desk.

"Why didn't you stop her?" he growled.

"Why should I have done that?" the accountant asked in genuine surprise.

Hugh's voice felt strangled in his throat. "No reason." He tried hard to remind himself that it wasn't Stephen Carter's fault.

"Anyway, I have to be out your way later today. I'll bring the papers with me. We can have a glass of that new bubbly of yours to celebrate."

Hugh wasn't aware of ending the call, but he found himself standing in front of the window, gazing out at the vines. Vines that he now owned—on both sides of the fence.

There was no joy. No sense of achievement. No sense of completeness.

Not without Zoe beside him.

He now understood that those feelings didn't come with a deed of sale. They'd come when he'd held Zoe in his arms. When they'd made love.

That was when all the loose threads of his life had tied together.

She drove him nuts, all that defensiveness and prickle. So furiously independent, so stubborn and determined. So full of grief and pain.

So *not* part of his strategy. His life was all about certainty, building security for himself, those who worked for him, and the community that he was a part of. Zoe Waters was a loner, a nomad—unpredictable and volatile.

Life would be simpler if he did as Zoe advised and tried to forget it had all ever happened—both the events of ten years ago and those of the past couple of weeks.

But when he thought about that kind of future—a future with someone easy, someone who didn't challenge him, who didn't make him face the darkest parts of himself, who didn't absolutely *need* him, he was left feeling hollow and flat.

Having Waterford meant nothing if he didn't also have Zoe.

Last time she'd disappeared from his life, Mack and his father had stood in the way, stop-

ping him from being with her. There were no
such obstacles now.

He'd lost too many people in his life. And
he'd already gone through the pain of losing
Zoe once.

He wasn't going to let it happen again.

He'd find her.

It wouldn't be hard. He knew where she was
going.

The first thing he'd do was let her know how
unimpressed he was about her running away.
That would be momentarily satisfying. Then
he'd make sure she knew she was never going
to need to run away ever again.

What happened after that? He didn't know.
Would Zoe be able to come back to Tanga-
warra? Maybe he'd just have to set up a new
Lawson Estate office in Napa Valley. Why not?
He was nothing if not up for a challenge.

He picked up his discarded keys and hat and
began to head for the tasting room. He needed
to let Morris know what was going on.

CHAPTER SEVENTEEN

"ZOE, THERE'S A DELIVERY HERE."

Zoe glanced up from the test equipment she was working with. "You get it, Luke. Ask them to take it round to the loading dock."

Luke, one of the new apprentices at Golden Gate, shook his head. "No, it's a personal delivery for you."

"Oh." Zoe wasn't paying much attention; all her focus was on the results in front of her. They'd just begun the harvest and grapes were tumbling into the winery by the truckload. Zoe was rushed off her feet testing sugar levels, overseeing picking and making sure things ran smoothly. This was likely to be her last vintage for Golden Gate—although she hadn't yet decided where she'd go next—but professional pride demanded it be the best she could possibly make it. "Can't you sign for it? I'm busy here."

"Sure."

A minute later, Luke returned with a foam packing box, just large enough to hold a single bottle of wine. He put it on the desk nearby. "Here you go."

"Thanks." Zoe finished her calculations and swept a stray hair back behind her ear, wincing at her sweaty face. The contrast of Tangawarra's wintery July with Napa's summertime August had been harsh on her. She frowned at the package. Zoe often placed mail orders for wine—it was important to see what others were doing and learn from different winemakers' styles. But usually she bought two or three bottles at least, never just one. She picked up the box and twisted it around. There was no return address—no mailing label, either.

She was about to set it aside to look at later when a niggling feeling made her pick up a box cutter and slit the tape.

Putting it down on the desk, she grasped the top with one hand. What if—

She couldn't bring herself to finish the thought.

Waterford was long gone now. In the three weeks since she'd returned to Napa, Zoe had continued on the emotional journey to say goodbye to her past.

Although she still made an effort to live her life as if her past hadn't happened, just as she'd counseled Hugh to do, she was no longer making an effort to force it to the back of her mind.

She knew now that it would simply wait to ambush her in a vulnerable moment.

Through many tears—not quite ten years' worth, but it had to be getting close—and talking with a therapist, Zoe had begun the hard work of reconciling herself with her losses. The fact that Golden Gate was at its busiest time of year was a help, too. At work she didn't have time to dwell on things.

Her ghosts hadn't disappeared—she knew they never would, as much as she wanted them to. Instead she was trying to learn to live with them in harmony.

Okay, maybe harmony was pushing it. If not quite harmony, then at least a level of peace that could allow her to get on with her life.

The only memory she hadn't been able to make peace with was the way she'd left things with Hugh. But he had Waterford now. He'd gotten what he wanted. Knowing that he would be satisfied with that, that he'd even now be making plans for taking down the fences between the properties—that would have to be enough. Besides, it wasn't as if she didn't know how to live with unfinished business. She'd had a decade's worth of practice on that one.

Her hand shook as she pulled the two halves of foam box apart. With a teeth-grating squeak they gave way, revealing a dark green glass bottle with a red foil capsule over the cork.

Her heart skipped and thudded in her chest when she saw the crisp white label.

The red ribbon and elegant black script of the Lawson Estate logo trailed across the top. The simple black lettering of the Waterford logo was printed across the bottom.

In between, stylish red writing announced the name of the wine.

Sara's Shiraz.

The world froze. Noise from the winery receded into silence, the almost overpowering smells of grapes and chemicals faded away entirely.

Twisting the bottle over, the label on the back contained only the necessary legal information about the wine. At the bottom, in small writing, it said, "Winemakers: Mack Waters, Zoe Waters and Hugh Lawson."

She turned the bottle over again. Tears stung her eyes and Zoe let them fall. She'd lost her fear of them somewhere over the past few weeks.

Her throat closed on her as she tried to swallow. She still remembered taking her precious, creased snapshot, worn around the edges with age and handling, to a photo lab and having it copied. And sealing that copy in an envelope, postmarked to Australia.

All she'd written on the back was Sara's name—
Sara Rachel Lawson—and her date of birth.

"You okay, Zoe?"

Luke's gruff concern snapped Zoe back to
the present. She swiped at her cheeks with the
back of her hand. She'd forgotten the kid was
still standing there.

"I'm fine."

"Don't look fine."

"Yeah, I…" Zoe didn't know how to even
begin to explain.

"You want me to get the guy who delivered
it?"

"Huh?"

"He's in the tasting room. Didn't look like a
courier to me."

It took a moment for the meaning of Luke's
words to sink in. She froze. Hugh was here? In
California?

"Earth to Zoe?" Luke prodded. "Want me to
get him?"

"Uh, no, I…" Zoe made her muscles release
and she slipped off the high stool she'd been
sitting on to do her work.

Luke shook his head at her, an amused grin
on his face. "Never seen you shook up like this
before."

The kid's cheek helped to unfreeze Zoe. She

shot him one of her well-practiced glares. "Isn't there something you should be doing, Luke?"

He shrugged, clearly disappointed that he wasn't going to continue to play a role in whatever it was that was unfolding. "I guess."

"Then go. Scoot."

He disappeared and Zoe's panic returned full force.

This was the last thing she'd expected, and yet, now that it was happening, she wondered why she hadn't prepared for the possibility. She knew Hugh—knew him for the man he was now. The time she'd spent with him had taught her about his tenaciousness, his persistence, his pride. She knew him well enough to know that leaving things unfinished the way she had was never going to be enough for him. If anything, she should be surprised that it had taken him three weeks to arrive.

So now what?

Somehow, Zoe knew, if she didn't go out and face him, he'd simply come back again tomorrow. Or maybe wait for her outside until she was forced to go home for the night.

And he'd accused her of being stubborn! It was the biggest case of pot and kettle Zoe had ever encountered.

This was putting a serious dent in her plans to forget him.

She had no choice. She had to go talk to him. What she would say she had no idea, but hopefully something would come to her.

She wiped her hands on a cloth, somewhat futilely—the grape juice stains weren't going anywhere in a hurry—then looked down at herself. Worn jeans, an old checked shirt, boots. Clothes she'd deliberately put on that morning knowing the hard, messy work she'd be doing that day. Oh, well. It wasn't as if Hugh hadn't seen her like this before.

Straightening her shoulders in an effort to feign a confidence she didn't feel, Zoe marched through the working areas of the winery and up the path lined with colorful blooms and manicured shrubs that led to the massive Golden Gate tasting room. A huge barn of a space, the room was designed for the busloads of tourists that stopped by each day, with multiple tasting stations, an interactive display about the winemaking process and a gourmet food deli off to one side that did a roaring trade in overpriced olive oil and handmade chocolates.

Stepping inside from the discreet back entrance, the noise was the first thing to wash over her. Clearly Golden Gate wasn't the first stop for the busload of tourists currently being overseen by Wil Shepherd. Laughter, heckles and loud questions from the audience punctuated his smooth, well-rehearsed patter.

Instinctively, Zoe eyes were drawn to the side of the room. She didn't need to be told that Hugh wasn't one of the group clamoring for more alcohol.

Her breath caught in her throat, even though she thought she'd prepared herself.

He leaned against an old barrel in boots, jeans and a red T-shirt, nonchalantly casual. The straw cowboy hat was missing today—maybe it hadn't been practical to bring on a plane. But those laser-blue eyes of his raked over the place, taking in every detail. In his hand was a small plastic tasting cup, a splash of red wine in it. As Zoe watched, he raised the cup to his lips, swished the wine around in his mouth and spat it out into the receptacle nearby. She could tell he took his time considering the wine, and if his face was anything to go by, in the end he decided he quite liked it. A rush of stupid pride went through her.

It was enough to get her feet moving again.

"So, what do you think?" she asked, pleased that her voice was steady.

He didn't seem surprised by her appearance, angling his head to one side as he turned to face her. His expression gave nothing away. "Good balance. Full bodied. A little strong on the acid, but that'll improve with time."

"That was this year's zin, right?" She knew from his description.

He nodded, holding up the empty cup and peering at the dregs.

"I'm quite proud of that one."

"Rightly so." His gaze went back to the crowd of people across the room, scanning them with a practiced eye.

Zoe swallowed. Were they just going to discuss wine? She could do that. "So what do you think of it?" She gestured around the wine room with one hand.

Hugh nodded. "Impressive. The scale of the place..." He trailed off. "If only we could get busloads like that coming out to the valley."

"It'll happen." Zoe had no doubt that Hugh's success would continue.

"Yeah." Hugh nodded, his eyes still scanning the room.

Again, Zoe was struck by his confidence. She knew he'd achieve whatever he set his mind to. They shared that same drive of determination and ambition. The difference was that Hugh went through life with the firm belief that he'd be successful. Zoe was never quite so sure.

They fell silent for a moment, watching the eager tourists take in Wil's skilful spiel.

Hugh shifted and his eyes met hers. "Did you get my delivery?"

Zoe's heart, which had been racing since she'd opened the box, kicked up another notch. Seemed like polite conversation was over now.

She gave him a watery smile. She did her best to blink back the unwanted tears, trying her best not to let Hugh see the effect his gift had had on her. "I did."

Wil was too involved with the visitors to notice Zoe, but the two winery hands who were helping to pour tastings for the group were shooting unsubtly inquisitive glances at her and her handsome visitor. Zoe didn't need her reaction to be workplace gossip, too.

"Let's go outside," she suggested.

Hugh nodded, put the plastic cup down on the barrel he'd been leaning against. "Lead the way."

Zoe headed for the employee exit, taking Hugh down the path to a spot that had been her favorite ever since she'd started working here. The whole estate was covered in beautifully tended gardens, almost all of which were open to the many visitors. Zoe's place was one that most people never found—an old-fashioned wrought-iron park bench under the shade of a massive olive tree and surrounded by an overgrown kitchen garden full of scented plants and herbs. Most people were attracted to the brightly colored beds of flowers under the dazzling California sunshine, but Zoe loved this spot for its muted greens and quiet shade.

The comforting scents of lavender and rosemary and the lazy summery drone of insects filled the air as they sat under the tree.

A practical consideration was at the top of Zoe's mind. "Did you do that to the whole vintage? Mack wanted—"

"No," Hugh interrupted before she could continue. "Don't worry. Your grandfather's customers got the Waterford Estate wine they were waiting for—and a note informing them it would be the last. They just got a bottle or so less than they were expecting. I kept one barrel aside and used that for Sara's Shiraz. It's not for sale."

Hearing him say their baby's name made Zoe's stomach flip.

Hugh somehow read her mind. He gave her a small, sad smile. "I didn't have a lot to do with making the wine, I know, but we did kind of finish it together. It seemed right to name it after her."

Zoe nodded, the image of the label swimming in front of her eyes. This time she couldn't contain the tears and a single, drop rolled down her cheek. She managed a weak smile as she shrugged at him. "I'm not afraid of crying anymore," she admitted with a hollow little laugh. "Not quite sure if that's a good thing, 'cause I seem to do it all the time, now."

He reached over and brushed away the tear with the back of one finger. "It's a good thing," he assured her.

She shrugged again. She wasn't convinced.

"I have something else to give you." He reached behind himself and pulled a long official-looking envelope from his back pocket.

Zoe frowned. She couldn't handle too many more surprises.

He held out the plain manila envelope and Zoe took it with a trembling hand. She held it gingerly, as if it might explode. If it did, she wouldn't be shocked. The past ten minutes had taken a surreal turn. She could still barely comprehend that Hugh Lawson was sitting beside her, here in Napa Valley. At Golden Gate.

"What is it?" she asked, frowning at the envelope in her hand. It looked so harmless and yet she knew it couldn't be.

"The deed to Waterford."

"The…what?" At first Zoe honestly didn't understand what he'd said. But as he repeated himself, the meaning of his words slowly beginning to sink in.

"The deed to Waterford. I paid off the mortgage. But…"

He reached across and took her free hand. He held it between his, playing with it, turning and twisting it around restlessly. Zoe's initial reaction was to pull away, but the look on his face stopped her. He stared down at her grape-stained hand, and he looked…*uncertain.* Insecure. Full of doubts.

She'd never seen Hugh like that before. *Ever.* Not even when they'd lain in bed and he'd grieved for their daughter.

"What's wrong?" she blurted before she could refine her thoughts into a more specific question. A hundred horrible scenarios flitted through her mind. He was giving her Waterford because he had lost all his money somehow and couldn't afford to run it. No. Worse. Because he had cancer and could no longer manage it.

Oh, God, if he was sick…if he was dying… she didn't want to hear him say it. It was a ridiculous conclusion to jump to, but she couldn't help herself.

"Zoe, when you left…" He bit his lip, as if speaking were painful.

"Don't," Zoe said, as her gut twisted. If he didn't say it, it wouldn't be real.

He glanced at her quickly, giving her a

crooked smile. "I have to, sweetheart. Just like you had to. I have to tell my story."

He looked back down at her hand in his and threaded his fingers through hers, clasping them together tightly.

"When you left—back when we were kids, I mean—and Mack and my father told me that you tried to kill yourself, I…"

Zoe frowned. For a moment she was overwhelmed with relief that he wasn't ill. But then the realization that he was dragging them through the past again made that relief extremely short-lived. "Hugh, I don't know—"

"Please." He squeezed her hand. "I've come halfway around the world. Let me say this."

Zoe could only nod. She swallowed hard. He'd been there for her when the dam holding back her emotions had broken. It was only fair that she repay the favor.

"My father was so angry when Mack told him about our relationship. He didn't let me talk, didn't let me explain. And the fact that we'd kept it secret just made it worse. Looking back, knowing what we know now—what Morris told us—I think he was mostly angry about history repeating itself."

Hugh still looked down, but Zoe could see his eyes were unfocused. Right now he was a long way from sunny California.

"I'm sorry," Zoe whispered, not sure what else to say.

The only sign he heard her was a quick squeeze of her hand. "He forced me to stay away from you—not to contact you, not to reply to your messages. Convinced me that it was best."

"I know." Zoe tried to sound comforting. She really had forgiven Hugh for that part of their past. Like her, he'd been doing what he was told—too scared to do anything different.

"And then a few years later he died. Left me with Lawson Estate to run. I've been working so hard to make it into a success and I told myself it was so that our employees could feel secure in their jobs, so that Tangawarra could thrive. But really, it was more about me. *I* wanted to feel secure."

"That's perfectly understandable."

He paused. "I just didn't want to lose anyone again." His voice was rough.

Hugh picked up the envelope that Zoe had left on the bench.

"I've always wanted to own Waterford—since I was old enough to have the idea," he said with a grim smile. "I convinced myself of all these business reasons it was important for it to become part of Lawson Estate—it was all part of the strategy. I thought if I could just buy more vineyards, make the business stronger, I could have more control over…well, *everything*. But I've realized…no matter how much I build the business, it doesn't actually give me control over the future. I think I worked that out when I finally held this." He waved the envelope containing Waterford's deed.

Zoe reached over and closed Hugh's fingers over the paper. "And it's yours now. You deserve it, Hugh. I want you to have it." She honestly did.

He shook his head. "No, Zoe, don't you understand? Now that I have it, it doesn't mean anything. I don't know what I thought I'd gain from it—satisfaction, revenge? I honestly don't know. But whatever it was, it's not enough. I want more and I need your help to get it."

Zoe wanted to pull away, wanted to escape the compelling blue of his eyes. But he held her hands firm and she could barely bring herself to blink.

"*My* help?"

"I know coming back to Tangawarra was tough for you. I know facing all that history, everything that happened was difficult."

Zoe swallowed hard and nodded. "Yes, but…" She managed a weak smile. "I'm glad I did. I needed to. I kidded myself that I'd moved on because I'd moved away, but really I was just carrying it all with me."

Hugh nodded and gave her an encouraging smile, silently urging her to go on.

"I've done a lot of thinking since then. I know I'll always carry my past with me, but now it's not because I've been ignoring it for years. Now it's because I'm beginning to face it and integrate it into my life."

Hugh released one of her hands to stroke a lock of hair back from her face. "You've been very brave, my love. But now I need you to be even braver."

My love? Before Zoe had time to think about Hugh's endearment, the meaning of his words sank in and her anxiety spiraled again. "Brave? Why?" Maybe that first instinct had been right—he *was* sick.

"You've stopped running away from your past. Now you need to find the courage to stop running away from your future."

"What do you mean?" she asked, although she already knew the answer. She only had to recall Wil's disappointed face when she'd declined his five-year contract, making up a feeble excuse about it being time to move on.

"I can't control everything, as much as I'd like to." He managed a rueful smile. "And you can't keep pushing everyone away. Not if you want to be happy. We both have a lot to learn. And I think we might be able to help each other with that."

Zoe shook her head. Her stomach ached at the thought of what he might be suggesting.

He continued, ignoring her silence. "And now you have to be brave enough to hear this and believe it, too. I love you, Zoe. I want us to be together."

It should have been a surprise, but it wasn't. Of course he loved her. Just as she loved him. That knowledge settled inside her easily. But loving each other was all tangled up with their past—could it possibly be something that would see them into the future? The idea of exploring that—of being *with* someone…

It was like asking someone terrified of heights to not just stand on the edge of a cliff, but also to jump off.

She leaped up from the seat and turned to the trunk of the olive tree as her vision blurred. She looked across the garden to the huge winery building and thought about running—even as she knew she couldn't do it.

"Hey."

She could feel Hugh's heat behind her even before he reached for her. His warm scent, stronger even than the herbs around them, flowed over her and promised safety, just as it always had. Was it powerful enough to override the constant nagging anxiety and fear she lived with daily?

His hands went to her arms, gently turning her to face him. His smile was as watery as her own. "It can be pretty tough on a guy's ego for a woman to burst into tears in response to a suggestion like that."

"I…I love you, Hugh." As the words tumbled out, their meaning filled her with both joy and terror. "But I don't…" She trailed off, scared to put voice to her fears.

"But what, Zoe? Talk to me."

Zoe fought for composure, struggling to put her feelings into words. "I don't know if I can risk it. I just can't…"

"Can't what, sweetheart? You can tell me."

"It sounds so stupid…but…you can't…you can't ever…d-die. I wouldn't survive."

His smile was sweet and filled with understanding. "You know I can't promise you that. But I promise to love you every second of every day until I do die—and I want that to be as far away as possible, so I swear I will take very good care of myself." He held up his hand in a Boy Scout salute and shot her one of those hundred-watt grins that had always made her heart melt.

Zoe knew her life would always be empty

if she let this opportunity go. She would never settle anywhere, never truly find peace. It would be her biggest regret—and that was after a lifetime with them. But taking this chance meant opening herself to the biggest hurt, taking the most perilous risk she'd ever faced.

Could she allow fear to rule her forever?

Fear of commitment had made her mother unhappy and unsettled.

Fear of success had made Mack's life lonely and filled with disappointment.

Fear of loss could easily make her own just as miserable. Unless she was willing to take a chance.

Her silence had taken its toll. Hugh's grin had begun to fade and a frown creased his brow. She reached up to smooth the lines away, never wanting for him to feel hurt or pain again. She knew she couldn't guarantee that. But she'd do her best to make it happen in any way she could.

She smiled. "I love you, Hugh. Let's get out of here."

The smile that lit up his face made her heart sing.

He brought her hands to his mouth and pressed his lips against her knuckles. "I would love nothing better. If I kiss you now, I won't stop, and I imagine Golden Gate has rules about public nudity. But you'll have to give me directions."

She took his hand and led him down the path that took them toward the car park. She deliberately didn't look back at the winery. They could survive an afternoon without her. "My apartment's pretty shabby, I have to warn you," she said over her shoulder.

"I don't care—if you live there, then I'll love it. As long as there's enough room for me to set up a temporary office until I can find something else, it will do fine."

Zoe stopped in her tracks. "You mean you're going to live here?"

Hugh shrugged. "Well, I figured that's what we'd do."

"What about Tangawarra? Lawson Estate?"

"I can manage remotely for a while. I might have to travel a bit—we'll have to see how it works."

Zoe thought for a moment. "Do you think Tangawarra's ready for me? Do you think they can handle their wild child returning home?"

"Is that what you want?"

"I think..." Zoe thought about meddling Patricia, interfering Stephen Carter, gruff Morris and the two goth kids at the supermarket. "I think that they're not going to know what's hit them."

Hugh laughed.

Zoe stepped closer and threaded her arms around his waist, resting her cheek against his shoulder. His arms rose and wrapped around her, pulling her tight to him. They were right in front of the Golden Gate tasting room—anyone could see, and Zoe didn't care in the slightest.

Hugh's chest swelled. "Oh, my love. I have no idea what's going to happen, but I can't wait to find out."

CHAPTER EIGHTEEN

Twelve months later

HUGH WAS OVER AT THE DAM with Morris when Zoe drove in. The two men looked deep in concentration as they examined the fencing. Zoe knew they were debating whether or not to improve the fences—now that there was a walking track connecting Lawson Estate's restaurant to the three romantic cottages being constructed on what used to be Waterford Estate, the safety of their guests was an important consideration.

The slam of Zoe's car door must have reached them, because Hugh looked up immediately, his face breaking into a nervous, questioning smile as he saw her.

It was a struggle to try to keep her face composed and not grin back—or, even more ridiculously, burst into tears. She did that pretty easily these days. In fact, running into Patricia in the street after her doctor's appointment had been exactly what she hadn't needed. But luckily the woman was totally focused on questioning Zoe about the latest developments of the Tangawarra youth council Zoe was setting up—the favorite topic of dissention in town this week—and it had given her time to pull herself together. By the time Patricia had got around to asking after her health, Zoe was able to give a polite, carefree reply.

Taking a deep breath, Zoe began to walk toward them, bare grapevines surrounding her. Winter this year had been temperate—or perhaps Zoe had just had time to adjust, because she hadn't felt the cold the way she had when she'd first returned to Tangawarra the previous year.

"Hey, there," Hugh called out.

At Hugh's words, Morris looked over and gave Zoe a nod.

Zoe couldn't take her eyes off her husband. His eyes were shadowed by that straw cowboy hat he loved, but she could feel his gaze on her.

They'd married on a hot summer's day at Lawson Estate, surrounded by vines and pretty much every person who lived in Tangawarra.

The reception afterward was still spoken about with awe—the spectacular gourmet food, beautiful surroundings and, even more reverently, the amazing wine that was served. Every vintner in the valley had brought their best bottle to toast the happy couple, and no one in the valley had ever been intoxicated on more expensive wine than on that night.

Everyone except Hugh and Zoe, that is. Drunk on each other, they scarcely touched a drop.

They had rarely left each other's side in the months that had followed. They travelled together to Napa Valley to visit Golden Gate—Wil and the staff there were still sad at Zoe's departure, but happy to see her embarking on a new life—and enjoy a short California honeymoon. They'd sat side-by-side in the architect's office drawing up the plans for the getaway cottages on Waterford land. Cleared out Mack's old house and moved in Morris's belongings. Morris now lived there, happily surrounded by grapevines.

They were so in tune with each other it was Hugh who had first noticed. Suggested that Zoe needed to see the doctor.

"Feelin' better, Zoe?" Morris asked as she drew nearer.

She gave him a smile. "I'm fine, thanks, Morris."

Hugh drew her into his arms as soon as she was within reach. He hugged her tight, his face pressed into her hair. "So?" he whispered. His words tickled her ear, the quiet tone in no way disguising his tension and eagerness.

Zoe swallowed, too overcome for a moment to speak. Eventually, she nodded. "Yes," she whispered back. "The doctor wants us both to come back next week for a proper prenatal appointment."

Hugh didn't say anything, but a quiver went through his body and his arms tightened around her even more.

Zoe's throat ached and the tears that had threatened since she'd received the news welled in her eyes. No longer afraid of their power over her, Zoe let a couple roll down her cheeks.

Hugh must have felt them because he pulled back.

"Hey, none of that." He wiped her cheeks with his thumb.

Zoe managed a watery smile. "Happy tears." Scared tears, too, but then she didn't need to tell him that.

Hugh's own eyes were bright. "Oh. That's okay, then."

Zoe noticed that Morris had wandered over to the other side of the dam, clearly picking up on the private moment. Zoe chuckled weakly. "Morris has made himself scarce. He probably knows what we're talking about, though. Bloody man knows everything that goes on here."

Hugh laughed, too, a funny strangled sound

that betrayed his emotion. "You're probably right." His smiled faded and he reached over to stroke her cheek. "What did…" His voice broke. He breathed hard. "What did the doctor say about…before? Will it…?"

The anxiety on his face made Zoe's heart ache. She shook her head. "He said there was no reason that it would happen again. But I'll be monitored closely, and I need frequent check-ups. We might have to go into the city every few weeks to see an obstetrician."

Hugh's jaw set firm. "We'll *move* to Melbourne if we have to. We'll find the best doctor in the country."

Zoe smiled as Hugh laid out his plans. Somehow, call it mother's instinct, Zoe knew everything was going to be all right. She was still nervous, of course—terrified, in fact—but even though it was far too early for such things, Zoe swore she could feel the little life curled up inside her, safe and secure, growing and waiting for the day she and Hugh could welcome him or her to the world.

Whatever happened, Zoe knew she had the strength to face it. With Hugh by her side, she could deal with whatever life sent her way.

They stood for a moment, arms around each other. A breeze rustled through the bare grapevines, and kookaburras cackled in the distance.

"Zoe's Zinfandel is still doing okay," Zoe said, looking over to the comparatively empty paddock to her right. The small, struggling new vines there—barely more than twigs in the ground—were a dramatic contrast to the strong, thick-trunked vines nearby. They'd planted the grapes only a few months before, the variety Zoe worked with in California. In a few years, once the vines had grown, she was sure Zoe's Zinfandel would be a star in the Lawson Estate range.

This year's first-ever Lawson Estate vintage with Zoe Waters as head winemaker had further cemented the company as the leading Australian wine producer.

Of special merit, noted wine journalists, was the brand-new, single-vineyard "Sara's Shiraz," made from the grapes that had formerly been used to make the little-known but highly prized Waterford Shiraz. Only a few dozen cases were made and they'd been snapped up by excited wine connoisseurs around the country. More than a few people had puzzled over the name, but Lawson Estate's publicist had been instructed not to explain it.

"You know our vines will be budding at the same time I'll start showing," Zoe realized with a laugh.

"Our own little bud burst," Hugh agreed.

"But they'll never be as fantastic as my beautiful Zoe. My pregnant wife," he added with more than a touch of wonder in his voice.

* * * * *